MY THING WITH TIMOTHY KAY

Misty Urban

www.BOROUGHSPUBLISHINGGROUP.com

PUBLISHER'S NOTE: This is a work of fiction. Names, characters, places and incidents either are the product of the author's imagination or are used fictitiously. Any resemblance to actual events, locales, business establishments or persons, living or dead, is coincidental. Boroughs Publishing Group does not have any control over and does not assume responsibility for author or third-party websites, blogs or critiques or their content.

ISBN: 978-1-957295- 58-9

To my little birds

ACKNOWLEDGMENTS

Thanks to the Tuesday critique group (we don't need a fancy name): Leslie Langtry, Susan Carroll, X.H. Collins, and Becky Langdon. You ladies inspire, rally, cheer, and always share your cake. Hand grenades on me.

Shouts out to local literary arts organizations like the Midwest Writing Center and Writers on the Avenue who work so hard to create community, lift writers, teach craft, and inspire art.

Cheers to librarians for everything they do, and they do everything.

Bows of deep gratitude to the independent bookstores and their visionary owners who are dedicated to creating communities, supporting literature, and nurturing art.

Thanks to the friends who pick up where we left off, and the family who always welcomes me back in. It's not easy to live with a writer and yet you do.

Much love to my little birds, who give the best hugs, and my real-life dreamboat, inspirer of all the fluttery feelings.

MY THING WITH TIMOTHY KAY

Chapter One

I hammered the last stake outlining the new flowerbeds for the front yard of the Desert Bloom B&B, and pushed sweat-laden hair from my eyes. The clock inside chimed four p.m. in Artesia, New Mexico.

That meant five o'clock in Hastings, Nebraska, where I'd lived for the eighteen years of my marriage.

And six o'clock in New York City, where my now ex-husband and his new wife had flown our teenage daughter to join them in Europe on the honeymoon the ex and I had always talked about taking, but never had.

Four to six. Happy hour, and I needed a dose of happy.

I shook the dirt off my trowel and tucked my tools into the cabinet on the front porch, turning my back on the empty yard, as sad and barren as my life.

Next month I'd turn forty, and all I could celebrate was my health. My husband was gone, my daughter was with him, and some kid from Omaha had been hired to manage the bank where I'd been fighting since college to climb the ranks.

My friend Bernie, an angel, had given me this chance to hide and heal, lick my wounds, and practice my landscaping skills at her B&B. Turned out I was failing here too, but I didn't want to tell her while she was up north in the hospital with her mom.

I had one thing going for me: I could still make a killer margarita.

Behind the double doors with their colored glass, Anahita sat cross-legged on the deep red couch in the reception room, settled in for the evening shift.

I wiped a last trickle of sweat from my hairline, and asked, "There's no one coming tonight, right?" If so, that was my cue to start on a nice buzz that took the edge off everything else.

Ana pointed toward the guestbook on its small lectern beside the door. "The guy in the penthouse is due tomorrow."

Bernie tried to maintain a historic atmosphere, so her registration book was a leatherbound, folio-size ledger ruled with green lines. A quill-shaped fountain pen stood in a fake inkwell. Ornate calligraphic script on the open page read "Mr. Golightly." He'd reserved the penthouse for all of September and into October.

I groaned. "Right, the Hollywood guy. Nice alias. What were the instructions again?"

"Don't drool. Don't use his real name. And have fresh ground organic coffee every morning. Dark roast, sustainably harvested, responsibly sourced." She nibbled her pen. "Taiye got coffee from the roastery, and Cristina's bringing her daughter to help clean."

"Glad you're dealing with Hollywood. Sounds like a pain in the ass."

Bernie didn't require me to deal with guests, one of the conditions of my escape.

"Want a drink?" I asked.

"Bernie bought me non-alcoholic spritzers."

Perfect. We headed down the hall connecting the formal sitting room, dining room, screened-in porch, and kitchen.

Happy hour had been the one thing my ex, Ritchie, and I did together. The nights he wasn't travelling, I had a cocktail waiting for us. He'd gripe about his day and his coworkers while I fixed dinner.

When she wasn't off at some activity, our daughter, Maya, joined us with a ginseng smoothie to gear up for a night of study. Happy hour and family dinner. I'd thought we were fine.

Happy, even.

Then two years ago, out of the blue, Ritchie asked for a separation. Shortly after, a divorce. Six months ago, we finalized the papers, and two months later, he married Lisa.

The kitchen ceiling sloped up to the back of the B&B, floor-to-ceiling windows shedding sun on the long eight-seater table.

Deep counters, banks of new appliances, and glass-fronted cabinets ran along the room on two sides. Ana hopped onto one of the high stools lining the kitchen island with its granite countertop and row of hanging lights. The move reminded me of my daughter, settling in for one of our chats. I missed her with a physical ache.

I grabbed a Proteau out of the double-sided fridge for Ana and collected tequila and a lime for me. It felt strange to refashion my old habits, like compensating for a missing limb. But while I'd missed happy hour, oddly enough, I didn't miss Ritchie.

"So the landscaping's going well?" Ana asked, pouring her spritzer into a glass.

"It's not astronomy." I sliced the lime and slid it around the rim of my margarita glass, then dipped the glass in the salt.

My vision for Bernie's yard seemed so pedestrian now that I had it staked out. Nothing more daring than a small depression for a rain garden, tiers of shrubs to fill the washed-out gully, vegetable beds, and fruit trees to offer food and shade. The only true beauty: the cottonwood full-grown beauty, in her prime, and after the summer rains her healthy green leaves rustled happily in the breeze. She was going to be the centerpiece of my garden.

Bernie had loved my sketches of flowerbeds that bloomed in every season, with paved walks around the old cottonwood, but right now her yard looked like an alien landscape, pocked with defeated holes and rocks.

"I told Maya about you and your program," I said, mixing my drink. "I'd like to interest her in science. Instead, she looked up Bahrain where there's an underwater park where you can dive a Boeing 747. Now she wants to put it on their itinerary."

Ana laughed. "At least you're not freaking out about her taking a gap year. My parents only let me come to the U.S. on the condition they get to arrange my marriage the minute I'm back home."

Talking about Maya's future made me nervous, but no more so than contemplating my own. If she didn't go back to Hastings, there was nothing for me. Ritchie had the house with the beautiful yard I'd added to year by year. I had a dead-end job, a cramped two-bedroom apartment with a short-term lease, and an olive tree I was barely keeping alive.

I looked up and dropped my tongs, sending ice cube skidding across the counter. "Whoa. Who's the creeper?"

Ana peered at the dark shape moving beneath the twisted cottonwood. "That's not Pete or any of the neighbors. I don't know that guy."

"I'll go tell him he's trespassing."

Ana clapped a hand over her mouth. "What if he's high? What if he came here to rob us? Maybe we should call the police."

"He's tall, but he doesn't look huge. I could run faster than he can." I hoped.

"What if he has a gun?" Ana's voice dropped.

That would be my luck. "Maybe you should get the phone. Just in case."

The glass doors slid on their rails without a hiss as I snuck outside. There wasn't anything in the B&B expensive enough to tempt a robber, but Bernie had sunk a lot of money and time into redoing the rooms with modern touches, filling the place with original art. She loved this place, and I was the Desert Bloom's protector while she was gone.

A stone clattered as I searched for something I could use as a weapon. Bernie had left me a pile of copper pipe she'd salvaged from her plumbing upgrade, but pipe meant I would have to be close enough to swing. The garden hose had a setting that produced a painfully strong stream, as I'd learned when watering my new bed of prairie dropseed.

He seemed around my age with broad shoulders that filled out his collarless button-down shirt, and he moved with the long-limbed, rangy grace of a natural athlete. He didn't display the jerky, nervous movements of someone on a controlled substance, but his dark scruff of beard, tousled hair, and wrinkled clothes looked like he'd been sleeping in the street for a week.

He looked good rumpled. I reminded myself he was a problem. Especially when he ran a hand over the thick grooved bark of the cottonwood, tilting his head to look up into the canopy. The pose, one I'd struck many times, unnerved me.

"*Hey*. What are you doing to my tree?"

He dropped his arm and turned toward me. A lot of people are taller than I am, but this guy loomed. I thumbed the switch that would turn my nozzle into a water cannon.

"Who are you, and what do you want?" His low voice held a silky quality, like he was accustomed to using it.

Did he think *I* was the one out of bounds here? I gave him my best stony glare. "That's my line."

"What are you doing?"

"Again, my question." My finger twitched as he moved toward me. He wasn't smelly or repulsive. His scowling eyebrows, thick and dark, were as unruly as his hair. I scowled back. "Why are *you* here?" I wasn't intimidating much, parroting his lines back to him like bad improv.

"I'm staying here tonight." He said this with confidence, as if he wasn't trespassing on Bernie's land, as if I wasn't holding an expandable garden hose.

"We take paying customers only. You're not sleeping in our yard."

"I'm sleeping inside." Annoyance darkened his face. Maybe he *was* on something and was getting to the paranoid stage. I'd heard people could become unusually strong while hallucinating, and he had the advantage in inches and pounds.

I aimed the nozzle. "Sorry, we're all booked." A lie, since the only guests were the construction worker on a project and the writer I never saw. "I have staff. A big guy. Huge. Who knows martial arts." I waved the nozzle to emphasize each word.

Taiye would shriek with laughter at being called big. He was as slender and light as a canary, and his martial art was tai chi.

My intruder kept walking toward the porch. I wracked my brain for backup. "And…we have a cowboy. Old rodeo style. Real tough. He'll—" What did rodeo cowboys do? "He'll *lasso* you."

Tree man's snorted laughter. "Give me that hose before you—"

"I warned you." I switched on the water to full bore.

A gentle spray showered him, droplets that shimmered like a golden halo before settling to earth.

"*You*—" Water dripped from his chin, and he reached for the hose.

Panicking, I cranked the switch. The gentle plume turned into a hissing jet that plastered his shirt to his broad chest. Muscles flexed when he threw up his hands to shield his face.

The stream had to sting. I didn't want to damage him and bring on a lawsuit, but every twist of the nozzle produced a new jet.

A hard, wet surface slapped against my back as his big arms clamped around mine, and before I could utter a curse, he'd snapped off the water and plucked the hose from my hands as if relieving a child of a toy.

Maya and I had taken a self-defense class before she left. I drew back an elbow to deliver the sequence of jabs we'd learned. Where would the solar plexus be on a guy this tall? Before I could aim, he stepped away, leaving my back cool and damp.

"I'm a guest here." His deep voice penetrated the rush of blood in my ears. "I'm registered. I put down a deposit. Or someone did for me."

"What? We don't have anyone arriving tonight." The only reservation was for the Hollywood diva posing with the silly name of—"

"Golightly." He wiped droplets from his thick eyebrows still knit in a scowl.

"Oh. Whoops."

Bernie was *not* going to appreciate my reception of her best-paying guest.

"Um. Welcome to the Desert Bloom Bed and Breakfast, Mr. Golightly."

Chapter Two

Hollywood—I couldn't call him Golightly in my head—stopped on the red cedar porch, dripping. "I can't come inside soaking wet."

A man with manners. I needed to find mine.

We couldn't have someone important—if indeed he was important—leaving a zero-star review of the Desert Bloom. "Um, can I bring in your luggage so you can change?"

If he'd knocked on the front door like a normal person with a set of bags, even a carry-on, I wouldn't've treated him like a trespasser. I wondered if it would help my case to point that out.

"My driver's bringing my bags over later. I came on ahead."

"A day early." His room wasn't ready. *I* wasn't ready. "Let me see if I can find you some clothes. Pete usually leaves a spare set."

Pete, the cowboy who took odd jobs as Bernie's handyman, didn't have clothes to match this guy's style, casual yet classy. His loafers were obviously expensive, and his linen trousers might have been creased from travel, not from sleeping in the street. He unbuttoned his long-sleeved shirt, also linen, and while he wrung it out, I stared.

His shoulders were actually *that* broad. He was all lean muscle, not the bulk made in a gym, but the shape of a man who was active. A light dusting of black hair covered broad pecs, arrowing past his defined ribs to the ripples of muscle banding his stomach. I swallowed, my throat suddenly dry.

Ana had disappeared. The kitchen was empty, our glasses

abandoned on the kitchen island. That was for the best. She wasn't supposed to be around strange men, much less nearly naked ones. I tore my gaze away from Hollywood as he pressed moisture out of his pants. He had long, strong legs, well defined thighs and calves, even nice feet. Since when were a man's feet attractive?

"Clothes," I croaked.

So he was handsome. That was why people went to Hollywood, because of their looks. Good thing I hadn't put out his eye. I stuck my head into the cupboard beside the bathroom. "Aha. Clothing. Should be close to your size. Until your bags arrive."

I froze with my hands full of denim as Hollywood picked up my margarita without even a hello. The nerve! His throat moved as he drank, and I stared. Again.

If that was a fake tan, it was well done. His skin was a delicious combination of gold and red and brown.

"That's a nice touch. Real tequila, one hundred percent agave." He set down the glass. "What's the twist?"

"Pineapple juice, because I ran out of orange liqueur." I narrowed my eyes. "Why did we have you arriving tomorrow?"

He shrugged. I refused to be bewitched by broad shoulders or anything else. Like his hands, which, when he took the pile of clothes, were as nicely shaped as his feet, his fingers long and nimble. The hands of a musician.

And probably famous. No wonder Bernie told us to keep cool and not drool. Too bad I was too parched to swallow.

"My assistant said I was booked for today. Maybe you got the dates confused?"

He was the one confused, but I held my tongue. The customer is always right. "Bernie might have written it down wrong. She was a bit distracted before she left."

Courtesy said I should turn aside while he dressed. I was partially courteous. While I pulled out the lime, another bar glass, and the tin of salt, I kept an eye on him. He was unpredictable, and I needed to be wary.

He shucked off his trousers as if he were used to undressing in front of strangers. Then again, the island blocked his lower half, so he wasn't being completely exhibitionist. Denim rustled as he pulled on the jeans, and the sound of ripping stitches followed.

"T-shirt's kinda tight."

"Beggars can't be choosers." I sloshed the last of the pineapple juice into his drink.

"People who are going to hose down guests before they enter should have spare clothes that fit."

"People who creep around houses instead of coming to the front door—" I turned and nearly dropped the glass, which would've been a waste of top shelf tequila. In his other clothes, he'd been a laidback cross between sophisticated and sexy-cool. In Pete's beat-up jeans and a faded coral pink T-shirt sculpting every line of that glorious chest, this man was a knockout.

Face. I focused on his face and took another hit.

His square jaw and high forehead were balanced by a strong nose and prominent cheekbones. And his eyes were intense, dark brown with flecks of green and amber. I'd been missing out if I hadn't seen every movie this man was in.

Down, girl. I'd had one or two hookups since my divorce, just to prove to myself that I wasn't going to die without ever having sex again, but I was a grown woman. Handsome wasn't the same as attractive. Nice-looking didn't make you a nice person. My ex-husband was proof of that.

"Here. Your own margarita." I shoved the glass his way. I needed to play nice. This guy was paying a premium for the suite that occupied the entire second floor above the main part of the house, and he'd booked it for several weeks. Bernie needed the income. "Tell me why you were molesting my tree."

"Your tree?" He raised those thick, scowly brows. "You planted the cottonwood?"

"You know what it is?" Not a city boy, then, at least not originally.

"That's a Rio Grande cottonwood. We call it alamillo. About fifty years old, with that size trunk."

"Nearer forty, I think. I'm hoping she has a few decades left in her."

"She?"

"So." I cleared my throat. He didn't act angry about the hose, so why was I still nervous? "Most guests use the front door."

With no sign of Anahita, we were essentially alone, and I had to deliver the news that we weren't ready for him. Would he throw a big Hollywood diva fit? Would I have to make up his bed? My cheeks heated at the thought.

"I meant to. But I was curious about the cladding on the house. It's unusual."

"Cladding?"

"That white stone on the outside. It's so square. I wanted to see if it went all the way around." He leaned against the bar, casual, relaxed in his gorgeousness. He was accustomed to making women nervous.

"That's cast stone," I said. "Artificial stone made of cement. It was a thing they did here when the town was first founded. Bernie kept it when she redid the house, which is otherwise stucco. It's unique, and, um, interesting, if you're into, you know, architecture. Or history."

His attention, the intensity, was alarming.

"It gave me an idea about my movie. So I walked around the house and met your tree."

Despite myself, I smiled. He smiled back, and it was devastating.

"Then I got attacked by a woman waving a garden hose."

Good, a timely reminder of my blunder. "I thought you were high or trying to sleep in our backyard."

"None of the above." He swirled his drink, and I braced myself for the do-you-know-who-I-am lecture, threats of civil action, emotional damages. I didn't have the resources to get into a lawsuit.

Then there was that moment when he stood behind me, his firm wet chest pressed to my back, his arms draped over mine. My T-shirt was still damp from him. I lifted my glass to hide the heat in my cheeks.

Mischievous crinkles formed around his eyes. "*Do* you know who I am?"

Ah, here was the game. I was smugly glad that I was so unplugged from mainstream culture, even though Maya complained all the time about how clueless I was.

"Of course." I sipped my margarita. "Mr. Golightly. You're a fan of Truman Capote, *Breakfast at Tiffany's*, or Audrey Hepburn."

That mind-slaughtering smile again. "My assistant is an Audrey Hepburn fan. I'm either Golightly or Doolittle. I don't get to choose. But you get points for knowing Truman Capote wrote the book."

"Oh, we're scoring points now? Well, you get demerits for sneaking around the backyard, more demerits for showing up on the wrong day, and you get docked extra because now I have to do your laundry."

I picked up the designer clothes he'd draped over the back of a chair. It was a carved iron frame, which his moist clothes wouldn't damage, but I didn't give him credit for noticing this. He was a pampered celebrity, and I'd be waiting on him hand and foot if I didn't watch myself. I'd had enough of that in my marriage.

He was one of those people who could raise one eyebrow. "Do I get points for liking your margarita?"

He'd want dinner, but fortunately, in a B&B, he was on his own about that. I held up two fingers. "You drank *my* margarita, and you made me waste water in the desert. You're in the hole, Hollywood."

"You hosed a paying guest. I'd say we're even."

True, he had suffered full-frontal assault and was being remarkably good-natured about it. This was the part where I should apologize.

Anahita, hijab in place, leaned in from the hallway. "*Psst.* Dale. I got Mr. Golightly's room ready."

"Oh, you darling." Game to Ana, who had guessed who he was

before I did. I was more than happy to hand over our guest and take a breather. "Mr. Golightly, this is Anahita, part of the Desert Bloom staff. She can help with anything you need."

Even damp, his discarded clothes smelled like him, a scent that was smoky, woody, and earthy all at the same time. He looked at young, gorgeous Ana with polite interest.

"Anahita," he said. "Arabic?"

"Persian," she said. "Dale can show you to your room. Call me if you need me, Dale." She disappeared.

Handoff back to me. I couldn't say I was disappointed as I stashed his clothes in the laundry room off the pantry. "Okay, then. Ready for the tour?"

"Dale." He rolled my name around his tongue like he was tasting a fine vintage. "Please tell me you're named after Dale Evans."

I grinned at him. "I'm named after my grandma, my dad's mom, and she was born in the thirties, so I guess it was a popular name then. This, as you've seen, is the kitchen. But we'll serve breakfast in here."

I steered him toward the formal dining room, with a long rustic dining table made of deeply stained pine. Potted plants of various sizes—my addition to the décor—clustered before the tall windows that would open onto a flagstone patio, as soon as I got it installed. One wall, painted in muted sunset colors, stood out as accent.

"That's a lot of Georgia O'Keeffe," Hollywood said, observing the art.

"This is the Georgia O'Keeffe room," I confirmed, softening despite myself. He knew his film history *and* art. "Every room has a theme."

"Who's in my room?"

"Wait and see. This porch is available to guests." The screened-in porch held a comfortable table for four, a pair of fat deep armchairs, and an artist's easel. He eyed the hammock appreciatively.

"This is the formal parlor, for guest use." This brightly colored room was a mix between Versailles and classic southwest with its

Edwardian furniture and vintage art. It held a wall of books and the baby grand piano Bernie carried with her through all her moves.

"This one's the informal parlor." This room, a more muted taupe color, held the flat screen TV and a table beside a shelf of board games.

"That wing is staff rooms, so nothing you need there. That wing is more guest rooms." I pointed in the opposite direction. "And you're in the Red Bluff Room up here."

I climbed the winding staircase to the upper part of the original house. The gambrel roofed room wasn't a second story proper but provided enough space for an expansive suite. The ceiling was high enough that Hollywood didn't have to stoop.

He wasn't breathing down my neck, but I felt him behind me on the stairs, warmth on my rear and my nape. "Well, this is straight out of *Amityville Horror*," he remarked.

The first movie was before my time and his, but his reference amused me. "It's the same style, what they call Dutch Colonial Revival. You like horror flicks?"

I didn't, and he ignored my obvious attempt at fishing.

"Which room is yours?" he asked.

"The Pablita Velarde room. In the guest wing."

"I don't know that artist."

"You should. She's one of the most important Pueblo artists of the twentieth century. She did work for the National Park Service, and she's in the Smithsonian."

"I'd like to see that room sometime."

I stopped on the tiny landing before the red door of the suite. Was he *flirting* with me?

A man who looked like he did had no need to troll for women. Maybe flirting was a reflex. A Hollywood survival mechanism.

Or did he think he was doing me a favor? A man like this pretending to have the slightest interest in standard issue nearly middle-aged average American female?

"For the art," he clarified, alarmed at my scowl.

"You can look her up. Or have your assistant do it. This will be your key. We have a spare in case of emergencies." I unlocked his door, then offered him the brass key, hoping he wouldn't touch my hand when he took it.

No such luck. His skin was warm and as smooth as silk. Clearly, not a man who worked with his hands. Before the blush could bloom, I opened the door to the Red Bluff Room, an airy suite with a muted mix of desert colors and enormous windows.

"Kitchenette, closet with extra linens here, that's the door to the bathroom, and those are the stairs to the loft jacuzzi."

That was a huge selling point. Bernie had the only jacuzzi suite in all Artesia.

"A whirlpool tub? That's not a waste of water in the desert?"

"Believe me, we reuse that water. Do you mind if I take a look at the plants?"

The room's elegant furnishings with the four-poster king-size bed, rolled-arm sofa, and counter bar table with its pair of high stools were all Bernie, as was the art. But I'd chosen the plants, all with red leaves to match the décor, a living touch to make the room welcoming.

"A telescope? Are you kidding me?" Hollywood went straight to it while I checked on the red aglaonema lining the nook holding the jacuzzi tub. The skylights and tall arched windows let in the orange-red glow of evening.

Anahita had laid out two plush bath sheets of Turkish cotton topped with a bar of castile soap and a set of soy candles in their round tins. I sniffed—she'd chosen the high desert label, a blend of sandalwood, cedarwood, and musk, with a hint of nutmeg. It smelled like *him*. How had she known? Was darling Ana as susceptible to this man as I was?

He turned away from the telescope and the bank of windows looking out onto the tiny patio, watching as I tested the soil around the coleus and dosed them with water.

"Are you responsible for the plants?"

"Yep. Bernie picked the art, but I do the greenery. Inside and out."

I busied myself with the rex begonia in the bathroom. A plant known as the red kiss: a splash of crimson sensuality in an otherwise chaste space.

My thoughts needed to remain chaste. I abandoned the rex and put my watering can away below the kitchenette sink. Hollywood examined each painting of red bluffs, all done in distinct styles.

"The art's amazing. Is that a Diné design?" He went to a woven blanket hung on the wall above a small divan, bright red with a distinctive diamond pattern.

He said Diné, the name the people called themselves, not Navajo, the name they were given by conquerors. Perceptive.

"It is, and that's a Maria Martinez bowl beside it. One of her redware works. Another Pueblo artist you should know," I added.

"You keep expanding my horizons." He watched as I rearranged the polka dot plant on one nightstand. "I don't think I have a single plant in my house."

I gaped at him. "Not one?"

"No. They require maintenance."

Ah. He was that kind of guy. No strings. Don't tie me down. "Plants are necessary," I said, pinching a deaf leaf off the polka dot. "They purify the air, for one thing. They brighten a space. They calm the sympathetic nervous system. And each has their own particular energy. Like a personality." I patted the polka dot and moved away.

His steady regard made my back prickle, made me remember how he'd pressed against me.

"Chocolates?" His eyes lit as they fell on the pair of Eldora truffles on the other nightstand. Everything in the Red Bluff Room was designed for two. "Green chile biscochito—is that a New Mexico thing?"

"It's handcrafted chocolate. You'll never taste anything better."

He handed me a truffle in its shiny foil package. "Hmm. There are two here."

"They're for you."

"I share."

I stared at his mouth as he tasted the chocolate. Such a nice shape to his lips, full but not pouty, as firm and attractive as the rest of him. Straight white teeth. His eyes widened, and the look that flickered through them set off the strangest tingle in the bottom of my stomach.

"I can't believe you would pass this up."

I needed air. This room was gorgeous anyway, but with him in it, that pure light falling through the windows and glimmering in his hair, those sexy bare feet…that enormous, soft-looking bed.

"Ahem. We've got other flavors if you'd like. Bernie stocks up every time she goes to Albuquerque."

He lowered his eyelids. That smoky look gave me more than tingles. "You could bring me a new flavor every night."

"That's Ana's job. I don't handle guests." The words came out of me on a whispered breath. What was with these come-ons? Could he just not help it? He probably burned through women in every town he visited, yet my body wanted to rise to his invitation with a joyous *yes*.

I backed toward the door. "So, Ana will be downstairs. Just call down if you need anything." He folded the foil from the truffle into a square and then placed it in the wastebasket. "Do you, um, need recommendations for dinner?"

He tested the door that led to a tiny porch with two aluminum chairs facing a small bistro table. "My assistant, Glenn, will bring me dinner, along with my bags."

He drew his phone from his back pocket and glanced at the screen, the first time I'd seen him consult it.

Didn't celebrities have to livestream their whole lives? He tucked the phone in his back pocket. His ass was as nicely shaped as the rest of him.

"Okay, Glenn," I said. "Will he—she?—need a key also?"

"They," he answered. "And no, they won't need a key." He

turned to face me. "The wet welcome aside, thanks for helping me settle in. Dale."

The way he said my name made me want to inch closer to him, hear him say it in my ear, whispered, hoarsely uttered in the midst of—

Get a grip on yourself, Dale! I stepped back as he stepped closer.

"I know your name, but you still don't know mine," he said.

Did it matter? "You're Mr. Golightly to anyone who asks," I said. I might not do guest services, but I understood discretion.

"My friends call me Kay."

He'd dropped the alias. That seemed important.

"All right. Nice to meet you, Kay."

Time to leave. For real. Time for my feet to turn around and carry me out the door and out of his intoxicating presence.

Finally, I made them obey me.

I wobbled down the stairs. It hadn't been *nice* to meet him. More like taking a hit from a rocket launcher.

This charisma must be what they called star quality, why people got picked out at grocery stores or walking their dog. An undeniable pull.

Mere pheromones, or some such. I'd gotten used to thinking of other men as off-limits during my marriage, but this guy was doubly, triply so. Good-looking. Even-tempered. *Tidy.* Keen intelligence with a dollop of easy charm, all of which added up to danger.

Call me Kay. I was *not* going to play drooling fangirl. But I was also going to take a quick, cold shower this evening. First time I'd needed to do that in years.

The doorbell rang, and since I was in the vestibule and Ana wasn't, I opened it.

This must be Glenn. They were shorter than me, with an asymmetrical cut to their brown hair and a firm expression on their young, pale face. They wore a man's blazer, slacks, a white Oxford shirt beneath a black lace-up bustier, and a pair of white high-top sneakers. They held up a paper bag.

"Is Mr. Golightly here?"

I let them in. "Upstairs. That way. Need help with the luggage?"

"Nope." It was a big black hard-side bag, the kind with the spinner wheels, expensive and well-used. Glenn hoisted it over the threshold with a thump. "And you are?"

"Dale Rose. Er, Wrighton." I was going back to my maiden name.

"You've been briefed, Dale?"

"Don't give out his name, don't be a fangirl, don't set him loose on the world without coffee. Anything else?"

Glenn smiled and held out a small card. "This is my number. Don't ask him any questions, ask me. We're at the Hotel Artesia. I don't know why he insists on sneaking off without us, but he likes to be alone, so don't let anyone bother him. I'll get you something autographed at the end of all this, for a keepsake."

"Don't worry about it. My collection of signed headshots of handsome actors is currently zero. I don't need to add to it."

Glenn stopped on the stairs, takeout bag in one hand, suitcase in the other. "You don't know who he is?"

This mystery was becoming annoying. "He's not Dwayne Johnson, and he's not Idris Elba. That's the limit of my Hollywood name recognition."

Glenn snorted. "That's awesome. I hope you said that to his face." That grin flashed again. "Let's hang out sometime, Dale."

Yeah, right. Like an ambitious youngster who moved in famous circles would want to hang out with a near-middle-aged woman with a failed marriage, dead-end career, and dirt beneath her fingernails from poking at the coleus.

Ana grabbed my elbow and pulled me into the breezeway, closing the door behind her. "Did Bernie tell you Golightly is Hugh Jackman?" she hissed.

"That's not Hugh Jackman." My Hollywood list was up to three.

"Looks exactly like him."

"Maybe from a distance. But I think Hugh Jackman has a wife and kids. He'd have a huge entourage. This guy is…" I hesitated over the word. "Alone."

I'd almost said *lonely*. Despite the hints about truffles and seeing my room, I sensed a deep reserve in Mr. Kay Golightly. He didn't let down his guard, and he wasn't letting anyone close.

And I wasn't trying to get close, to him or anyone. So this would work out fine.

Chapter Three

I was doing sun salutations on the cedar patio when Kay ran up from the gully behind the house. He stopped under the cottonwood to stretch, and I paused in upward dog pose. His damp shirt clung to every swell of muscle in his chest and arms. His legs in black running shorts were equally muscled and nicely curved. So was his ass.

He headed toward the porch, and my chest thumped. A damp bandana held back his thick hair, and his mirrored sunglasses hid the expression on his face. I moved into plank pose. *Stop ogling the guests, Dale.*

It had been so, so long since a man upped my heart rate. I felt like an adolescent again, knocked over by the rush of pheromones.

"Smart move, running while the sun is still low," I said from downward dog. "It's going to hit mid-eighties today."

Dumb, Dale. Was I going to chat about the weather with him?

"I grew up in the southwest," he said. "I'm used to heat." Sweat gleamed on his throat and arms. He had a morning's worth of dark scruff across that jaw.

He stepped onto the deck and, conscious of my butt in the air, I moved back into plank pose. He picked up a metal canteen bottle from the small patio table and gulped water.

The man was a walking commercial, sweat gleaming on serious muscles. An image designed to stir admiration. And longing.

"Where in the southwest?" I asked from upward dog.

"Las Vegas."

"Viva Las Vegas." *Lame, Dale.*

"How about you?" He sat at the patio table, stretching out his legs. Was he going to watch me finish my asana sequence? Sit here and talk to me?

I moved into triangle pose, glad I'd chosen the yoga pants that sculpted my behind and sucked in my thighs, and the tank that showed my flat stomach and arms. Separating from Ritchie had put me on a crash diet that melted my long-marriage weight gain, and muscle had started popping out on my shoulders and arms when I started doing heavier landscaping work.

"Illinois, then Nebraska, then here," I said.

"Sounds like an interesting story." His voice was low and raspy. Maybe he was one of those actors that did a lot of voice work.

I'd resisted searching for him online because I wanted the mystery to last a little longer. See what he would tell me on his own. He didn't seem like a man who was forthcoming. And I didn't see the need to outline the larger failures of my life.

"It's not that interesting. I grew up in Springfield, went to Hastings College, got a job there after college, and then came here to help out a friend."

"Family?" he asked, breaking into the water bottle again.

I wasn't going to talk about my ex. "My daughter is in Europe, doing the obligatory post-graduation lightning round of cultural capitals."

Maya had texted that they were in a boutique hotel in Interlaken and the hiking had been awesome. I'd peeked at her social media accounts and wished I hadn't. Ritchie stood with his arms wrapped around Lisa, blonde and slim in her name brand hiking gear. Everything he wanted that I wasn't.

I still didn't understand why this East Coast, boarding-school beauty had fallen for my ex, who was greying at the temples, soft around the middle, and seventeen years older than she was. But it was obvious why he'd fallen for her.

I'd suggested going to Europe many times. He insisted we scrimp and put our money away for later. Then he divorced me, spent his half of our savings on a classic car and a motorcycle, and took his new wife on the trip I'd always wanted.

He wanted her. Not me. I was the one who got left.

I hid my face in child's pose and decided to stay there a while.

"Maybe I'll get the full story over a margarita sometime," Kay said.

I sat back on my heels, a nervous twinge darting through my lower belly. That sounded like an invitation. "I'd rather hear about California. I'll bet you have a really interesting job."

He cleared his throat. "Speaking of which, did you have plans for today?"

I rose and waved toward the stack of flat paving stones and the hose I'd used yesterday to spray him down. I wondered if he'd told Glenn why he was wearing someone else's clothes. They'd been neatly stacked on the washing machine when I came to the kitchen to check on his coffee.

Not that his coffee was my job. I didn't do guests. *Look after* guests.

"I have to level my beds for the gravel that's coming in a day or two."

He surveyed the cratered-moon yard. "What are you building?"

"Standard xeriscape. Rocks and stones, some lavender and fountain grass for interest. Up front, aloe and artichoke. The usual." It was all regular and boring, and I felt embarrassed saying it out loud.

"I suppose you can't water the desert."

"You can, if you do it right. If you look at some of the pueblos around here, the existing ones as well as the ruins, they figured out irrigation hundreds of years ago. See that?" I pointed to the tall adobe brick reservoir hugging the laundry room. "Bernie built three of these for her catchment system, plus there's another tank under your feet. Thirty thousand gallons of captured rainwater."

This was where most people would look politely bored. Kay looked interested. "What do you use it for?"

"Everything. We filter it for the tap and use the rest for laundry, cooking, and your jacuzzi. Eventually, the Desert Bloom will use very little city water."

There would also be water for irrigation. I stared out at the yard, seeing again my impossible dreams. There was so much I wanted to try: a greenhouse behind the reservoir so Bernie would have fresh veg year-round, flowerbeds to catch runoff from the patio, all native, drought tolerant plants. Fruit trees for shade, privacy, and birds. All of it well beyond my small expertise.

I pointed at the draw Kay had run up. "One problem is that arroyo. So much soil washes away after a rain. There used to be a creek that fed into the Pecos River, and I'd love to come up with some way to turn it back into a riparian zone. For the biodiversity, but also, the roots would channel some water back into the artesian wells, which are what made this town famous a hundred years ago."

"Sounds amazing," Kay said. Ritchie had always gotten bored when I started chattering about land features and drainage.

I slumped my shoulders. "Yeah, well, I have no idea how to go about any of that. I'm sticking with something simple for now." Bernie had told me to go nuts, but she was also paying for all my tools and materials. Anything adventurous I tried and failed at would end up on her bill.

I'd learned a lesson about wanting things beyond my reach. Things I couldn't have.

"Is that what you do? Landscaping?" For some reason, he was still sitting outside, talking to me, instead of going inside to clean up and continue his day.

I reknotted my ponytail, looking down in embarrassment. "My degree's in accounting."

"I have coffee!" Taiye slid through the glass doors, twirling a tray, a bright white apron cinched around his waist. Taiye believed in hospitality with flair. He was one of Bernie's former students, now in graduate school for hotel management so he could return home and run the family property in Salvador, Brazil. "Black for Mr. Golightly, cream and sugar for Dale. You want breakfast out here?"

"I'll come in and help," I said automatically, but Taiye shooed me away.

"Stay. You two look so cozy. Cristina is here." He fluttered his eyelashes at Kay. "Or would Mr. Golightly rather eat inside?"

"Here's fine." Kay leaned back in his chair, shoulders tense. He was used to people fussing over him, but he didn't seem to like it. "Dale, join me?"

I stood there stupidly a moment. The prom king, inviting the nerdy girl to join him. That plot worked in romantic comedies, but in real life, it was a disaster. "Why?"

"I have a question for you." Kay picked up the large ceramic mug and sipped. His expression softened, pleased. I sighed with relief. We had the right coffee.

Kay nodded at Taiye but addressed me. "Is this the big guy who was going to scare me off yesterday when you thought I was trespassing?"

"Big? You said I was big?" Taiye squealed with laughter.

"Well, I thought Golightly was a robber. Or a homeless addict. I was trying to make him go away," I said, sliding into the chair across from Kay.

"I'm a big, scary *man*." Taiye clapped his hands and ran into the house. "Cristina!" Spanish followed, too rapid for me to understand all of it, but I gathered he was letting Cristina in on the joke.

Kay took off his sunglasses and set them on the table. I sucked in my breath. His eyes were more striking when he was laughing at me and those crinkles came out around them.

"Is the coffee okay?" If I was on guest duty now, I might as well do the job right.

"It's great. Thanks. You don't want to see me on cheap coffee. Or no coffee."

Maybe I should. Maybe if I saw him cranky or sullen or mean, I wouldn't be sitting here absurdly excited at the idea of having breakfast with him. He should have been disgusting and damp from his run. Instead, the smoky mesquite scent of his sweat stirred tendrils of something I thought had dried up and died long ago, or at least gone dormant.

Taiye brought out two heavy, hand-painted stoneware plates steaming with crunchy tortilla strips, fluffy scrambled eggs, and a rainbow of crisp-tender vegetables. He snapped out a cloth napkin and laid it ceremoniously across my lap. Kay took his napkin with a polite smile.

"I got it. Thanks."

Taiye bowed—overdoing it, but graceful—and retired to the kitchen.

"The napkins are made of recycled plastic bottles," I said as Kay tucked in. "And the dinnerware is recycled clay. Bernie wants to make eco-friendly a selling point for the Desert Bloom."

Had I forgotten how to make conversation? I shoved food into my mouth. It wasn't like this was a date.

"Tell me how an accountant gets into landscaping," Kay said.

This interest in me again. I didn't know what to make of it, and I wanted to know more about him. "To get outside and away from a desk. You don't have a desk job, I'm guessing."

"What did Glenn tell you?"

Kay ate like a man who didn't spend a lot of time over his food. I, on the other hand, savored every bite. Eating food I didn't have to cook myself was such a luxury.

"Glenn said to call them with questions and not pester you, and if I was good, they'd get me an autographed something when you leave."

I didn't mean to sound flip. I liked Glenn. They were the kind of smart, sassy, self-possessed person I'd want Maya to hang out with. Maya was too timid, too eager to please. I chalked it up to her being adopted, but a new thought made me pause with a fork-load of omelet halfway to my mouth.

Maybe she'd learned from me to be concerned about pleasing others, worried about what other people thought. She'd watched me trying to make her dad happy and never quite succeeding.

The delicious omelet tasted sour in my mouth.

"I'm not giving you an autographed anything," Kay said. "If you want to know what I do, I make movies. Part of my sequel is being filmed around here."

"Artesia is going to be in a film?"

He polished off his plate and leaned back in his chair with his coffee, still uncaring that he was sweaty and damp. I liked a guy who didn't mind being dirty.

"We're doing our studio work on a sound stage in Albuquerque. The film industry in New Mexico has been growing over the past few years. My art director came out here a few months ago and fell in love with the place."

A few months ago would have been before I arrived. "Loved Artesia? Why?"

He raised that brow at me again. "New Mexico? Land of Enchantment?"

I squirmed, but his teasing wasn't trying to make me feel stupid, like Ritchie had so often done. "I've heard the ads. I haven't seen much of the state yet."

"You should. It's incredibly varied here. You have the Chihuahuan desert, which we plan to use for our alien landscape. Then you have Lincoln National Forest, and Lake Brantley, and the Pecos, like you said. Drive a few hours and you have incredible mountains, drive past those and you have White Sands. All these completely different landscapes within a few miles of one another. We can do all our location work right here."

I didn't know anything about movies beyond the candy options our local theater offered with the kid's popcorn and soda. But Kay's grin made me feel like I'd swallowed sunlight.

"Don't forget Carlsbad Caverns," I said.

"I wish." He nodded. "But the National Park Service would never let us film inside the caves. They only allow outdoor, very low-impact filming. I checked. We might visit one day to get some ideas. My production team could whip up a cave in a few days if we wanted one."

"You should go to the Caverns because you can," I said. "Biggest cave in the Western Hemisphere, and one of the most unique limestone caves in the world? This time of year, you should be able to see the bats."

He lowered his eyelids as he studied me. "Have you been? You could come with us."

I let the invitation sit on the table a moment, afraid to touch in case it disappeared. This wasn't the practiced come-on I thought he'd been giving me last night. In fact, I was beginning to think his suggestions last night weren't a practiced come-on at all. They were something else—but I didn't know what.

"So, this film. You're the—?"

"Director."

"Oh." I tucked omelet into my mouth. "The guy in charge."

"I wish. The guy in charge is the producer, or in this case, a whole boardroom full of studio execs who want to tell me what's going to sell to their demographic. Even though they hired me to make the movie."

I could read his face this time. Irritation.

"So. Everyone is coming to Artesia to make this movie?" That would be good for the town's business. And Bernie had more rooms.

"The crew will bring the trailers and equipment next week, and the actors and their staff will come shortly after. I'm here to do some last scoping of the area before my DP shows up. He's wrapping filming in Vancouver right now."

"Ah." I nodded, but he saw through me.

"DP is director of photography." The smile deepened the crinkles around his eyes. "I can give you the crash course in Film 101 if you want."

"I'm happy buying a ticket and eating my popcorn. I don't want any of the magic to go away if I see behind the curtain."

He leaned forward. "You're not curious at all?"

I was intensely curious, but only about things having to do with him, not movies in general. And curiosity, as I well knew, was a dangerous game. I shrugged and reached for my mug.

He sipped his coffee. "You said something yesterday about that artificial stone being a look around here."

"Mm-hmm." I settled back in my chair, wrapping my hands around my mug. "It's unusual because the Spanish settlers used adobe, and the natives had mud and clay bricks. But the Anglos wanted the timber-framed houses they'd known from back East.

"Adobe brick making, there's a trick to it. The settlers couldn't get the right mix, so they fell back on cement. There's a dozen or so houses in town that have the original cast stone exterior, all on the Register of Historic Places. And there's a nice historic district you can walk through, with sculptures and such."

His eyes were as dark as his coffee, unreadable. "Care to show me?"

I choked on my coffee, surprised by a wide, rare burst of pleasure. Also alarm. "Don't you have, like, an entourage of people? And wouldn't you rate a tour by, I don't know, someone official?"

"I'd rather you show me. If you can get away from your work." He nodded toward my piles of dirt.

I'd be delighted to get away from my work and avoid spending the morning laying ground for designs that held no inspiration. But I needed to steer clear of this guy. He came from a world far different from mine. A world of make-believe, where women were preternaturally beautiful and people jumped to fulfill his every command.

Safer to stay on my side of the street, watching from afar for things I might want and would never have.

I stopped short. What was this sudden concern with safety?

I could, of course, stay here and be desolate Dale, licking the wounds of rejection, missing her daughter and wondering how I was ever going to haul myself back to the empty cavern my life in Hastings had become.

Or I could take a morning off to stroll through Artesia, a town I was genuinely coming to love, with the most interesting man I'd met in, oh, ever. Who made my heart skitter and my breath skip, but more than that, I liked him in a way I couldn't define. I liked his quiet steadiness, his flashes of dry humor, his awareness of the world around him. He might live in Hollywood, but he didn't have the ego. He did, however, possess a sensuality that kept derailing my train of thought.

If you want to dance, you gotta pay the band, my dad always said.

Desolate Dale could pay the band later. For now, I could be someone else. I was free of my marriage, free of my kid, and Hollywood had come calling.

I had to start figuring out who post-divorce Dale was sometime, and I could give her a brush-with-fame story to tell at cocktail parties, if I ever went to cocktail parties again.

I put down my mug. "Give me fifteen minutes to shower?"

"I need half an hour." He smiled. "Should I call my driver?"

"No, if I'm your guide, we do this the normal people way. I drive us downtown and park the car, and we walk like the other tourists. Bring water and a hat."

He lifted his coffee mug to hide his mouth, but the crinkles around his eyes gave him away. "Are you going to be this bossy the whole time?"

"You want to back out? Find a nice friendly local to hire?"

His eyes flared. "I want you."

My heart did a backflip before I grabbed it and told myself that didn't mean what it sounded like. I had the odd sense I'd dreamed this moment before. Kay in a damp bandana, morning sunlight gleaming in his dark hair, in causal scruff and sweaty running clothes, sitting across the patio table from me. Relaxed, yet with that alertness about him, the guard that was always up.

In dreams, you woke up before you hit the ground.

I smiled. "Then let's do this."

Chapter Four

I wished I dared a snap of Kay's expression when he came out the door of the B&B and saw me sitting in my Jeep. I'd chosen bright red, with removable top and doors, and customized rock rails for when I decided to veer off road.

I'd gotten the Ford Fiesta in the divorce, a car Ritchie had selected. As soon as the papers were signed, I gave it to Maya and bought my Rubicon. Plunging into the wilderness for backcountry camping or day-long hikes suddenly seemed like something I might want to do.

"I am currently reframing my opinion of accountants." Kay said, admiring my upgraded tires.

I grinned at him. "This is for landscaping work."

He'd traded the sleek, sophisticated linen look of yesterday for a pair of cargo shorts with multiple pockets and a pair of worn-in hiking sandals. His battered T-shirt bore a smiling chili pepper wearing a sombrero and the slogan Twisted Gringo Salsa Co. I laughed.

"Nice shirt."

"Thanks." He slung his metal canteen into the cupholder and lifted himself into the Jeep with an ease that made my insides flutter like the gills of a fish. Ritche complained that the Jeep was an embarrassment and a hazard. Kay just climbed in and buckled his seatbelt.

Then he took out his phone, and the gills deflated. He was going to spend the whole time on the phone with other people. He was a busy Hollywood type, after all. A *director*. Why had he asked *me* to take him around to look at locations? I didn't know anything about Artesia that he couldn't learn by asking around.

"We're leaving now," he said into the phone.

"Let me talk to Dale," Glenn demanded.

"No," Kay said, surprising me.

Glenn sighed. "You can do your job when I can do my job, Kay. Remember?"

"You can hook up to my Bluetooth," I told him.

He tapped at the phone screen, and Glenn's voice crackled from the speakers of my Jeep. "Hi, Dale."

"Hi, Glenn. How's the hotel?"

"Not as nice as your B&B. Kay got his morning coffee?"

"He didn't complain about it." Kay hung onto the overhead handle and stared out the window at the passing houses and buildings, muscle ticking beneath the stubble of his jaw. Interesting.

"But we're happy to try a different brand if he wants," I offered.

"He'll let me know," Glenn said briskly. "Okay, if you're out and about in public, there are a few rules. Ready?"

"Do I need to write this down? Is there something I need to sign?"

"We'll do the NDA later." I was joking, but Glenn wasn't. "For now. In public call him Golightly, don't call him Kay. Don't post any pictures to social media. Don't talk about him with your friends. I mean it, no hashtags, no livestreams, no selfies, nothing. Got it?"

"Is he under deep cover? In the witness protection program?" I slowed in the school zone, though the kids were behind the building, enjoying a noisy recess.

"We need to control the pre-movie buzz," Glenn said. "If anything leaks to the public, it can be a shit storm. People make entire careers of trying to tell fans what a movie will look like before it comes out. Kay doesn't want that, we don't want that, you don't want that. Right?"

"Right," I said meekly, stopping outside the hospital as an

ambulance, lights flashing, wheeled into the emergency room entrance. "And here I thought he just had to, you know, hide from the paparazzi."

"That's a whole different shit show," Glenn said. "The tabloids are dying to know about Kay's sex life. There are literally entire channels devoted to gossiping about him. TikTok, Insta, Snapchat—"

"Please stop," I said. "I won't do anything. I promise. No pictures. No leaking. In fact I can walk ten feet behind him and pretend I'm by myself."

Kay turned to look at me. "Don't do that."

"Your background check was clear, so I believe in you, Dale," Glenn said. "I'm checking your DMV records right now, okay?"

"Glenn did a background check on me," I stage-whispered to Kay.

He shrugged. "Studio rules."

"And now I have to make sure your license is valid," Glenn said. "Wow, not a single speeding ticket. Who's the other driver—Maya Rose?"

My heart clenched. "My daughter."

"Well, this vehicle record is squeaky clean. Okay, have fun, you crazy kids," Glenn chirped. "I'll have lunch ready at the hotel when you're done."

"We can get lunch on our own," Kay said.

"But Dale needs to sign the NDA, so might as well bring her here. See ya." Glenn hung up.

"Your movie requires an NDA?" I asked. "I thought that was, like, for corporate secrets."

"Same thing, according to the studio. Glenn's not kidding about leaks."

I drove past Eagle Draw Park, a long stretch of wooded greenery and walking trails, taking Kay on the scenic route. He looked out the window and I waited.

"How old is your daughter?"

I gripped the steering wheel. How I wished we could avoid this discussion. That I could just be fun Dale, with no baggage and no scars, strolling around historic Artesia with a Hollywood director, feeling great in my wrap front maxi dress that I'd chosen because it was cool, comfy, and casually dressy, a bright yellow cotton blend with a hibiscus floral print.

Too late for that.

"Maya's seventeen. She's in Switzerland right now with her dad."

He startled. "You're married?"

"Divorced," I said, knuckles turning white.

"Is he dying of cancer or some wasting disease?"

"Not to my knowledge." I blinked.

"Was he hiding all along that he's gay?"

I laughed despite myself. "No, he suddenly realized he wanted to be married to a pretty young blonde, not to me. Why do you ask?"

"I'm trying to figure out why a guy would leave you." He paused. "Do you still love him?"

"Wow. That's a bold question."

"Sorry. I like stories. And not superficial stories, the real ones with earthy grit and pain, the human drama and conflict and moments of triumph. That's what I do, you know. Tell stories."

"Well, my life would make a boring Netflix series. Cliched, garden-variety plot, man dumps wife after a long marriage, buys classic car, takes new wife to Europe." Leaving old wife groping to understand what she'd done wrong, and who the hell she even was anymore.

I pulled us round the corner, enjoying how well the Jeep handled. My vehicle was the only thing in my life that did exactly what I told it to, every time.

"I'd rather hear the story your movie is telling."

He tugged on a worn ballcap with the logo of the Las Vegas Aviators and slid on his mirrored sunglasses. "Did you see the movie *The Visitors?*"

I nosed the Jeep into a slot before the Artesia Historical Museum and Art Center. "Rings a bell, but don't be offended if I didn't see it. I don't watch many movies."

"Special-effects-heavy action movie in which a down-on-his-luck pilot defeats an alien invasion and gets the girl." He swung open the door and stepped out. "But the aliens managed to leave the beginnings of a colony behind, so now I get *Visitors 2*."

"And you are utterly thrilled about it."

"The script isn't terrible. But I'm in a battle with the producers to follow my vision for the film, which is more about a metaphor for global climate disaster and less about a way to CGI every inch of the screen."

He regarded the stone encasing the front of the museum. "This isn't the cast stone on your B&B."

"No, this is cobblestone. Hauled from a riverbed south of here. And I only know this because I visited this museum before. I wanted to get a sense of the place before I started on Bernie's yard. Make sure my designs fit with the vibe she wants."

"Same reason I'm here." He held the door for me, something I couldn't ever recall Ritchie doing.

We strolled through the exhibits on historic Artesia, the history of cattle ranching, assorted Indian artifacts, and the art gallery displaying fashions of the 1900s. I loved museums, even teeny ones, but Ritchie hated them. It was strange to have someone at my side, reading the signage with me. We lingered at the antique fire truck, as red as my Jeep.

"The everyday," Kay said. "That's what I want. The stuff that seems ordinary here, but that you can't find anywhere else."

The skin over my shoulders prickled at his words. We waved goodbye to Nancy, the volunteer docent, and as we headed up the street, I wondered if Kay would know everyday if it hit him in the face. Nothing about this guy was ordinary. Above average height, above average intelligence, and a masculinity that emanated from him the way the heat of the fall sun reflected off the pavement.

We paused before the Lukins House, a Queen Anne style encased in sand-colored cast stone. The yard was a sad, flat expanse of dead grass. At least the designs I'd shown Bernie were better than *this*.

"If you want out of the ordinary," I told Kay, "there's an elementary school in town that was designed to be a fallout shelter. It's completely underground. Though it's not open anymore, and I don't think they give tours, so—"

"Glenn can get me in." He palmed his phone and typed a quick message.

The utter confidence that his request would be granted—and his assistant would do the legwork—silenced me. Just how big was this guy? How far beyond my realm of normal was I right now?

We stopped before the Sallie Chisum Robert House, where the caretakers had put in a simple xeriscape with grey gravel and a few native shrubs, very low maintenance. I inspected the long-leaved palm, though I couldn't get excited about it. The yard I'd designed for Bernie would blend in with everyone else's.

"Now Sallie Chisum has a dramatic story," I told him. "They called her the First Lady of Artesia. She ran her uncle's ranch for a while, then came here and tried farming. She was known for her hospitality, and for helping orphans and women, so it makes sense the domestic violence shelter is next door."

Sallie Chisum had worked hard, made a mark, and left a legacy. I wondered what my legacy would be. Everything Dale Rose owned dissolved in my divorce. My landscape designs could be my legacy, little lasting oases of peace, nourishment, and serenity, if only I had the guts to build what I really wanted to build.

"And every man who visited her uncle's ranch fell in love with her." Kay read the screen of his phone.

"It helps when you're beautiful."

"You would know," he said.

There he went again with the comments that threw me off balance. Did he just naturally hit on women? I led us down Main Street toward the highway and the hotel, casting a nervous look over my shoulder at the car down the block.

"I don't want to alarm anyone, but there's someone following us. Silver Toyota Rav4 with tinted windows. And the driver is a lot bigger than Taiye."

Kay looked around. "Is he Black?"

"He *happens* to be Black," I bridled, "but I'm not worried *because* he's Black. I'm worried because he seems to be following you."

Kay broke into a grin. "Stand down, that's Madz. My driver."

"Madz?"

"Short for Madzinga. He's from Zimbabwe. He came to LA to be an actor but decided he'd rather be near movies than in them."

I strolled over to the Rav4, idling in the lot of the gas station. The driver's side window scrolled down, and a tall man flashed me a smile with a silver line of retainer crossing his teeth. He had a black boxed beard, no mustache, and a pair of gold studs in his ears. Was everyone who worked in and around movies supernaturally gorgeous?

I stuck out my hand. "Madz? I'm Dale. How's my driving?"

"You're doing fine." He laughed. His handshake was warm and firm.

"Want to join us?"

"Oh, no. Kay hates when I play bodyguard." His accent charmed me, a softness to his syllables and a different emphasis on the vowels. Despite the heat, he wore a black T-shirt and black leather jacket.

"Do you want something to drink? We're headed to the Fat Straw." I waved at the shop. "They do blends, boba, macchiato, whatever you want."

His eyes brightened. "They do a breve? Steamed half-and-half, not milk."

"Got it. Breve for Madz. Should we get something for Glenn?"

Madz's grin turned mischievous. "Yeah. The Love Potion. Coconut water and muddled strawberries."

I squinted at him. "Are you trying to get me in trouble?"

"They'll like it, I promise." He nodded to Kay. "Lunch at the hotel at one. I can drive you."

"We'll walk," Kay said.

Madz scrolled up the window, leaving an inch for air.

"So. Now you've met my entourage," Kay said as we crossed the street.

It struck me that, though I thought I was alone with Kay, we were being watched the whole time. How could a man seem lonely if he was never alone? "Are you one of those helpless Hollywood types who can't pour water from a tap all by themselves?"

He held open the door of the Fat Straw. It seemed a habit. I *was* in a different world.

"Those types don't last long in Hollywood," he said. "Don't worry, you're in. They love you."

Was he teasing? Or flirting? Either way, I felt self-conscious. "Unless I blow it at lunch."

"Something tells me you're not going to blow it," Kay said.

Women looked him over as we stood in line and ordered our drinks, but he appeared not to notice. He stood closer to me than a causal friend might, close enough that I felt his body heat like a stroke of his hand across my skin. I was really glad I'd worn a pretty dress.

We strolled along Main Street and paused before the larger-than-life bronze sculpture of Sallie Chisum reading a book to two young children. Kay pushed up his sunglasses to study it. Her bronze skirt flared as if blown by a breeze, but not a hair of her coiffure was out of place.

I'd heard somewhere that Sallie Chisum divorced two husbands. She ran a business, raised kids, helped her community, and survived a lifestyle not meant for the tender. Bet she never sat around feeling sorry for herself, sad, sobbing Sally.

A tug on my hand made me look over. Kay hovered above my straw. "Can I?"

Before I could think of a protest, he took a long slurp of my iced coffee.

"Hey." He'd done the same last night with my margarita. The gesture, so innocuous and yet possessive, made me splutter. "You— you— drink rustler."

He grinned. "I wanted to see what Vietnamese coffee tastes like. Regular coffee, as far as I can tell."

I stared at him, knocked over by that grin. The man was a wrecking ball. "Rude."

Wrapping his hand around mine, he leaned down to steal another sip. His eyes held mine. "Tell me to stop and I'll stop."

I didn't share my food. I didn't let people eat from my plate, and I didn't let people drink from my glass. The only person I would split a dish with was Maya. And yet Kay putting his mouth where my mouth was going to be didn't outrage or disgust me. It felt—

Like he was testing to see how far I'd let him venture into my territory.

He hadn't yet reached the line where I wanted him to stop.

The brown in his irises glowed with streaks of amber and jade green. His gaze made my throat close and my face heat. If I dipped my head, I could kiss his cheek. His dark stubble looked soft and his bronze skin even softer. I *wanted* to kiss him.

"I'm not still in love with my husband," I blurted.

He straightened and pulled his sunglasses over his eyes. The copulatory gaze was over.

I sipped my caramel cold brew to try to stop myself talking. "To answer your question from earlier." I clamped my lips over my straw, right where his lips had been. It was like I could feel him.

Kay stood silent, listening. The steady murmur of traffic held us apart from the rest of the world.

I turned and started walking. "I'm not bitter." Much. "I don't wish him harm. I did love him, for a long time, and he is always going to be in my life, because of Maya. But our marriage..." I paused, groping for the words I hadn't been able to frame before, not even for Bernie. "It feels like graduating college or leaving a job. It happened, I learned a lot, I gained some things and lost some things. And now that part of my life is over."

I gulped air, my chest expanding, understanding something I hadn't realized I felt. I was done with Ritchie. The separation gutted me and his falling for Lisa was a betrayal and I still hurt for the future I'd thought we'd have, but I didn't miss *him*.

Kay touched my arm, drawing me up short at the "Do Not Walk" sign.

"What's next?" He didn't sound flip or flirtatious, simply curious.

"That's what I have to figure out. Typical post-divorce narrative, I guess."

"Designing it as you go," he said. "Like your landscaping."

"Yeah, for sure." Another thing I didn't know how to navigate. It was time to bring the Dale Confesses All portion of the program to a close. "How about you? I'm guessing you're not a parent."

"Not a parent. Not an ex-husband, either." He contemplated his coffee. "My longest relationship is with my best friend from film school. And beyond that, my mom."

"There's nothing wrong with that," I said, but I read between the lines. He was one of those untamable men, a commitment phobe. A man who didn't want to be tied down. He'd be looking for a quick fling and then no contact after, no sexting, no nudes, no long distance. In, out, fun, done.

Maybe that was exactly what I needed right now.

We reached the Artesia Hotel and waited while Madz parked the car. The building's blocky aesthetic, like Cubist adobe, drew tourists, and the xeriscape harmonized well, large granite rocks standing among shrubs of native grass, with a few trees I thought might be aspen. The place looked fit for a Hollywood director: chic, sleek, and cool. But I wanted something warmer for Bernie's place. Inviting, relaxing, and luxurious.

"My first name is Timothy," he said.

I blinked. "But Glenn calls you Kay. Madz called you Kay. *You* told me to call you Kay."

"People who know me well do. But my first name is Timothy."

"Timothy Kay." He'd told me to address him how his friends addressed him. Even though I'd greeted him with a garden hose. The name rang bells of familiarity.

Which quickly turned to alarm. "Wait, Timothy Kay *Visitors*? That blockbuster alien invasion movie with Chris Stevens trying to look scruffy and that gorgeous little actress, Regan Forrester, in skintight—" I groped for words. "That was you?"

"I directed," he confirmed. "Or was listed as the director, anyway."

I stepped back. "That movie was everywhere last summer. I think I saw action figures in the toy aisle. You—you're *big*."

He frowned. "It's a job," he said. "And I got lucky."

"Okay, I need a minute to process." I forced a weak smile. "I see why you have an alias. Like all the really famous people." I took another step back, which unwisely put me in the pull-up lane where cars could appear any moment. "You know, I have a lot to get done today. I should go."

He stepped toward me, his hand twitching as if he meant to reach out but stopped himself. "Don't run," he said softly.

A warm breeze combed through the grasses and swirled around my calves, lifting my bright yellow skirt. The light draped a golden casing on everything, the building, the tamed rocks around us, his glowing skin. The sky above us deepened into a flawless blue dome, limitless. New Mexico was so beautiful it hurt my eyes.

Behind him stood another bronze sculpture of a horse rearing while a cowboy roped the legs of a downed steer, dancing just beyond the reach of its lethal horns. It felt significant, but what was I in this scenario—the frightened horse, the daring cowboy, or the steer about to be trussed and sent off to the beef market?

He waited for my answer. *Don't run.*

What was I afraid of? He wasn't inviting me into his life. He was inviting me to lunch.

Lunch with an A-list Hollywood director, while I was in this dress. What a brush-with-fame story. So far from depressed, dumped Dale.

"Okay." I moved toward him. The sky didn't crack and fall. The great stones set among the landscaping didn't tremble.

He smiled at me, and I saw the danger. I didn't even know what my new world looked like yet, but this man could pull that world off its axis.

Madz joined us, taller than he'd looked in the car, and we entered the lobby with its sleek, contemporary Southwestern look, crisp straight lines, and an accent wall the color of fired clay. It felt strange, like walking through a carnival exhibit of funhouse mirrors, to be with someone famous who looked, in his T-shirt and sunglasses, completely normal. We passed the restaurant, walls of adobe brown and upholstery in sunrise yellow, and Madz opened a door tucked at the end of the hall.

I hadn't suddenly entered Hollywood, just an average two-bedroom hotel suite. The desert colors harmonized well, the contemporary lines of the place were unobjectionable, but it didn't have half the character of Bernie's B&B.

"Hi, Dale." Glenn strode in from the patio and snapped off the women's soccer game playing on the TV. Today they were wearing a frilly white button-down blouse, black vest, and skinny black tie paired with tailored black men's trousers and the white high-top sneakers. "Have a fun morning?"

"You can leave on the game," Kay said.

"No distractions." Glenn pointed to the carryout containers from El Dorado stacked on the faux granite counter of the kitchenette. "Dale, I didn't know what you liked, so I got you three different dishes. Don't worry, Madz will take what you don't. Man eats for five."

Madz patted his belly and grinned. The black T-shirt was tight enough to suggest that the ridges on his stomach were from muscle, not fat.

"NDA's here." Glenn handed me a clipboard with a pen and a

stack of paper with tiny print. "Sorry, the Heads insist. And by heads I mean the studio and the executive producers who pay Kay's salary and therefore mine. Don't worry, we're not going to ask for your firstborn."

They grinned. "Speaking of firstborn. I checked Maya's Insta feed. Don't worry, not a weird stalker, just have to mark the boxes. Looks like the three of them went to see the waterfalls around St. Beatus Cave today, and tomorrow they're taking a cruise across Lake Thun." They held out their phone.

The waterfalls were gorgeous, cascades of lacy white foam plunging down rocky slopes lined with brilliant green. Maya wore the widest smile. Lisa's designer tank showed a great deal of cleavage, the effect aided by how tightly Ritchie held her around the waist. He'd grinned like in our wedding pictures. A long time ago.

I turned to my paperwork. Maya hadn't texted me yet today, but she'd had time to post pictures. I wouldn't scold. She was enjoying time with her dad, seeing new places. I was *not* going to be the mom who clung or pestered her to report to me.

Kay peered at Glenn's phone. "Looks like fun.".

Glenn moved to the counter and started plating entrees with a speed that made me suspect prior serving experience. "You can tell me to buzz off, but my wife and I are trying to adopt, so I have questions. Did you go to China to get her, or someplace else?"

"Maya was a private adoption," I said to my clipboard. "A friend of mine from college." Glenn waited for more, but I wasn't prepared to share. I'd sign the agreement not to say anything about their movie, but they didn't need to know everything about me.

"Dale's not going to tell you her life story in one sitting," Kay said. He wandered out to the patio and looked around.

Did he sense I was being guarded with him? But no more than he was. How long had it taken me to learn his real name?

Glenn marched a plate and cutlery outside to him. "A lot of US agencies only want hetero couples or singles. But I hear international is even harder."

I accepted my own plate and joined the others at the patio table, waiting for the weirdness of it all to hit me. I was dining with a famous director and his entourage. I was—

No, I realized as Glenn sorted out mini flautas and we all grabbed cups of salsa and queso, I was dining with a movie crew. Kay wasn't a celebrity to be pandered to; he was a man doing a job, and this was a working lunch. While I read the eight hundred pages of my NDA, or pretended to, Kay ate with the same dedication he'd shown at breakfast, while Glenn caught him up on what sounded like a hundred conversations from just that morning about production logistics. Glenn's phone buzzed continually with incoming notifications. So did Kay's, both of them vibrating in the center of the table. Madz agreed Artesia's artificial stone casings had the look of an alien colony hidden in the desert. They talked about filming locations, the dystopian sight of the Artesia skyline at night with the lights and steam from the tall cylinders of the Navajo Refinery, and whether the permit at filming in Lincoln National Forest would come through.

Kay included me, but the innuendos fell away. His gaze never lingered, and he didn't once steal from my plate.

Glenn included me, too, quizzing me on the history of Bernie's B&B (she'd run it for three years, since she retired from New Mexico State University), what security measures there were in place (cameras, I thought?), and who else was staying there (the construction worker who had the night shift and the writer we never saw). But they made it subtly clear that my play time with Timothy Kay was going to be limited.

"Kay's going to have his own trailer on the filming site," Glenn told me. "He might not be at his room when the days get long or there are night shots, but we'll still pay for the room."

"Thanks." I wouldn't fantasize about seeing more of Kay over the scheduled six weeks of his reservation. That was dangerous and silly.

We polished off the chips and queso, then Kay pushed away his plate.

"Book all the tours this week if you can," he said to Glenn. "Include Dale on the visit to Abo School."

"Does Dale *want* to go to Abo School?" Glenn bent over their phone, tapping rapidly.

Kay looked at me. My stomach turned over, and not because the enchiladas had been pleasantly spicy. "I'm curious," I admitted. "But I don't want to be in the way."

"You're not in the way," he said softly.

Glenn rose. "Dale, okay if Madz takes you back to your car? We've got a lot of work to do here." When Kay started to protest, Glenn narrowed a blue-eyed stare at him. "I'd rather hang out with Dale, too. But you have seventy thousand missed messages, a call with the producers this afternoon, and locations to nail down before Des gets here. Des is the DP," Glenn explained to me, taking Madz's plate. "Canadian by way of Bermuda. He's utterly brilliant and he makes Kay look good. I'll get you clearance to visit the set."

I was being shown the door, not rudely, but efficiently. The movie crew had work to do and the local sightseeing was done. I stood and smoothed the skirt of my dress.

"I'm okay walking back to the Jeep myself. You have your key," I said to Kay. "We'll leave the light on in case it's late."

"I won't be that late." He said this like I had any claim to his time. Any reason to know where he was, or why.

He had no claim on me, either, yet I hastened to inform him, "Well, I'll be leveling soil and laying landscape fabric. Watch out for the garden hose."

He smiled, eyes crinkling, and walked with me to the door of the suite. Glenn was busy inside the living room, yet I sensed their ears on us. "Will I see you later tonight?" he asked.

"I'm there most nights." All my nights, and now he knew exactly how boring I was. I slid on my sunglasses. "Thanks for lunch, Glenn. Nice meeting you, Madz. I'm sure I'll see you both again."

I hoped to. I hoped to see *him* again. Maybe tonight. Why did my toes curl at the very thought?

"I'll see you out." Glenn followed me out the door and closed it behind us. We walked together down the hallway toward the lobby of the hotel, dotted with people. There wasn't a special glow about walking with the employee of a famous person. No, the aura I'd sensed earlier was Timothy Kay, Director.

On the sidewalk outside the front foyer, Glenn turned to me. "Dale, you can tell me to buzz off again, but you should know. Kay doesn't do relationships."

"I—" I swallowed my denial that I had any interest in him. My interest was a cartoon sign flashing above my head, obvious to anyone. "I don't think either of us is going there." I was pulling myself together after my divorce. We inhabited different planets. There was no relationship budding here.

Glenn shrugged. "I just wanted to warn you. He's straight, as far as I can tell, but he doesn't date much, and he doesn't stick with them long. In all the time I've been with him, he's never had anything long-term. I don't want you to…" They hesitated.

Don't want you to be stupid. Don't want you to get your hopes up.

"Appreciate the heads up," I said, hoping the glasses hid enough of my face.

Glenn smiled. "You're a big girl. I like that about you. And I think that's why he likes you too."

I gave myself a stern talking-to as I walked through the historic district back to the museum and my Jeep. So I felt attraction. Big deal. I was a divorced woman who'd gone without touch for years before my marriage ended, broken by only two small incidents since then. Timothy Kay was extremely sexy. It was simple math.

With a sum of zero, anyway I looked at it. I might have invested in the rugged Jeep that could go into wilderness, but all the same I wasn't going to drive off a cliff. I wasn't going to be stupid like I'd been with Ritchie and ignore the red flags waving wildly before my eyes. I would be friendly, I would be relaxed and approachable, and

I would stuff the coils of desire into a sturdy clay pot and make sure the lid was shut tight.

Chapter Five

Kay didn't look like a hot Hollywood anything when he wandered into the backyard that evening. He looked tired.

Anahita and I sat on the porch, sipping cool drinks, watching the low-slung clouds catch the coppery glow of sunset and listening to the birdsong. She had her star charts, and I had a plant catalogue over my knees. I was daydreaming of Maya's grin, the enchanting drop of water from the caves of St. Beatus. I could put in a waterfall next to the cedar plank patio, structure a graceful trickle for Bev's guests to enjoy while they soaked in the sun or cooked at the grill. I could reuse the copper pipe and recycle water from Bev's cistern. I'd lose volume to evapotranspiration, but it was well documented that the sound of water soothed the sympathetic nervous system. A water feature would set Bernie's yard apart.

I had no idea *how* to build this, of course. But for reasons I couldn't explain, I hadn't spent the afternoon leveling beds and rolling out landscape fabric. I'd read up on subirrigation techniques, then canceled the order for decorative gravel and placed an order for a dozen fruit trees.

"Here comes your creeper," Ana whispered, checking that her hijab covered her hair. I'd told her who Kay was, hoping I wasn't violating the NDA I hadn't read. We'd spent our dinner, roasted quinoa piled with vegetables from my outdoor pots, speculating whether Bernie would have a future in the celebrity hosting niche, like they did in Taos.

As tall as I remembered, with darker scruff and shadows under his eyes, he stood a moment looking up into the cottonwood, head cocked toward the bubbling series of notes.

"Western kingbird?" he called.

"If you say so." I was still learning the New Mexico flora and fauna, but I loved that Kay knew birds. "He's been singing to us all evening."

Kay walked towards the porch, navigating my furrows of dirt and staggered holes.

"Still against using the front door?" I grinned at him.

"I wanted to see what you got done. Looks—interesting."

"If you find piles of dirt interesting. How was your afternoon?"

"I fought so many fires, I still smell like smoke." He faced the sunset with us, and I took the liberty of admiring his broad shoulders and sculpted body. He looked good for a man who worked a phone all day.

"All of them out?" I leaned my head back on my deck chair. I'd decided to reinstitute happy hour as a tradition, and I hoped I would always find people I felt happy with.

"One of my supporting actors wants a pay raise, the company providing our trailers is one short, the catering company is having staffing issues, and the actor playing my army general was allegedly involved in an episode of public intoxication, so I got a dozen calls about whether I intend to keep him on the movie." Kay folded his lean frame into the chair next to me. There were other chairs scattered around the patio, and a pretty stone bench flanked with my potted limes, but he sat next to me.

He was here. He'd spent the day working with his crew on his movie, and now he was here, where he wasn't a famous Hollywood director, just a regular guest at the Desert Bloom.

"Non-alcoholic spritzer?" I offered. "Or Taiye stocked us with a Brazilian beer that is named, weirdly, Ithaca, if you like dark beers. We also have Devassa. Or a nice tall glass of water tinted with lemon, if that's what you want."

He rolled his head toward me, massaging his neck. "Or the rest of your margarita?"

"What is it with you stealing people's drinks? I'll make you your own."

"How about you give me that one and make yourself fresh."

Our fingers brushed as I handed him my glass, and a warm flush raced across my collarbones. I made a show of sighing and stomping into the kitchen. In reality I wanted to stand next to his chair, my hand touching his, plugged into him like a car at an electric charging station.

He chatted with Anahita while I fixed the drinks. The sound of his voice sent a happy, alert hum running through my body. I reveled in the sensation. Pete the cowboy handyman had kindly demonstrated that I was still capable of having sex, which had been one of my chief fears when Ritchie left me, but I didn't find casual hookups much of a turn-on.

My response to Kay was dangerous. He was the first time I'd *wanted* a man again.

Though not just any man. Him.

"Time to assume my post." Ana gathered her scrolls of star measurements as I returned to my seat. "I'll be up front if you need me."

"Did Glenn feed you dinner?" I asked Kay.

He nodded. "More Mexican. I've missed southwest food, non-LA-style."

"If you want something else, let me know." I said it automatically, trained by years of mom mode to attend to dietary needs.

He raised those thick eyebrows of his. "And you'll make it for me?"

"I'll tell you where in town they serve it." I sipped my drink, stunned by the recognition of my freedom. With Ritchie divorcing me and Maya growing up, I'd been officially discharged from my full-time live-in position as maid, cook, and laundress for a man. I didn't have to take care of anyone but myself.

Too bad Pete had taught me that causal was disappointing. A short-term position as lover sounded good in theory. No strings, no commitments, no demands. No expectations but that I wildly enjoy myself, consequence-free.

With someone who wouldn't turn me inside out and then set fire to my remains, which I had a feeling Kay would do.

"Want to watch a movie?" he asked out of the blue.

I looked at him over my glass. "Don't you deal with movies all day?"

Those eye crinkles were going to kill me. "In my line of work, watching films is research. It's one of the fun parts of my job."

I sipped my drink, considering. Say yes, and I would get to spend more time with Kay.

No. I had to lock down my attraction for him. No foolish staring and sighing, no schoolgirl crush.

"I have washing up to do," I said. "And, to be honest, I think Glenn warned me off you."

He shot me a look, his brow furrowed. "What did they say?"

"That you don't do relationships."

His cheekbones stood out above the dark line of scruff. "As far as Glenn knows, I don't. I can see why they'd think I'd be a bad bet."

"Good thing for me, I'm not running back towards coupledom," I said, licking salt from the rim of my glass.

He watched me, or rather, my tongue. A splash of heat, not remotely connected to alcohol, bypassed my belly to pool somewhere deeper.

"I'm going to go occupy that incredibly long, incredibly comfortable looking couch in the sitting room," Kay said. "If someone wants to watch a movie with me, they can come in. If someone brings popcorn, I might let them pick the movie."

I dawdled in the kitchen, stacking the dishes, scrubbing the countertops, telling myself I should email Maya. Run my new ideas past Bev. I really ought to wash the dishes. Instead I pulled out popcorn and heated oil. A few minutes to pop a batch didn't give me enough time to line up all my very good reasons to steer clear of Timothy Kay. They kept slipping away as I reached for them.

Sure, divorcée Dale could go sit in her room. Daring, didn't-play-it-safe Dale could watch a movie with a hot Hollywood director. Who did I want to be?

He smiled and lifted his head when I stepped into the small, informal parlor with a tray full of popcorn and iced tea. He was scrolling through a menu of choices on the TV screen but sat up and removed his feet from the couch to the floor, leaving room for me to sit down.

"You're in the mood for Audrey Hepburn, I take it." I passed him a bamboo bowl full of popcorn. "I've never seen *Charade*."

"I was thinking *Unforgiven*," Kay said. "John Huston. Consistently ranked one of the best directors of the twentieth century."

"I don't think I'm in the mood for 1960s portrayals of white settlers valiantly fighting buckskin- and feather-wearing Indians whose land they stole." I settled into the extra-long couch. It *was* supremely comfortable, with deep cushions.

"But you're okay with 1960s gender roles." He watched with amusement as I tucked my feet beneath my knees, Anahita-style.

"As portrayed by Audrey Hepburn and Cary Grant? Yes. And no, I'm not turning in my feminist card." I passed him a glass of iced tea. "It's decaf. And you should know in advance that there is a ninety-nine percent chance I will fall asleep on the couch during the movie. Maya says it's like a trained response. It drives her nuts."

"I'll let you know if you snore." He tugged the string on the table lamp, dimming the lights as the opening credits rolled.

Alone together, in the shadows. A hot prickle crept along my neck and down my spine.

"What are you watching?" Ana poked her head around the door from the hallway, reminding me that we were not, in fact, alone. The frame filled with the wheels of a speeding train and, through them, the shape of a body tumbling from a train car. "Nope, never mind," she said and withdrew.

"You have to admit it's an interesting camera shot." Kay stirred his tea.

"And that shot really, really wants us to know that man is dead." The screen showed a closeup of a man's face frozen in surprise, fake blood smeared across his brow.

"Are you going to comment the entire time you're not asleep?"

"Yep. It's a gift honed over many years of practice, beginning with a lot of drunk late-night *Mystery Science Theater 3000* viewing during college." I handed him a napkin.

"I knew you were perfect," Kay said, munching popcorn.

I let that comment slide. Likely more offhand, reflexive flirting. Though he hadn't dropped a single innuendo in from of Glenn, or Madz, or Ana.

"I'm glad Anahita's not watching this," I said as the camera zoomed in on the barrel of a gun. "I thought this was a romantic comedy with—hey! Doesn't the little creep squirting her know that coat is Givenchy?"

"Audrey Hepburn made Givenchy, and he made her," Kay remarked. "You don't see those kind of collaborations these days."

"There are no Audrey Hepburns these days," I said. "Cary Grants, either. This dialogue is delightful." I grinned as the actress, wrapped in a hair scarf and enormous sunglasses, commanded Grant to stop blocking her view of the Swiss Alps.

"You remind me of her a little bit," Kay said.

I let my jaw drop, exaggerated. "Did you take out your contacts?"

"Dark hair," he said.

"And there the resemblance ends."

"Okay, so your face is a bit rounder—"

"And I don't have those cheekbones. Nobody in the world has those cheekbones."

"Your eyes have more green." He sat forward to inspect my irises. I stared back, mesmerized. "It's like there are emerald sunbursts in there." His breath moved over my cheek, and my breath snared in my throat.

He sat back. I swallowed hard and turned toward the screen. *Down, girl.* I'd said I wasn't going to act on the attraction. Remember?

"Now this shot," Kay said. "Of her walking through the empty apartment. You can tell exactly how she feels about her husband betraying her. And then she's in the shadow, waiting while she hears footsteps. Obvious, but it works."

Audrey Hepburn looked elegant and resigned as the jilted wife, while I'd looked fanatical and ungroomed. "But now Cary Grant is in shadow. So you don't know if he's come to help or if he's another menace."

"Oh, very good. Now Walter Matthau. Does the camera tell you to trust him or wonder?"

"Definitely a dodgy mustache. Don't trust him, Audrey," I called to the screen.

Kay laughed. I clutched my bowl to keep my hands on my side of the couch. He was nothing but temptation, that lean, warm body, that focus. Too much intensity for real life.

I shoved popcorn in my mouth. "I love how she's always eating. That's one thing we do have in common."

Kay handed over his bowl. "Any left to share?"

I refilled his bowl and passed it back. "Oh. Here we go with the iconic little black dress and pearls. And the old pass an orange to the person beside you without using your hands game. Terrific foreplay."

"There's a reason it's a classic," Kay said.

We both watched as Audrey Hepburn and Cary Grant shared the wide-eyed copulatory gaze that Kay had tried on me earlier that day. My body flushed, remembering his lips around my straw, the sun on his hair, his face so close to mine.

I cleared my throat. "Is she inviting him up to her hotel room? On the first date?" The characters climbed into a tiny elevator, the chemistry between them nearly crackling out of the TV. Or maybe that was me buzzing.

"Bet you'd let Cary Grant see your Pablita Velarde paintings," Kay said.

"Not on the first date."

Audrey batted her enormous eyelashes and cooed at Cary Grant.

"How is he possibly resisting her?" I demanded. "Even if he is also a villain out for her dead husband's money."

"Maybe he wants her to know who he is before he makes his move," Kay said. "He doesn't want to be a fantasy."

His remark stuck in my head as Cary Grant walked in on the villains and the twists of the movie proceeded. Kay lounged in a state of attentive relaxation, remarking on camera angles, lighting, closeups. I held my breath as the two leads enjoyed a romantic dinner cruise down the Seine. We laughed at the scene of Cary Grant taking a shower in his suit.

Kay didn't try to make a pass. He didn't try to touch me. He didn't have to. Everything about him thrilled me.

As the movie closed, everything tied up neatly, I sighed. "That hit every beat. Gorgeous settings, beautiful people, sparkling dialogue, romance heightened by danger and suspense, Audrey Hepburn in Givenchy. Why don't they make movies like that anymore?" I turned to face him.

He leaned forward, and my breath caught in my throat. "Because most of us want to explore new territory," he said. "Do something that hasn't been done yet." He stacked our popcorn bowls inside the larger bowl and stood. "Need help with the dishes?"

"Um, no. Because I am the staff, so washing up is my job, and you are the guest." I took the bowls from him and marched into the kitchen. I wasn't technically on the payroll; Bernie was letting me stay here for free in return for labor. I just needed a breather so my taut nerves could unfurl from ninety minutes of sustained arousal.

Recessed lights shone softly in the kitchen, reflecting on the quiet night outside the windows and doors. I flipped on the light above the kitchen sink. There weren't many dishes, but Timothy Kay, Hollywood director, tossed a dish towel over his shoulder and leaned against the counter, waiting.

The man looked good in any pose, but this I hadn't expected.

"What? A woman cooks for me, I help clean up. It's manners."

"All right. Well done, Mama Kay. You taught your boy well." I filled the sink with water from Bernie's new cistern, glad to find it clear and clean smelling. I squirted in biodegradable dish soap, curiosity getting the better of me. "So. Who's the last woman who cooked for you?"

A slight ripple went through his body. He cleared his throat. "Regan Forrester."

I froze over the dish cloth. "The actress? In your movie?"

"Ah, yes."

"Were you—did you…" Jerkily, I picked up a plate.

"It was just dinner." He looked relaxed but his vibe was alert, his gaze steady. "I heard she'd been attacked by her boyfriend, so I went by her apartment to make sure she was okay. She was cooking dinner and invited me in."

"So she was okay." I settled on that, since it was none of my business who he had dinner with.

"The boyfriend—ex-boyfriend—is currently in jail, and she'll come with the others to start filming next week."

"That was—nice of you. To check on her." I didn't know anything about Regan Forrester other than that she was a sultry raven-haired beauty with pouty lips, bedroom eyes, and a body made to model expensive lingerie. That was the kind of woman Timothy Kay had dinner with. Not women pushing forty who had crow's feet and curvy hips and grey hairs poking among the black.

"She'd already signed on for the sequel, so you could say I was checking on my investment."

I scowled at him, seeing through the ruse. "You were concerned for her."

He shrugged. "She was going through something at the time. She

63

seems back to her usual self, though."

I plunged my hands into the sudsy water, letting the heat give me strength.

"So. I imagine lots of women make you dinner."

"Not as many as you think. The women I meet are all part of the industry, and they get caught up in the life. It's easy to do."

"The life of the rich and famous, you mean?" I rinsed a dinner plate and handed it to him.

"The image-making. To be on camera you have to work really hard to look a certain way, and now, in the age of constant media attention, they have to curate their whole life according to an image. It's time-consuming, I imagine it's exhausting, and you never have something that's all to yourself."

I nodded. "I got worn out just dressing up and getting my hair done for office parties or events at Ritchie's firm."

I bit my lip. *Way to bring your ex into the picture, Dale.*

He put the dried dish on the shelf with the others. "The job can become your life and leave no time for anything else. I signed on for that—I did it to get where I am—but once *The Visitors* went big, I realized…"

He paused, looking out at my unfinished yard, where the leaves of the giant tree moved in the night wind beneath bright stars and the salt-white glow of the Navajo refinery.

"I want a life that my job is part of, not the other way around. I need to find more of a balance. So that might mean spending more time with people. Though I don't think I'm any good at it."

I smiled. "You passed today. I totally pegged you as socially competent. At times even charming. Except for when you keep stealing my drinks."

His smile was crooked, completely endearing. "You're different. You're not impressed by the job. I can leave it at the door."

I frowned. "I didn't know who you were. That's different from not caring."

His fingers brushed mine as I handed him another dripping plate.

"Can we go back to the part where I'm charming?"

I scrubbed hard at a pan. "Nope. I'm not feeding a giant Hollywood ego. Even if I am totally off-brand when it comes to your type of women."

He stepped close and braced his elbow on the shelf above our heads before dipping his head my way.

"I suppose you haven't noticed," he said, his breath brushing the hair above my ear, "that I'm having a hard time keeping my hands to myself."

It wasn't quite Cary Grant's line to Audrey Hepburn in the film, but I tingled all over, recalling their romantic float down the Seine, the couple's first smooch, how I'd tried so hard not to look at Kay as Audrey Hepburn declared she loved Cary Grant in all his guises.

I looked up at him, his eyes steady, all traces of green swallowed by the dark. "Who's the last woman you kissed?"

He winced. "Regan."

He'd kissed her. That gorgeous, shapely, young, every man's fantasy of a woman—

"It didn't go anywhere." He didn't need to explain, and yet he did. "For a minute she seemed like—the type of person I'm drawn to. But then she pulled out of it and was back to being Regan. You'll see when you meet her. She knows what she has to do, and she's up for the game. I don't like games."

"All games? Like, board games, or sport games, or games of strategy, or—"

"Are you going to kiss me or not?" The low rasp in his voice scraped my nerves to full awareness.

"It seems unwise. For a first date."

"We've had several dates. Breakfast, then walking around town, lunch, a movie—not to mention last night—"

"When I sprayed you with the hose?" I wrinkled my nose. "That wasn't a date."

"That was the meet cute."

"The what?" I busied my hands in the soapy water, scrubbing a plate I'd already cleaned.

"When the girl and the guy meet in a ridiculous way and it seems like they're not going to get along, but there is obvious chemistry. And then they're thrown together by circumstance, or he does something to get her help—like, he wants to learn about cast stone on houses. And she starts softening."

I flicked soap at his neck. I was too much of a mom to go for the eyes. "That is not what's happening here."

"And then they wash dishes together," he continued, taking the plate I thrust into his chest, "and she can't stop from wildly kissing him—"

"Good *night*, Kay. I suggest you head up to your room. Since I will be retiring to my room. Alone," I added when he opened his mouth.

He grinned. "You're right on script. He has to earn her attention. She doesn't just fall into his arms, overcome by his charm, or because he's a hot shot Hollywood director—"

"Good night, Mr. Golightly," I said loudly.

Still he watched me. He might as well have run his hands over my body, I felt his attention so keenly. "What about my truffles?"

"On your pillow. Anahita will have seen to it."

"What if she didn't?"

"For heaven's sake. Coffee and chocolate? Really?" I jerked open the cabinet door, grabbed three truffles out of the box, and slapped them into his hand, withdrawing my fingers as quickly as possible.

"Mmm. Peanut butter, bourbon, and blood orange," he said, examining the wrappers. "How will I decide which one I like best?" He unwrapped a chocolate, opened his mouth very wide, and chewed theatrically. I wanted to laugh, groan, and climb him like a beanstalk, all at the same time.

"Yep." He licked his finger, making a drawn-out gesture of it. "Found my favorite."

I sucked air through my teeth. "I'm going to bed now."

"Breakfast tomorrow?" he called as I turned my back.

"Cristina will make it, Taiye will serve. I will be working in the yard." I stomped out of the kitchen, and he followed.

"Glenn set up a tour of Abo School tomorrow. Will you come?"

In the vestibule, I turned to face him. "Glenn warned me off you."

That shrug, those eye crinkles. I could read him already. "I'm a big boy. I make my own decisions about who I want to spend time with."

"I'm busy." I pulled open the door to my wing, where the staff had their rooms.

"See you tomorrow, Dale," he said softly, and that husky voice slithered down my back, leaving little trails of fire as it went.

I needed to pull myself together, ground myself in reality. No losing my head over light flirting. I took a cold shower, distracting myself with thoughts of Bernie's cistern, how I could recapture this water and reroute it. Toweled off, sleeping attire on, and opened my laptop to read up on drip irrigation systems. Instead my search bar reflected "Timothy Kay."

There was no dirt on the man. No gossip or tabloid speculation, just a short, standard bio duplicated across several sites. Born in Las Vegas, raised by a single mom, graduated from a Las Vegas film school, worked his way up in Hollywood and won major awards with a visually gorgeous dystopian film about kids trying to reach a moon colony. The pictures were of two types, him at some charity event rubbing elbows with other powerhouse directors, Steven Spielberg, Ang Lee, Alfonso Cuaron, Seth Britten. Or him on the red carpet, lean and gorgeous in a black tux, sometimes alone, more often with a smoky brunette who'd obviously had work done. The captions identified her as Lana Kay, his mother.

One recent picture caught him on the red carpet with Regan Forrester tucked up beside him, smiling in a red dress, skin gleaming, hair perfect. His was the pat smile he always gave the camera, but he had a hand on her back. They looked good together, two exceedingly attractive people in expensive clothes.

That was the reality check I needed. What I didn't need was to go on Maya's socials and look at the pictures she'd posted. Yet I couldn't stop myself. That snap from Glenn had haunted me all day.

They were all having a great time. Nobody had the awkward look that said something was missing, that a gorgeous young blonde next to Ritchie felt strange or wrong.

I wouldn't have been in the picture anyway, if it were the three of us. I would have taken the picture, or been on one side of Maya, or in the background, a flash of calf or the back of my head. My husband's arm had fallen away a long time ago.

I closed my laptop and lay back in bed. *That* was who I was. I wasn't the ponytailed, Jeep-driving landscaper I pretended to be for Kay, the reason he was watching classic movies with me. I was the woman whose husband had lost interest, who couldn't afford to take her daughter on expensive trips and had to follow her social channels to see what she was doing. I was the woman who currently didn't have a home, staying in a friend's house to lick my wounds. I was a failure, I was a mess, and I was broken. Nobody could be drawn to that.

A-list Timothy Kay hung out with movie stars and dated actresses. He might flirt with me because I was around, but I had nothing to offer him, and we both knew that. I really didn't care to put myself in a position where yet another man had to kindly tell me I wasn't enough for him.

Chapter Six

I spent the night building up my defenses, mortaring together the solid reasons why I couldn't spend more time with Kay. On the yoga mat, I examined them in the red-bronze light of a New Mexico morning while the birds chirped and the cottonwood leaves swayed in the breeze. I knew who I was, the earthy woman who played in dirt all day, watching a lizard dart among the ceramic pots of the peppers, peas and beans, and a few late-season tomatoes I had growing along the patio. Timothy Kay was a star.

We were from different planets. I grew attached, I knew that. I grew suckers, roots, and vines. I was neither portable nor hardy. And he didn't do relationships. He told me, his assistant told me, the internet told me. Nothing lasting was going to grow in a bare few weeks of filming, and I would want more. I always did.

I wouldn't flirt. I wouldn't dangle. I wouldn't throw myself in his way and get run over.

Kay came up the slope from the gully, glistening with sweat, his shirt and shorts plastered to every muscled curve of a runner's body, and my reasons snapped like the anchor lines releasing one of those hot air balloons that frequented the New Mexico skies.

Yep, I was already in trouble. Time to make a full retreat to my little Dale burrow-hole and be wise, like that lizard, safe from being flattened. I knew how this equation worked out, and it ended with a negative value for Dale.

He touched my cottonwood tree as if in salute, then dropped into one of the teak patio chairs and chugged his water. He leaned his head against the chair and closed his eyes, soaking up the morning sun.

I restrained the impulse to cut short warrior pose and crawl into his lap. "Rough night?" I asked instead.

"Rough morning. My special effects makeup artist came down with a virus, and I was planning on starting with the alien colony scenes. Reorganizing the shooting schedule is a nightmare at this point. Bound to throw off the budget."

"Hmm." Must be nice to live in the Hollywood bubble where a nightmare was changing a few hundred work schedules and adding a couple million dollars to a budget. Whereas my idea of a nightmare, depending on the moment, was Maya getting sick while abroad, Maya getting abducted by criminals who would force her into a sex trafficking ring, Maya's boat capsizing in Lake Thun, Maya being stranded in the Alps.

He glanced at me with a half-smile. "I realize these are not real-world problems."

It unnerved me that he read my mind. I ended my sequence and joined him at the small table. "I'm sure it's not easy. You said the movie was big."

Here was where most men, my husband included, would fob off the invitation to talk. Ritchie would never show weakness or suggest he wasn't one hundred percent on top of something. If there was a problem, he would fix it. End of story. Kay looked thoughtfully into the leaves of the cottonwood.

"There are a thousand people I have hired or booked for this film. Probably fifteen hundred more on payroll once the visual effects are in."

"Wow. That is huge."

Wearing a cotton apron decorated with peach slices, Taiye set two coffee mugs before us and winked at me. I curled my fingers around the New Mexico peace sign on my coffee cup and tried to imagine how it must feel to have that many people depending on you. The only person depending on me was Maya, and she had both feet out of the nest already. She was on the front porch, ready to fly away. She might go all day today without texting me.

Taiye brought out two plates of huevos rancheros topped with sliced avocado and shredded cheese, and Kay tucked into his breakfast. "It's bizarre to think I did my first film with five people and a budget of forty thousand dollars. And now—I'm here."

"I want to see it." I wanted this peek into his mind. I wanted to know everything about him.

We talked about this, Dale.

His warm grin made eggs and salsa slide around in my belly. "I'll give you a private screening if you want. It was called *Inside*, about a couple of guys just out of college who realize the investment company they're working for is run by aliens trying to take over the world."

I bit into my tortilla. "Nice metaphor. Financial conquest."

"Yeah, it had a more psychological element to it than the *Visitors* franchise. My buddy Seth and I started working out the concept in film school. It went on national release and actually did okay. Opened doors, which I guess was the point." Finished, he pushed his plate aside.

"Was it?" I asked. "The point."

He looked closely at me, lifting the coffee mug to his lips. I would *not* stare at his mouth. "You're right," he said. "The point was to tell the story the best way I knew how, and to learn from doing it. Which is what happened. The success thing…it doesn't change the nature of the work, or the goal. It just means you get more attention, bigger budgets, and studio heads trying to make you tailor your story to their marketing demographics." He cradled his coffee. "You said you're an accountant?"

Back to me again. He was so curious about everything. I liked that about him.

I nibbled on a slice of perfectly ripe avocado. "I work at a credit union, specializing in small business loans. Helping dreams come true."

Kay's look of interest made my job suddenly sound cooler than it was. "You must hear a lot of stories."

I nodded. "Loan officers have to be personal therapists too. You need to make sure the person is committed, has the passion and resources to succeed. You have to be there with encouragement and direction when they meet obstacles. And you have to get them through every struggle—employee theft, bad landlords, regulations, tax codes. Then there's the inevitable family drama. Jealous relatives, resentful spouse, it all gets poured out on my desk."

I put down my fork. I'd loved my job. Then the kid from Omaha came in to streamline and wanted to turn me into a police officer, only focused on profit line, return on investment, timely payments. He rejected most of the loans I wanted to back. That was too many disappointed faces for me.

"Our jobs are alike in that respect," Kay said. "Everything drops in the director's lap. Rivalries, hurt feelings, harassment, sick days. I'd rather fight with producers over budget." He sat back. "I'm not very good with the people part, but I love their stories."

I dragged my last bit of tortilla through the salsa. "If you like stories, then you like people, I think. What I love about landscaping is finding the pieces to put in place to make the vision come true. I can take this space that seems dull or dead and bring it to life."

That's what I wanted to do with Bernie's yard. *Needed.* I needed to show her, myself, the world, that I could rebuild. Regenerate. Grow in new ways.

His gaze, careful and steady, touched each part of my face. "Bringing a vision to life. That's the part I love too."

His attention made me feel jumpy beneath my skin. I stacked his plate on mine. "Except you handle casts of thousands and are super famous and I—am not." Time to remember the very wide differences between us. Whatever connection I felt, it was illusory.

He rose and grabbed our napkins, following me into the kitchen where Taiye stood at the stove. Something moved in the dining room, where the guests were supposed to eat.

Kay thanked Taiye for the huevos—those manners again—then turned to me. "You're going with us to Abo School, right?"

Lockdown, Dale. I flapped a hand toward the tortured back yard. "I have a lot to do."

"I don't like small dark spaces, especially underground spaces," Kay said. "I need you to hold my hand."

I stared at him. There he went, hopping over my carefully structured defenses like a desert mule deer.

How did that brush-with-fame story end again? Oh, yeah, Dale hid in her room until the Hollywood hottie went away.

"Besides," he pressed, "I want to ride in the Jeep again. So much cooler than the Toyota."

His smile wiped away my risk calculations like an eraser board. This connection between us wasn't a Hollywood illusion. Whichever version of nowhere it was headed, it was real.

I could spend more time with Kay.

Daring Dale was going to get us all in trouble.

***

The Rav4 sat outside the sandy concrete block labeled Abo Elementary School and Fallout Shelter, parked next to a Nissan Leaf with the City of Artesia logo on the side. Madz and Glenn stood beneath a metal canopy, talking with a glossy young woman in a black sheath skirt, a white lace top buttoned over a white tank, and four-inch black heels. Madz wore the black leather jacket I suspected he wore everywhere, and Glenn wore a bright blue blazer and trousers with a bow tie and suspenders.

"Everyone else got fancy," I muttered, shutting off my engine. I'd grabbed a pair of dark red palazzo pants, a high neck tank top, and a pair of heeled sandals to try to bridge the height difference between Kay and me. Divorce had been good for my wardrobe in that I'd gotten rid of everything that was old, ragged, or reminded me of

Ritchie, and had to buy new.

Kay wore a battered pair of cargo shorts and a brown T-shirt with a screen print of a bison and the slogan Buffalo Soldiers 1866. I loved his scruffy tourist look and was starting to wonder if he was making an attempt to dress down or if this was him in everyday life.

The young woman from the city wasn't fooled. She made a beeline for him, reaching out a perfectly manicured hand.

"Mr. Kay. I'm Summer Reyes from community development. We're delighted that you're interested in one of our historic sites."

"Thanks for going to the trouble," Kay said.

"Oh, it's no trouble." She produced a historic-looking set of keys. "We have law enforcement officers in here every couple of weeks to train for school-shooter scenarios, so you'll see some of their equipment. Just step around."

She smiled at him. Her lips were gleaming red, her teeth gleaming white, her cheeks perfectly blushed, her brows perfectly shaped, the kind of flawless young woman with whom Kay would be daily surrounded. Her glance skimmed me as if she could tell my best effort involved off-the-shelf tinted moisturizer and luminizing powder because I had to fake my glow.

But I'd left dingy Dale at the Desert Bloom. I smiled at everyone. "Thanks for letting me tag along. This is my first fallout shelter."

"Mine too," said Madz.

"I love being a first." Kay's expression was unreadable behind the glasses, without the smile or the eye crinkles. My pulse kicked up.

"I already know I'm going to like this better than Carlsbad Caverns." Glenn took out their phone as Summer opened the door on a building that looked exactly what I imagined a Cold War-era bunker would look like.

"Abo Elementary School was built in 1962 and designed to function as a fallout shelter as well as the nation's first underground school." Summer launched into her speech. "With the White Sands Missile Range and Walker Air Force nearby, as well as the refinery, Artesia's citizens felt that they could be targeted in the event of a

Soviet nuclear missile launch."

"How did the students like being underground?" I asked.

"We'll get to that. This is one of three entrances. Note the construction: steel reinforced cast concrete walls. The twenty-one inch concrete slab of the roof—" She pointed to the canopy. "—was the playground. These doors are eighteen hundred pounds of steel, designed to withstand a thermonuclear blast."

"If people get inside in time," I murmured.

Summer glared at me, marking me out as the problem student. I straightened. I was the good girl, high grades, overachiever, the pleaser and the perfectionist. I was giving Summer, and Kay, the wrong read on me.

"The space was designed to shelter over two thousand people," Summer said as she stepped inside. "That's the decontamination shower. There's a freight elevator to bring in supplies. Emergency rations were kept in stock at all times, along with medicines. There's a generator for electrical power, a storage tank for fuel for the generator, and an air-conditioning system that could filter out radioactive particles."

She flipped a switch, and sets of lights punched down a broad stairwell and into the hall beyond, exactly like a creepy movie.

Kay moved close to me as the others moved ahead. "I'm guessing more than two thousand people lived in town at the time."

Timothy Kay wasn't a model student. His bio said he'd flunked out of two universities before he graduated from the Las Vegas Film School. He didn't care about good grades.

"Can you imagine being a student in class when the missile launches, and your family doesn't make it in in time?" I shuddered. "You're crammed in here with two thousand people you don't know, and you have no idea what happened to the people you love because you can't go above ground."

His eyes caught the light overhead, growing brighter as the bulbs warmed. "We should write that movie."

"I heard there was a morgue." Glenn looked around, taking

snapshots.

"Dale wants to know about the water supply," Kay said.

Summer looked at him with approval, ignoring me. "Great question. The school had an independent water system but during normal operations relied on municipal water and used the auxiliary system for the air conditioning."

"This isn't small or enclosed at all," I commented as we emerged into a long, broad hallway with wooden doors at regular intervals and scuffed laminate tile on the floor. "It looks like every other elementary school I've been in."

"The below-ground space is nearly thirty-four thousand square feet, covering ten acres." Summer rattled off the numbers. "A second hallway runs parallel to this, with eighteen of the twenty-eight rooms designated as classrooms. Let's step into this one and you can see the original blackboard."

"Original acoustical tile too." Kay pointed to the ceiling.

Summer beamed at him. "One of the praises sung of Abo was that it was very quiet. People felt the students could focus better without the distraction of outside windows."

"I'd miss the daylight," I said. "It has to be claustrophobic after a while."

"I'll hold your hand." Kay tangled his fingers through mine. I sucked in air.

"Parents tried to get their children into Abo," Summer continued. "For children with asthma, the increased air filtration proved beneficial. And despite the concerns about psychological impacts, educational experts concluded that Abo students performed as well as or better than their above ground counterparts."

"I'll bet they were just as naughty." Kay's breath stirred my hair against my neck. Sensation punched through me, like those lights powering on..

"When did it stop being a school?" Glenn backed into the hall with Summer and Madz following.

"In the mid-90s, maintenance costs were increasing, and the cost of asbestos removal would have been prohibitive, so the new elementary school was built next door." Summer's voice faded as they moved down the hallway. "It wasn't hard to get it listed on the National Register of Historic Places, because it's one-of-a-kind, and the original mechanical equipment is still in place."

"It's still spooky," I whispered to Kay.

"I'll bet it gets really dark underground. Turn off the light and see."

"You're just trying to get me alone in the dark."

"You bet I am."

His eyes held a challenge. He was luring me onto ground I knew was a minefield.

He smelled like bergamot and cedar, with just a hint of lemon. I flipped off the classroom light.

The lights were still on in the hallway, so the dark wasn't absolute. But we stood in deep shadow, and in the hush his breath caught. The air between us moved as he stepped closer, and I turned toward where I thought his mouth would be. His lips slid along my jaw, mine catching his ear, and my guilty giggle turned to a murmur of approval as he corrected and brought his mouth to mine, catching my lower lip between his. Time halted. The world stopped turning.

Now *this* was a kiss, like tasting Dungeness crab after knowing nothing but crab sticks. The texture, the heat of his mouth, his coaxing lips, my racing heart, all combined to make me dizzy. I dove my hands into his unbelievably soft hair and fell into a giddy spiral that went on and—

"Seven minutes are up, children," said the outline of Glenn in the doorway.

I dragged in breath and waited for him to leap away, for embarrassment to hurtle through me like the blast Abo was built to withstand.

Kay touched the back of my neck, thumb brushing my jaw, then sliding down my arm to catch my fingers once more.

I feigned interest in the rest of the tour, but my head replayed that kiss in full Technicolor glory. I wanted more of that, much more.

The tour wrapped, and Glenn sprung Kay's to-do list on him before the steel blast doors had closed behind us. We stood beneath the steel-reinforced concrete canopy, designed to protect from a nuclear missile, and I sensed that the others, all without trying to notice, were as intensely conscious of Kay's hand around mine as I was.

"I was going to take Dale to lunch." Kay squeezed my fingers. I was afraid the top of my head might float away like one of those hot air balloons.

"You've got a video call with set production to finalize some designs and a call after that with Hyun Ki to work out the animation timeline." I couldn't tell if Glenn had decided not to like me or was just nipping any distraction in the bud.

Kay turned to me. "Dinner, then?"

My hot-air balloon heart bobbed on another swell.

"Char needs your signoff on costumes, Glenn said. "I scheduled that call for tonight."

Kay walked me to my Jeep, and though I needed my hand to get my keys out of my purse, I didn't want to pull away first.

"Don't forget about me," he said.

I pulled myself into my seat—I'd removed the doors to please Kay—and the heat from my neoprene seat cover seared me back to reality. Nothing but a severe blow to the head was going to make me forget Kay. I wanted to kiss him all day, every day, forever.

So much for my careful defenses.

I slid on my sunglasses. "See you at the Desert Bloom, Mr. Golightly."

Then I drove away before the hot air balloon could come crashing down on all the sharp rocks below.

Chapter Seven

Kay returned while Ana and I were finishing a late dinner of chicken and rice. He walked into the kitchen like he belonged there, like the whole house was his and there weren't demarcated spaces for guests and staff. Like he was one of us.

"Survived your day," I said lightly.

He looked tired again. I wanted to slip my arms around him and kiss away the furrows on his forehead, rub the tension from the back of his neck.

I hadn't just thrown myself at him at Abo School. *He'd kissed me back.*

Ana slid off the stool to fix him a plate, but he shook his head. "I've eaten, thanks." He sat next to me and sipped my drink. "This is delicious. What is it?"

"Sharbat zafaran. Basically, saffron. It's Persian," Ana said.

He savored my drink, and I could summon no outrage. His big body was close and warm. He smelled faintly of pepper.

He turned on his stool to face me, his knees lightly brushing mine, and the hair on the back of my neck lifted.

I was in entirely new territory here. Exactly where I said I wouldn't go.

"I was thinking *To Catch a Thief* tonight," he said. "Hitchcock, Grace Kelley, your crush Cary Grant. It's more rom com than thriller, but I thought you could give me some notes."

The urge to touch him was unbearable, to run my fingers along his cheekbones and nose, test the texture of his growing scruff, trace the shape of his ear. I tucked my hands beneath my thighs, relieved to have an out.

"Normally I would never turn down Cary Grant, but Maya texted me to schedule a video call. She's getting up early to catch me."

He nodded, but I saw him realize that, if he were in my life for real, he could be ditched at any moment for Maya. She would always come first. She had always come first, even when I was married.

Maybe that's why I was divorced.

He wandered into the small parlor and clicked on the TV. "I'll be here if you want me."

Oh, I wanted him. That was the problem. I took a glass of water to my room and flipped open my laptop so I could soak in the face of my sleepy daughter and ooh and ahh over hundreds of pictures of Alpine scenery that she was exploring with my ex-husband and the woman he had chosen over me.

Timothy Kay might kiss me, but he would leave too. I was dispensable Dale.

"And today we have to go skiing." Maya sprawled on the tiny hideaway bed of their suite. Behind her, the sun rose over the mountainous lakes and darling Swiss architecture that I had only ever seen in commercials.

"Skiing in the Swiss Alps, boo hoo, poor you."

Maya made a face. She hated to ski and had ever since she fell on the breezeway at Mt. Crescent when she was five. Ritchie made her get up and continue all the way down the hill so she wouldn't be afraid of falling, he'd said. Maya had refused ever since then to put herself in a situation where falling on skis was possible.

I would have argued with him about making her go. Lisa never objected to anything Ritchie wanted. I could have told her that bending over backward to please him hadn't worked out for me, but she had the advantage of youth and blonde hair.

"And then tomorrow's Lausanne?" I wouldn't mention that I had mapped the metro system, pinned the police station, and had the numbers for both the US Embassy and the Bureau of Consular Affairs stored in my phone. I called this research, but Maya would call it micromanagement.

"And Dad will want to ski some more, and Lisa will want to shop, and no one will want to go to the cathedral or the art museums with me." Maya sighed. "Or take the train through wine country, which is my top pick."

I bit my lip before I said those would be my top picks too. I wasn't going to say a single thing that might sound judgmental or make Ritchie accuse me of playing favorites. I was mentally girding myself in case Maya decided to attend Hastings College after all and wanted to stay with Ritchie and Lisa in the house she'd grown up in, in her childhood bedroom. I would not take it as rejection from her either.

We hadn't ironed out a custody agreement, deciding Maya was old enough to decide for herself. But when I moved out, she more or less came with me. I was the one who helped her study for finals, research colleges, let her best friend stay on our couch when he fought with his parents. In fact he was at the apartment now, keeping my plants alive.

The top pick was my way of organizing family trips. Everyone chose the thing they most wanted to do, and then we tried to fit in everybody's top pick. Of course, my top pick usually shifted to make room for someone else's, like the two activities Ritchie couldn't choose among, or the three attractions that were a tie for Maya. I'd never resented this. It was simply what moms were expected to do.

But now, I could have my top pick all the time. In everything. A dizzying thought.

"So. Highlights so far?" I knew what my highlight of the day was, but that was something I couldn't tell my daughter.

She perked up. "Adam's parents filed for his legal name change, so he doesn't have to wait till nineteen."

I blew out a rush of air. "Maya. That's *huge*. I'll bet he's happy."

She nodded. "Yep. Now that his counselor cleared him for

medical transition, Adam's parents are coming around. They're even letting him start hormone therapy." She made a face. "Though they're making him pay for it."

"I'll have to raise his housesitting salary, then."

It hadn't been a surprise to me when, at age thirteen, Maya's best friend since their Toddler Tumbling days asked me to use the name Adam, not Adele, and refer to him with male pronouns. At fourteen, Adam with his pierced nose, flannel shirt, and buzz haircut had cried in my arms when his parents wouldn't get him puberty-blocking medications for fear that he was "going through a phase."

For all their high school dances, Maya and Adam had been each other's dates. One wall of my otherwise empty apartment was filled with eight-by-tens of Maya and Adam standing inside a plastic arbor or balloon arch, Adam in a tux and waistcoat that matched Maya's flowing, frothy dress, both of their grins a mile wide. They were the best of friends, and Adam was practically family.

At graduation, when Ritchie and Lisa handed me the invitation to their wedding and then said they had to cancel our dinner plans for an event in New York, Adam's parents let Maya and I crash their reservation at Odyssey. We dressed fancy, went out, and toasted the enormous changes in all our lives with mocktinis for the kids and vodka with extra olives for me.

I wondered if Ritchie had ever noticed when *I* changed, lost my sparkle, turned into dull Dale. Was that the reason he left?

"Have you talked to him?"

"Adam? Email only. He doesn't want to do calls until he's been on the testosterone longer." She hesitated. "I think he's worried I won't like him anymore."

"Are you worried?" I asked carefully.

"Heck, no. He's *Adam.* I love the big nerd."

"Well, you can tell Adam that I love him too. Especially since he's managed to keep my olive tree alive."

Maya laughed. "I miss you, Mom. Wish you were here."

"Pretty sure Lisa wouldn't appreciate that. Or your dad."

Maya sighed again. "I know we talked about this. You said to let new things grow. But I resent him. I can't help it. Everything is so different and—I liked how it was."

My heart contracted. Of course she liked how it was before, because our lives had centered around her. I'd made sure of that. Now her father was changing the dynamic.

With me, there was no question she was first. If I built a life with anyone else—if I tried to pursue another relationship—he would have to accept Maya at the center, not an accessory. And what guy would want that?

Especially, say, a Hollywood director accustomed to getting exactly what he wanted five minutes before he asked.

Still, I was jealously glad that she missed me. And grateful that she still needed me, even a little bit. If Maya liked Lisa better, like Ritchie did, it would end me.

I held out my arms. "Love you a billion."

"Love you a billion trillion. Bye, Mom." She blew a kiss at the screen.

The Desert Bloom was quiet when I closed my screen, but I was too worried to sleep, worried that Maya and her dad wouldn't be able to reconfigure their relationship, worried that I wouldn't be able to reconfigure me.

Also, like an adolescent with a crush, I was dying to see Kay.

I carried my glass to the kitchen as an excuse to peek. He was stretched out on the couch in the parlor, one hand tucked behind his head, the other holding the remote to his chest. Blue light flickered over his face, highlighting his cheekbones, the strong arch of brow and nose and jaw disguised by stubble. He was terrifyingly appealing. Without taking his gaze from the screen, he sat up and shifted his feet off the cushion, stretching out the arm with the remote, inviting me in.

I didn't have the sense to keep my distance. I crawled onto the couch beside him and then, when his arm came around me, rested my head on his shoulder.

He felt solid, warm, present. *Real,* for all that the simple fact of his being here was a fantasy, a detour from my real life.

"How's Switzerland?" His lips moved against my hair, and tingles raced to the base of my spine.

My normal reflex would be to say "Fine" and leave it at that. But Kay was *listening,* not going to fix or solve or tell me I was imagining things. He listened with his whole body, and he loved stories.

"Things are strained," I admitted, surprised I felt comfortable enough to confide in him. "I'm not sure she's hitting it off with Lisa. That's the new wife."

He stroked an index finger down my arm as if testing whether he were allowed to touch me. The little hairs from shoulder to wrist lifted into the air, trembling.

"People say divorce is easier when the kids are older, but I don't think it's ever easy," he said.

"How did your mom do it?" It wasn't a secret that he was raised by a single mom; it was right there in his internet bio.

His hand moved back up my arm. Tingles shot through my chest, like an experiment with electrical circuits.

"She didn't have much of a choice. It was be a single parent on her own, or be a single parent with a man who showed up when he was high or drunk or needed money."

"Are you in touch with him?" I dared to splay my fingers across his chest. Firm, warm muscle beneath the fabric of his T-shirt.

"No." His heartbeat was slow and steady, like the pendulum of a clock. This was a guy who didn't rile easily; he was still and deep. "My mom keeps in touch with him, though. He was exotic to her, Shoshone Indian, straight off the res, completely wild—this is how she tells it."

His finger paused at my shoulder and stroked the ends of my hair in its ponytail. The electrical current built. "They'd get high and be wild together. Then one day she came home from her waitressing job to find him passed out on the kitchen floor while I had a broken leg.

I was five. My grandmother had this enormous alamillo in her front yard—that's a—"

"Cottonwood." My heart thumped. A random connection, yet it felt meaningful.

"I wasn't supposed to climb it, and of course I did, and I fell, and my dad couldn't help me. Mom had to find someone with a car to take me to the hospital because she was afraid the ambulance would cost money." He shrugged. My body lifted with his. "That's when she kicked him out for good. Told him not to come back till he was straight. She got sober, my leg healed a quarter of an inch shorter than the other, and all the kids teased me because I didn't have a dad *and* I walked with a limp."

"I never noticed a limp." My heart squeezed for young Timothy Kay, hurt and scarred. No wonder he refused to let his emotions show to the world.

"So you turned out all right. And your mom seems great," I said. "She's got the red carpet nailed."

"You internet stalked me?"

"Of course. I investigate all our guests. It's due diligence."

That was an outrageous lie. I couldn't tell him the first thing about the writer. All I knew of the construction worker was that his wife and kids were still in Honduras, waiting for visas.

"Then you know the writer is working on a book based in Roswell, and he's already been in here to pitch me three different script ideas."

"Any of them good?"

"Not my kind of project," Kay said politely. "I told him to keep trying to get an agent. He was a little annoyed with me."

We watched the screen, its gorgeous backdrops, its beautiful people, and I was aware of nothing but Kay beside me. The fabric of the couch, normally so soft, prickled against my sensitized skin. Nothing in the internet bios said anything about Kay's father. He'd given me behind-the-scenes information.

"You know, Hollywood could use a lot more, and a lot better, indigenous representation. I'm just saying."

He shrugged again, his shoulder rolling against mine. "Sure, from someone who knows about or was raised in the culture. Not a Pretendian. I'm a Las Vegan all through."

"Pretendian." I muffled a snort. Maya made fun of my snorts. "I know what you mean. We're pretty sure that my mom's grandparents were Chickasaw, but to keep their home they had to pass for white. If anyone guessed, they'd be sent to the rez with the rest. My grandma remembers her parents talking about it, but she sensed it was a big secret. And then she married a white guy and had the house with the white picket fence and the two kids in Springfield, so I could say I'm one-quarter Chickasaw, but it only matters on a DNA test."

"Then you get it," Kay said, stroking my arm.

On screen Grace Kelley and Cary Grant fell into a passionate liplock. The heat between us was so thick in the air that I could feel it, like the moisture in the air after a summer monsoon. Every minute with Kay was another lure cast out, another fishhook lodged in my chest, slender and barbed.

"I forgot this movie is set in the French Riviera." I needed distraction. "Is this where Grace Kelley met Prince Rainier?"

"So legend has it. She wasn't impressed. But he eventually persuaded her to marry him."

"Real life fairy tale," I murmured.

Kay ran his fingers over my scalp. "Only works if you're a prince."

I widened my eyes at him. "Trust me. All *you* need to do is point."

His eyes were a smoky haze, shifting bars of gold in the deep brown. "Needs to be someone worth pointing at." His voice was low, scratchy. "And she has to want that too."

Did I want that? Him? I'd said I didn't, but I couldn't think of why when his mouth moved toward mine. I cupped his jaw to keep him close. He tasted of saffron and chili and essence of man. I hadn't imagined how good kissing him felt, and this time, no one would appear at the door. He wrapped his arms tight around me, hauling me against his body, and I slid my hands into his hair, stepping into a shadow world of heat and silk and whirlwind and the faint scent of ginger.

We swam to the surface at the same time. The way he met my stare made me burn hotter, brighter. He looked at me as if he too couldn't believe what sprang to life between us.

He looked at me like he'd been waiting for this—for me—for a long, long time.

"Are you going to put truffles on my pillow tonight?" His voice was a gravelly rasp.

Now I remembered why. I was in a fantasy realm here. When he returned to Hollywood and his real life, and I returned to mine, all these hooks he'd set in my heart would pull tight and then tear me open, and I would be destroyed Dale all over again.

Pete had proven I still knew how to have sex, which was nice of him, but we'd understood the terms of the hookup. This was different. Kay wanted something from me, and I didn't know what that was. I didn't know what *I* wanted, except not to run a knife through wounds that were just beginning to heal.

"I'm not ready," I whispered.

"You said you weren't on the rebound." He ran a finger above my eyebrow, then down my nose, tracing the lines of my face. Even that gentle, unassuming touch made my insides turn over.

"I'm not. When—if—I start something, it's going to be new." Not attempting a do-over or trying to rewrite Ritchie. I ran my thumb along the blurred line where his beard met smooth bronze skin. His lips were damp and warm, the pounding of his heart swift but steady. "I don't want to use you when you are so—*so*—delicious."

Light glowed in his eyes. "For the record, I am absolutely fine with being used, if that's how I get you."

A hookup. A holiday fling. A taste of the local color. That's all he wanted. He was in Artesia for six weeks, so why not explore?

I told myself to slide away, collect my dignity. Instead, my treacherous fingers curled into the hair at the nape of his neck.

"Can I still kiss you?" he murmured, leaning forward to brush my lips with his.

"It seems unfair. A tease."

He stroked his hand through my hair, setting my scalp on fire. "Tease me all you want, Dale. Do your worst."

I kissed him for an hour. Days. An infinity of mindless bliss, the same gleeful swirl of lust and delight. Tension coiled in him, the same way arousal clawed up inside me, but I could dance against the edge, knowing I wasn't brave enough to tip over. And then the exquisite agony when I came up for air, not knowing when, if ever, I might get to kiss him again.

"You," I panted, staring into his eyes, "are my top pick."

His smile was a slow curl, deep with promise. Sex with him, if I ever dared risk it, was going to blow my mind.

"I like being top pick," he said.

Chapter Eight

I told Kay I couldn't go to Carlsbad Caverns with him because I had a tree delivery scheduled, and because Pete was coming over to help me drive irrigation pipe.

It was the world's weakest excuse, and we both knew it.

Kay sipped his coffee while I relished Taiye's fluffy frittata with a mound of pico de gallo on the side. I hadn't even pretended an excuse to join Kay for breakfast, simply slid onto the patio chair across the table from him when yoga was done. The morning sky still held a trace of sunset, blood orange bands climbing to a scrim of blushing clouds.

"I wish I could help you drive irrigation pipe," he said over his coffee.

My cheeks went as hot as that rising sun. If Kay actually wanted me, for whatever reason and whatever duration, I was being a white-knuckled idiot for holding back so hard. How could the sting of ending a film-shoot fling possibly compare to the shame and humiliation of ending a two-decade-long relationship with my husband?

Timothy Kay couldn't actually want *me*. If a real-world guy like Ritchie had lost interest after getting the best of me, why would a walking fantasy like Kay look once?

Really? the little voice needled. *Ritchie got the best version? That was Dale living her best life?*

I choked down egg. I felt better at the Desert Bloom than I had in years, tanned and strong and sleeping as hard as a teenager. I was away from my desk, building something with my hands. I wasn't driving twice a day past the street to my old house, feeling the surreal sensation of trying to map a new route home into my brain.

After kissing Kay on the couch last night, I'd gone back to my Pablita Velarde room and researched designs for a water feature for Bernie. I had no idea where that new ambition came from, but I was determined to make it happen.

"I like your shirt," I told Kay. The sepia picture showed four Indian chiefs toting long rifles, beneath it the slogan "Homeland Security: Fighting Terrorism Since 1492."

"I don't buy 'em, I just wear 'em," he said, stealing the last bite of frittata from my plate.

I was dying to ask who bought him shirts with off brand humor. There was so much I wanted to know. Why he was just like Carlsbad Caverns, one part of him open to the public, dramatically gorgeous, beloved by millions, and the rest of him inaccessible, deep, intricate, and unexplored.

I rose when he did, and he leaned down and kissed me as naturally as if we did this all the time, as if he had every right to kiss me and I had every right to kiss him back.

***

Pete arrived an hour later, when I was sweaty, cursing, and losing the battle to wrestle the sections of irrigation pipe into the places I wanted them. Pete was tanned, rested, unshaven, and could pick up loads four times heavier than I could carry.

"So what's going on with you and Golightly? Ana said you're hooking up."

I yelped as I pinched my thumb between pipe. "No. That is not what's happening. I've been...helping out, looking after the guests." Which wasn't my job.

"Ana saw you snuggled on the couch last night, all cozy. And

Taiye saw a smooch this morning."

The shovel slipped from my hand and grazed my foot. Fortunately, I'd put on my steel-toed boots. "We're not hooking up."

"Well, why not?" Pete had brought his post hole digger, the old school clam-shell kind, and he strode with it toward the gully where my array of stakes and flags flapped in the breeze. "We had fun, didn't we?"

I was glad I was behind him so he couldn't see my face. Pete had been an experiment, arranged somewhat drunkenly on both sides, to see if I could have sex with someone not Ritchie. We had promised not to get weird afterward, and I had learned that sex with someone I wasn't attached to was even less satisfying than sex with someone who had lost interest years ago.

"I'm just saying." Pete shoved the clamshell into my starter hole, working loose the soil. "If you like him and he likes you, why not go for it?"

Because Kay was different. He called up some primal response in me, some drugging hypnosis I hadn't felt since my first crush when I was fourteen, when the captain of the math league had been able to obliterate my nervous system by just walking past me in the hall.

Kay wouldn't be a fling. I would fall for him, hard. There would be weirdness.

So why not fling myself over the cliff? Why not be like Wile E. Coyote in the cartoons my brother and I used to watch on Saturday mornings, take a shot at the thing I wanted, strap myself to that firecracker? Why not enjoy that exquisite, breathtaking feeling of falling, being suspended in midair for a brief, heart-stopping moment?

Because why rang the doorbell an hour later.

Taiye hollered that he was neck-deep in dishes and Cristina was upstairs cleaning Kay's room. I walked around the house to find a slim young woman standing on a porch amid a pile of luggage, clutching the strap of a vintage designer bag across her chest as if it were the only thing holding her together.

She wore ripped blue jeans and a loose button-down shirt with the tails tied to show a flat, coppery stretch of belly. Her black hair was pulled into a messy ponytail. When she lifted her sunglasses to look at me, then Pete, her intense green eyes stabbed me in the chest. She was beautiful in a way that seemed almost unearthly.

"Holy shit." Pete sounded like he'd been whacked by those emerald eyes too. "You're her."

"Yeah." Her laugh was breathy, nervous, her voice low and sexy. "Ah. Is, um, Mr. Golightly here?"

"Not right now," I said.

Her gorgeous face fell into a look of despair. "I thought he was here. He's not?"

"He's staying here, he's just out right now. What did you say your name was?"

I remembered what happened when Wile E. strapped himself to that firecracker. He ended up flattened at the bottom of an arroyo, burned to a crisp.

"Are you for real, Dale? You are in the presence—" Pete paused for effect. "—of *Maxim*'s sexiest woman alive. This is Regan Forrester."

***

"What are we supposed to do with her?" I hissed.

"Girl, you *look* at her. Just soak it up," Taiye said.

Pete didn't need to be told twice.

"It's rude to stare." But I couldn't help it. Regan Forrester, movie star, sat stretched out in the deck chair on Bernie's back porch, the chair that her ex or possibly still boyfriend Timothy Kay sat in during our evening chats. The sunglasses were back on her face but her sandals were off, revealing perfectly shaped feet with a flawless pedicure. Pete, Taiye, and I huddled among my piles of dirt, planning our strategy.

The noon sun beat down on the bandana I'd pulled over my hair to keep it out of my face and absorb the sweat. "Do we even have a room for her?"

Taiye nodded. "One left, the Helen Hardin room. It's fancy enough."

I liked that room and had chosen plants for it that complemented Hardin's paintings with their bold shapes and vibrant colors. She didn't want to share Kay's room, right? He'd said that their—whatever connection they'd had, captured in all its red-carpet glory—hadn't gone anywhere, hadn't he?

Why would any guy not want a woman who looked like this? And how could she, if she'd kissed Kay even once, walk away from him?

Well, she hadn't. She was here. Several days before shooting was scheduled to start.

"I know." Taiye snapped his fingers. "I'll make her an agua fresca. Dale, I'm using your pineapple."

"Not my—" I cut off my yelp. I might not know Hollywood, but the way Taiye and Pete were behaving, this tiny little stick of a girl was a name. "Are we sure she wants to stay here? Kay's entourage is at the Artesia Hotel, and they—"

The two men stared at me like I'd sprouted alien eyestalks on my head.

"She stays here," Pete said firmly. Taiye, mouth open, nodded hard.

Taiye brought her a sunshine-yellow drink in a tall frosty glass and flirted with the security of an openly gay man who adored beauty and knew his attention wouldn't be mistaken for sexual interest. Regan played along, but to me her smile was strained, tired.

Pete leaned on the post hole digger and stared. I had to kick the clam shell every time I needed to move him to a new spot. It was back to work for dusty Dale, back to the dirt of her real world.

"How long do you think she'll stay?" Pete wanted to know.

"They're scheduled to shoot on location here for six weeks, with an extra two weeks for the B-roll in case they need more footage.

Hand me that shovel."

Six weeks of Kay in proximity with this emerald-eyed girl. She wasn't just a standard beauty; she had some magnetic quality that was mesmerizing.

Kay had it too. It's how he'd pulled me in so quickly. There was no way these two incredibly beautiful, potent people wouldn't be drawn together.

I stabbed at a clump of soil with my shovel. I'd missed my chance with Kay, if I'd ever had one. Did I wish now I hadn't held back, caught up in my own agonies over rejection and looking like an idiot?

Yes. Yes, I did. But, on the other hand, Kay wouldn't be comparing me to Regan Forrester. So there was that small mercy.

"Look, I've got the digger right here," Pete said at my shoulder. "Or you want to keep skewering the ground, show it who's boss?"

"I'm ready to drive pipe." I wiped away sweat from my forehead. "Where's the mallet?"

I'd saved the copper pipe for the greenhouse and instead hunted up recycled HDPE plastic and reclaimed PVC pipes for my suddenly expanding ambitions, which Bernie had approved with delight in a late-night email. I'd decided to terrace the gully with native trees and shrubs, planting a grid of vertical cylinders with holes that would capture and release rainfall into the soil in a controlled drip, rather than washing down the dirt slope. Pete held the pipes while I pounded them into the ground, and the physical exertion was exactly what I needed. The manual labor cleared my mind and let me pummel my regrets, worries, and fears.

I'd never really had a shot with Kay. I knew he was a fantasy. *Whack.*

My daughter was moving into the adult phase of her life. I hoped our bond would hold, but she would choose her internship and then her school, and then she'd have a place of her own, and I would no longer be in her day-to-day life in the ways we'd known. *Whack.*

And Ritchie. The man I'd loved and been faithful to for twenty years, who'd hid that he was unhappy, who watched me shape myself into excruciating forms to try to please him, who'd cut loose and had a pretty and shapely new wife that he took to Europe, to places I'd love to visit but might never see. *Whack, whack, whack.*

"So I've got a thing for lunch," Pete said as I paused my swinging and wiped my forehead, realizing I was steaming hot. "But I'll come back and help you put the trees in this afternoon?"

"Fine." My arm dangled like a noodle, the mallet suddenly very heavy. I felt beat up. "I could use a break."

He strutted off, making sure the girl on the porch had time to take in the full effect of him: his muscled, compact body, cocky stride, the way his shoulders stretched at the worn T-shirt and the jeans outlined his lean hips and toned ass. Regan's expression didn't change behind the sunglasses, but her head turned to follow his swagger.

I headed toward the porch, smiling politely at our movie star guest. She pushed up her glasses and smiled back nervously.

"I think, um, he's making us lunch?" Regan pointed inside to the kitchen, then looked at the small table set for two with Bernie's best napkins, two colorful chargers, and a sweating pitcher of cold water flavored with lemon and mint, which was exactly what I wanted right now.

"For you. I won't bug you." She wasn't inviting me to join her. Or if she did, the invitation had to be a trap, like when the cool popular girl in middle school invited you to join her lunch table, only to make you sit in a splat of ketchup. I didn't get the vibe that Regan Forrester was a mean girl, but she was miles above me on the cool ladder.

She plucked at a string hanging from her jeans. "I feel weird eating alone."

"Um. Okay." She sounded so plaintive. "I'll just wash up."

Taiye bustled around the stove, wearing his favorite citrus apron. "You have to quit serving me like I'm a guest," I told him. "And we're a bed and breakfast, correct?"

"I like our rhythm. I provide the food and style. You do the chatting. I am not going to make our beautiful sad little movie star go out in town when she doesn't want to be seen." He handed me two vintage green stem glasses.

"How do you know she's sad?"

"My excellent intuition." He pointed the spatula toward the porch. "Go."

"You're sure you don't mind about this?" I asked Regan as I stepped through the doors. She did look sad, now that Taiye mentioned it.

She came to the table with a graceful saunter, a sinuous way of dropping into the chair. I supposed performers had to be aware of how they moved, how they spoke, how their every expression created an effect. Kay had something of the same studied manner. How much of him had I seen, and how much was the Hollywood persona?

That was the thing. Nothing about Kay said persona, and Regan dropped hers as Taiye brought out a steaming platter of golden-brown quesadillas. "And avocado salsa? Omigod, how did you know I love this?"

"So," I began, "did Kay know you were coming today? I find it hard to believe he'd go off to Carlsbad instead of staying here to meet you."

"Timothy?" Her hand froze with a scoop of salsa on a wedge of tortilla. I'd violated rule number one: don't give out his real name. "He—ah." She crammed the wedge in her mouth and chewed. "He didn't know I was coming early."

"That explains it." I took my own overlarge bite of tortilla. It was crisp and delicious. "Kay might forget something, but Glenn never would."

"Glenn?"

"His assistant. You haven't met?"

"No, Tamara handles all that. She's *my* assistant." Regan took another enormous bite. Either she had a healthy appetite, for all her tiny size, or she hadn't eaten in three days. "But she just started her honeymoon, and my manager's out of the country, and my mom's off on a spa retreat trip with her Sober Sisters. That's her recovery group. She's got this whole network she started in rehab."

Regan set down her wedge of quesadilla and stared at it. A spatter of tiny freckles dotted her nose. "And, um, my ex-boyfriend gets out of jail today. His sentence was commuted for good behavior, and because there was such a campaign of people saying I'd accused him unfairly and set him up. So, I didn't want to be in town and have every single reporter asking me how I felt about that."

My throat closed, and I worked to swallow my bite of food. "Kay said he'd attacked you."

She shrugged, as if this happened regularly. "He was, like, drugging my food because he knew I wanted to leave him. And after Beth—I mean, after I kicked him out of the apartment, he broke in and, um, I ended up in the emergency room, and he went to jail."

"Cripes," I croaked.

"Yeah." She forced a fake laugh. "Usually when I want out of town, I go visit Beth in Minnesota, but her husband just made partner in his law firm, so they're in Cancun." She inspected her plate, the bright colors of the salsa standing out against the fired pottery. "And I know filming doesn't start for a few more days, but it looked like Timothy was having so much fun here, I thought, why not? I've never been to New Mexico."

If Kay was in my life and I needed emotional support, I'd run to him too. He was the most solid man I'd met. "He'll be glad you're here."

Why was I trying to be supportive of my rival? I'd done the same with Lisa, actually stepping in when her wedding planner was overwhelmed and it was clear Lisa regarded me as the expert on all things Ritchie. What did I gain by helping the man I wanted to move along to the next best thing?

"Mmm, maybe?" Regan returned to her food. "He'll probably make me run my lines. He got so mad with me filming *Visitors* when

I'd get anxious and forget the script."

"I can't imagine Kay being mad at anyone. It's not easy to get under his skin."

She lifted her eyebrows. Dark black brows, distinctly angled at the outer edge. Even without makeup, she was perfect. "Then he's never been mad at you."

Warm quesadilla flopped over in my stomach. No, because I'd known the man for a few days. Yet he'd burrowed under my skin, fast and deep.

Now that this exquisite creature was at the Desert Bloom, my chatty breakfasts with Kay and our nights curled up watching movies on the couch would end.

I'd been a fool to think I could stop myself falling. I already had.

Regan watched me and widened her eyes. "We're not together. He told you that, right?"

I didn't have the power over my expression that she had, and now she knew my embarrassing secret. The landscaper falling for the man who ran the show.

"He said at some point there was, um, interest." Did I *want* to humiliate myself further?

"That wasn't me." Her ponytail swished over her shoulders as she shook her head. "I mean, um, there was some buzz for a while, but it fizzled." She grinned, and I was charmed despite myself. "He's all yours."

If only. I didn't have to respond to that, because Pete strolled up.

"How's the power lunch? Done yet?"

He smelled soapy fresh and wore a different battered T-shirt and worn jeans, but his sandy hair, still wet, looked like it had been tousled with a comb, and his light beard had been pruned back to stubble.

Regan leaned back with a smile I guessed was one of her masks. "Dale's really easy to talk to. She reminds me of my friend Beth." Her smile turned impish, the mask slipping. "Actually, I think my friend Timothy had a crush on Beth for a minute. And you two are a lot alike."

My lunch pirouetted in my belly instead of settling property. When Kay flirted with me, just the two of us, I could play along with the fantasy. In the light of day, with other people discussing what may or may not be between us—or with Glenn's cool eyes watching—I just seemed like a sad fangirl with no chance in hell.

It was nice to pretend for a minute that he was attracted to me. But sitting before me, with no effort at glamor or allure, was the kind of creature that Kay was surrounded with daily. And Pete's riveted stare was the reality check I needed.

"The delivery guy from Sun Country is here," Pete said. "Meet you out front?"

As he sauntered around the side of the house, Regan leaned to watch him. I shifted to allow her an unrestricted view.

"So, Pete?" She looked at me.

This girl talk I could do. "Available. *Very* available. He doesn't do serious, but he's a lot of fun."

She pursed her lips. "I wouldn't be…you and him?"

Damn it, this girl was perceptive. It was a little like sitting with Maya, who read me like a book. Or maybe I simply hadn't the slightest ability for mystery and allure.

I shook my head. "Nope."

She leaned back in her chair. "I'm always serious. Too serious. And I just kind of blew things up with my manager. We were on for a while, and then we tried again, and then she got mad at me and left for Europe, and…" She shrugged and let out a puff of air. "I hope she'll still be my manager. I really love her. But we are not going to make a power couple, sadly."

So she was available too, and she'd be working with Kay. He admitted he'd been interested in her, even if she didn't feel the same. What if those flickers returned in all those hours of him staring at her unearthly face?

"Pete's good with the recently rejected. I have to take this delivery." I stood.

Taiye came to take my plate from my hands. "You can't be done yet. I'm making cocadas for dessert."

"Those quesadillas were amazing," Regan gushed. "And I *love* cocadas. We ate them every day in Bahia."

Taiye fanned himself. "You know Bahia? You know my home. Where did you go? What did you see?"

And they were off, exchanging notes about places Regan had seen that Taiye knew well. I bowed out, envious that Regan had this connection with Taiye that I didn't, that she visited these places I would love but could never afford to see. New Mexico was exotic for me.

And the appearance of Kay's lead actress, this smoldering beauty, reminded me of what I'd forgotten, strolling around Artesia with a famous man on my arm. Hollywood was more exotic still, a land apart.

He lived there, and I lived here, and a very wide stretch of desert lay in between.

Chapter Nine

I'd finished laying hose for my brand new, spur-of-the-moment drip irrigation system when Maya texted me to set up a video chat. She'd had a miserable time on the ski slopes and a building catalogue of little slights and frustrations before that. Ritchie put Lisa first in everything. He thought Maya should be headed straight to college, not taking a gap year, and she should focus on something other than social work or music. I hadn't been able to detect this unease from the big grins on social media, and while I was relieved that she was finally confiding in me, I was increasingly anxious that her big trip would be a big fat disappointment.

I thought about calling Ritchie to ream him out. Of course he would try to please his new wife on their honeymoon, but I had warned him about this when he first proposed the trip. He couldn't make Maya feel like the afterthought, the third wheel; she was still his daughter.

But Ritchie had always been about pleasing Ritchie. It had been the prime directive of our life together. The only time I really overruled him was in adopting Maya.

"How's Adam?" I asked after she listed her woes.

She slouched, deflated even further, and pushed her long black hair out of her eyes. "His mom is ready to do family counseling while he transitions, but his dad isn't. Says he doesn't need some expert telling him how to treat his own kid." She gnawed a fingernail. "Should I be there, Mom? What if he needs me?"

"Did he ask you to come home?" Ritchie would throw a fit about the cost of changing the ticket if Maya wanted to cut her trip short.

I shook my head to clear it. I didn't have to worry about Ritchie's feelings anymore. I could focus on my daughter.

I could focus on *me*. The things I wanted.

"Adam told me to stay and have fun and spend as much of Dad's money as I can."

I laughed. "I'm with Adam. Enjoy what you can."

"I miss you so much, Mom." Maya sniffled. "I *really* wish you were here."

I tucked her into bed and closed my computer, then headed outside with a brick in my chest. Part of me wanted to fly straight to Switzerland and sweep Maya away. Her whole life I'd fought the urge to leap in a solve her problems for her. I worried she needed extra protection because she was adopted, because our town had so few Asian Americans, because she was slight and small and shy, because I needed to prove my worthiness and parenting abilities in a way that biological parents didn't.

But she was seventeen. She needed to be equipped to handle her own challenges. I was here to be backup but not her show runner, not anymore.

Pete leaned against the pillar of the arbor, thumbs in his pockets, chatting with Regan. The pose showed off his muscled length, and Regan seemed to be enjoying it. I wondered if I'd been as obvious, basking in the glow of Kay's attention. According to Taiye and Ana, I had been.

I dragged my big canvas bag full of compost toward my first tree hole, taking a deep breath. If I made a failure of her yard, I was wasting Bernie's time, money, and her trust in me. The compost, dark and crumbly, gave off the loamy scent of ready soil, promising loads of mineral nutrients and microorganisms to feed my trees. The scent shot to my brain, parting the clouds of worry. Everything else in my life was ass over teakettle, as my dad would say, but if I could do this one thing, build one place of refuge and comfort and nourishment, that would mean something.

I started with the desert willows I'd slated for the northern boundary. At full size, the trees would screen guests relaxing in the backyard but wouldn't grow so tall they'd hide Bernie's gorgeous house from view. As I grabbed the trowel to dig out the sides of my hole, something turned over in my brain.

Bernie had offered me this project of landscaping the Desert Bloom as an out when being passed over for promotion at work capped a truly exhausting string of months. But she was wiser than I thought, giving me an opportunity to grow something new. Now I didn't want to go back to my desk job, arranging numbers in different lines to try to please my boss. I wanted to play in the dirt.

But what if I wasn't good enough at that too? I was taking an awful risk on Bernie's dream, trying things well beyond my comfort zone. What if I crashed and burned again, piling yet another failure on top of all the others?

No wonder I'd clamped myself down around Kay. He was the

biggest risk of all. He made me feel alive in a way I hadn't felt in, oh, years.

And living things, like this slender sapling, could be killed.

Regan came to stand beside me as I slipped my utility knife out of my tool belt and started cutting slits in the root pouch of the first willow.

"Won't that, like, kill it?" she asked.

"No, this material is fabric that will degrade in the soil, but see how the roots are coming through already? The slits help the pouch break down so the roots can get established."

Pete came over, following Regan. "You need to trim the roots before you set it in."

"Nuh-uh. See how these branch outward?" I tweaked one strong but flexible root, touching the feathery fingers at its end, eager to anchor, feed, grow. "A root pouch avoids that girdled effect you get from a plastic container. These little babies will dig right in."

Regan dropped into a crouch. "I've never planted anything. Except lima beans in third grade."

I hooked my knife back in my belt. "It's the best feeling ever."

"Not *ever*," Pete said.

"Try it and see," I told Regan. "Here, take my gloves. I don't want Kay yelling at me because makeup has to redo your manicure. He's already bugged because his special effects supervisor is sick."

"Alex is sick?" The gloves hung off Regan's tiny hands. "I hope it's not serious. He's got, like, five kids."

I lifted the tree by its root pouch, focusing on my task. I'd needed that reminder that Regan knew Kay better than I did, that she was part of his world. And I wasn't. "Okay, hold it on this side. Now lower it into the hole. Yep, center it, just like that. Now hold the bole—that's the trunk, right here—and we'll fill in a good amount of compost, then backfill the hole with dirt."

Pete grabbed the shovel and flexed. I didn't blame him for showing off. The rich compost tumbled into the hole, showering me with that rich, abundant smell.

Pete held the top of the tree while I showed Regan the next steps. "We'll add more compost on top. Now tamp the soil—not too hard, you don't want to compact it, roots need some air. Only fill up to the root flare—that's right here. Now, put this stake in the ground, and we'll give our little guy some support while he roots in. It's really best if you can go without staking, but it gets windy here."

"I'll do that." Pete took the wooden stake from Regan and flexed some more as he drove it into the ground.

I tied a piece of hemp twine loosely around the tree and patted the slender trunk. "There you go, baby. Grow big and strong."

Regan sat on her heels, regarding the tiny tree with wonder. "That *did* feel great. It's amazing that you know how to do this, Dale. You're really good at it."

My chest felt strange, like there was extra air in it. I *could* do this. This could be my life. I could imagine ever bigger, bolder designs, and I could build them, brick by brick, tree by tree.

Regan was sweet underneath all that glossy beauty, and I could see what Kay liked about her. But he'd also said she knew the game, how to be a celebrity, how to fashion the image, how to exist under the lights and the constant watchful eyes. I didn't know that game. I didn't even understand the rules.

"I couldn't do what you do," I told her. "Act in front of a camera? It was hard enough standing up in front of people for math league."

"Yeah, well, it's just pretending. I *am* good at that." She clapped her hands. "I see more little trees in bags. Let's get going here."

We worked late into the afternoon, moving next to the hackberry for the corner where, once grown, its crown could blot out the spires of the Navajo refinery. I could envision the finished garden in my mind, an oasis of peaceful color that would shelter Bernie and her guests from the modern world and its grinding wheels of commerce. I explained pollination to Regan when we put in the two desert broom cherry and she helped with the pomegranate, figs, lemon and grapefruit, plums. She wanted to put my lime tree and apricot in the ground, too, but I was keeping them in containers so they could be brought onto the screened porch during the colder nights of winter.

Regan chatted and asked question after question, and by the time we got to the osage orange, meant to keep curious wildlife from wandering up from the gully, I realized Regan had pulled out the history of my marriage and divorce, Maya's childhood, and every stage of their trip through Europe so far. She was easy to talk to, for a larger-than-life movie star.

"I want kids," she said, patting the last trowel of compost around the root flare of the orange. "My ex didn't. And things get crazy with filming and promotion, right now I have to take the biggest projects I can. But once I'm established and have, you know, the right coparent, I want, like, six kids."

"Me too," Pete said. When we both stared at him, he grinned. "I grew up with a bunch of cousins. And now whenever one gets pregnant, the girls need to pop out another to keep up."

"Two at minimum." Regan stretched, arching like a kitten. "Six preferred."

A prickle moved over my skin, like someone had blown warm air onto the back of my neck. I looked up. Kay stood on the porch, staring at us. He looked at Pete, at Regan, then at me.

My breasts tingled. I rose, brushing dirt off my jeans, and my heart thumped as he stepped off the porch and started towards us.

"Kay's here." I tried to make my voice light. "You go say hi to him, Regan, and I'll water the trees."

Regan stripped off my gloves and ran a hand over her hair. "Does he look mad?"

Was she primping for Kay? Had she, at the very sight of him, decided she wanted him after all? Well, why wouldn't she?

"Kay doesn't do expressions," I said as he moved within earshot. "So I can't tell."

She stood and faced him. He looked back and forth between us, and I wished he wouldn't. The comparison couldn't do anything for me.

"Regan." I loved that deep, rich vibe of his voice. "I'm surprised to see you." He didn't look surprised. He looked his baseline, calm, steady, aloof.

Regan lifted her chin and chirped. "Hi, boss."

Pete twitched, like he couldn't stand her attention on another man. I pushed him. "Grab the garden hose for me." I needed something to do with my hands.

Kay's gaze flickered from me, my hand on Pete's arm, back to Regan. "You're early," he said. "Where are you staying? Glenn and Madz are at the hotel."

Glenn and Madz stood on the back porch talking with Taiye, who should have been off shift by now but had obviously stayed to snoop.

"Actually, um." Regan glanced at me. "I'm going to stay here. They have a room."

Kay narrowed his eyes. He didn't like this news, and I wondered why. Glenn had mentioned that Kay liked to sneak off alone, away from all the other movie people. Did he want to be alone, or did he want to smooch strange women out from under the eyes of his watchful entourage?

"Why?" he said, his gaze moving to me.

I might be up for more smooching. His mouth fit so well with mine, and he was so warm and solid in my arms. I wanted to kiss him right now with a longing so strong it ached.

"Um, this is a bed and breakfast?" I said. "We rent rooms for money."

"But *here*," Kay said, as if the Desert Bloom belonged to him.

"Well." Regan pushed her ponytail over her shoulder and shifted her stance. It was subtle, but the pose gapped her shirt to show her cleavage, an outthrust hip outlined in her jeans. "It just looked like you were having a great time. I needed a break."

Pete was drooling. Madz was staring. Kay let out a breath.

"Ah. Kevin gets out of jail today. Glenn said something about it."

She deflated, the provocative pose giving way to slumped shoulders. "Yeah."

I wanted to ask why she thought Kay was having a great time here. Had he called her? Did they talk? But I also wanted to hug her. She was a young woman who'd been abused and manipulated, and the man who'd hurt her was back in the world free to live his life, while she lived hers looking over her shoulder, wondering if he'd try to attack her again.

"She's welcome here," I said, doing my best to puzzle out Kay's forced calm. He was annoyed about something and determined not to let on, but I couldn't guess what it was.

"Des flew in today," Kay said. "Met us at the caverns, in fact."

"Des!" Regan charged toward the porch. I grabbed the hose from Pete before he dropped it and ran after her.

"Give me that." Kay reached for me. "You're not allowed."

"Excuse me, my trees need water." I held the spray nozzle like a shield.

"Show me." Kay smiled, and my heart gave a sharp kick, stealing my breath. I hadn't felt dizzy about a boy since the math league captain, whom I had adored with all the intensity that first-time adolescent hormones could produce.

I simply stood there while Kay plucked the hose out of my numb fingers. It wasn't his celebrity status that knocked me over. It was simply the man, the scent and shape of him, his dry humor, his quick intelligence, that slow sexy smile that made my insides turn to warm, sparkly mush.

"I want to see what you've done," he said.

All of his friends were on the porch, and he was with me. It all felt so normal and possible, even if the people on the porch were very beautiful.

I led him to each plant, and he showered the fresh dirt with exactly as much water as I instructed, the precious water drawn from our cistern. He wanted to know why I'd picked the trees I had, so I talked about bloom times, shape, shade, color. He made me explain the drip irrigation system I'd laid for the new beds and show me the irrigation pipe I'd pounded into the ground.

We ended at my hedge of desert willows, and he looked around. "I can see it, Dale. It's going to be incredible. Like nothing else around here."

"Regan helped," I blurted. *Why* was I trying to bring her between us? To test his reaction? "Girl's not afraid to get her hands dirty."

His eyelids lowered in that sleepy, sexy look that did me in. "I like a girl who can get her hands dirty."

I stepped backward, and he hooked a finger in the waistband of my jeans, coaxing me toward him. He cast aside the hose to put both hands on my hips. I battled the rush of instant heat, trying to stay steady on my feet.

"I wish you'd been with us today. You'd love the caverns. There's absolutely no way to describe them."

"I do want to see Carlsbad," I whispered, suddenly short on breath. But I didn't want to see them as part of an entourage. I wanted to wander them hand in hand with Kay and kiss him in the corners, like we had at Abo School.

Wasn't that what he was doing here, at the Desert Bloom, with me? Sneaking away from his entourage? Getting a taste of the real world, like the princess Audrey Hepburn played in *Roman Holiday* before he had to go back to being royalty?

I hitched in a breath as Kay lowered his lips into my hair. The bandana I'd tied to hold my hair back had slipped, and his hot breath against my sweaty curls lit me up from within.

"Dale." He pressed a kiss to my temple, then inhaled, like he was breathing me in. "I'm not into Regan."

I groped for a response. "Well, why not? Look at her."

He dropped a kiss on my cheekbone, then in front of my ear. "If you saw what I see—there's no comparison."

He moved his mouth over mine, and I rose to him like he was giving me air. We stood in the dirt of my freshly planted trees and he kissed me, and my defenses crumbled to dust. He pulled me against him, chest to chest, thigh to thigh, and I curled my hands into his T-shirt and clung. I leaned into his solid heat and kissed him like he was glorious new territory and I could map every inch of him with my mouth.

If this was the taste of the gritty real world that he wanted, then I was. All. In.

He lifted his head, his eyes glazed. It took a moment for the roaring in my head to subside.

I blinked and looked over his shoulder. Glenn looked irritated. Regan looked astonished, then gleeful. Pete jerked his chin and gave me a thumbs up.

Taiye fanned himself with his hand. "Girlfriend, take it to his *room*."

I hid in Kay's shoulder, and he quivered with laughter. "*You* turn around and face them," I muttered. How had I completely forgotten that everyone I knew in Artesia stood on the porch, in full view?

A new face stood with them, a tall man with thick black dreadlocks pulled back in a knot. A tight athletic T-shirt outlined every curve of a supremely muscled torso and dark brown arms, which below the sleeve of the shirt were covered in tattoos.

"Good to see you, Des." Regan stood with an arm slung around the newcomer.

"Who's Kay in the clinch with?" Des gave her a brief squeeze.

"That's Dale. She works here. We love her," Regan said.

"Then I need to meet Dale." Des munched on something wrapped in parchment paper—one of Taiye's cocadas. His deep voice held a trace of an accent. French Canadian, I guessed.

Kay gripped my hand firmly and brought me to the porch for introductions. I tried to be nonchalant. I was full of dirt from my hair to my boots, my jeans smelled like compost, and I had a lightweight flannel tied around my waist.

Des walked around to study my profile. "Kind of an Audrey Hepburn vibe," he remarked.

Kay looked smug. "That's what I said." Glenn rolled their eyes.

I agreed with Glenn. "There will never be another Audrey Hepburn."

"If I light and shoot you right." Des grinned. "Madz, my man." He held out a fist to bump Madz, then kissed Glenn on the cheek. "Miss me, Glenda?"

Glenn crossed their arms over their chest and scowled. "The ranger made us crawl down a chimney."

"Wow, you got the real tour," I said. So this was life for the special people: they got to go places regular people didn't. "Did you get to see the Lechuguilla cave? I heard it's not open to the public."

"The Big Room was impressive enough. That's our alien den." Kay nodded at Des.

"A few more crystals, dripping water," Des agreed. "We need to send those pics to Samira in Albuquerque so she can build that into our set."

"Enough shop talk." Regan clapped her hands. "Dancing. Dinner, first, then dancing." She looked at me. "There's a place here, right?"

"Um, maybe?" This was a town of ten thousand people, not LA with its thriving nightlife. "The Adobe Rose Restaurant has nice outdoor seating, and they might still be doing their concerts in the courtyard. We'd need reservations, though, and it's usually—"

"On it." Glenn already had the phone to their ear. "Hi, I'm looking for a table tonight? Party of..." They scanned the porch, taking a headcount.

Kay looked at me. "What about your friend? The girl who works here?"

"Anahita? She's at Apache Point observatory. It's her night on the big telescope."

"We all need a night on the big telescope," Des said to Kay.

Kay bit back a laugh, confirming my suspicion that there was some sort of continuous innuendo going between these two colleagues and friends.

"Eight it is," Glenn said. "Nice even number."

Me and the movie people. That did not compute. "I should probably stay here tonight. In case Maya calls or something. And I signed this nondisclosure agreement—"

"Don't say anything about the movie." Glenn tapped at their phone. "If someone asks you if you're in a relationship with Kay, you say no comment. If someone asks you about the movie, you're not in a position to know."

"But if someone asks if you're in a full-contact spit-swapping clinch with Kay, you can say, very recently—" Des cut off when Glenn punched his arm, not lightly.

"If anyone spills about this movie before filming has even started," Glenn growled.

Regan put on an innocent look. She pulled out every stop, big green eyes, tiny pout. "Look around. Who's going to care? Who's going to even recognize us?"

Pete hovered close to her shoulder. "And if anyone bothers you, I'll take 'em out."

Glenn checked their smart watch. "Our reservations are at nine. Music goes till midnight. Kay, you have calls booked all day tomorrow, so don't be hungover. Break for hair and makeup, everyone, and we'll have the cars ready to leave at quarter till."

"Break for hair and makeup," I muttered, feeling like I'd wandered backstage into a cast party.

Wasn't there some firm and clear line between the people like me and Pete, the real-life people, the landscapers and cowboys, and the people like Regan and Kay and Des the DP? They made the magic happen, created the illusions. We bought the ticket and munched our popcorn and then left the theater with a brief high, taking the exhilaration of fantasy back to our workday lives. For those who made the magic, where did the illusion end?

Kay traced a knuckle beneath my chin, and my knees about buckled. "Do you have a little red dress?" he asked.

"I thought it was supposed to be a little black dress. With pearls."

"Yes, if you want to get Glenn going." He grinned. "But I like red."

Regan popped up at my elbow. "Let me style you, Dale. You know how you're really good at planting things? I'm really good at *this*."

Like Dad said, I was going to have to pay the band eventually. Did I want to sit on the sidelines, or did I want to dance?

"I'm not sure I have anything red with me," I said.

Kay stepped back with a slow, not at all subtle wink. "I guess we'll see."

I led Regan to my room, heart pounding with fear and elation and a sudden certainty. It was too late to stop myself falling. All I could do was enjoy the exhilarating rush before I hit ground.

Chapter Ten

I sat in a candlelight glow at my favorite restaurant in Artesia with a table full of beautiful, hilarious people, and a Hollywood director sat in the seat beside, his arm across the back of my chair.

If this was an illusion, I didn't want it to end, ever.

"And for you, sir."

A black-clad young man hovered behind us. The Desert Bloom crowd had our own dedicated server and a secluded table, cordoned off behind the arbor at the end of the outdoor seating area. The potted trees glimmered with fairy lights, the band played a soft rumba, and mesquite smoke floated from the grill. I wondered if Glenn had dropped a hint or if someone recognized Regan. We'd gotten the best table, the best service, and lots of inquisitive looks, but the fairy arbor was as good as a bouncer announcing the VIP section, a special place for the exalted, and no one approached.

I'd never been seated in the VIP section before.

"I'll have what she's having." Kay flicked a finger toward my poco grande glass, blushing pomegranate red and sweating lightly in the heat, much like me.

"Chimayó cocktail? New Mexico specialty." The server approved.

"No, I mean, I'm sharing her drink."

"And the callouts to Nora Ephron movies?" I tried to give him a stern look, but all I felt was flirty.

Regan had rooted through my luggage and located the one just-in-case dress Bernie had coached me to buy from a local boutique, a soft navy midi dress with pleated skirt and flutter sleeves. Regan tore out the bodice insert to show my cleavage, picked out a scarf to cinch my waist, and unapologetically lifted a pair of heeled strappy sandals from Bernie's closet. She'd done up my hair in soft curls, slapped on makeup that made me look twenty-six, then strolled off to toss together her own look.

When she came out of her room in a solid sheath mini dress in deep cranberry, showing off every one of her knockout curves, I'd feared Kay was going to come to his senses. Instead, he'd tugged me into the Toyota with Madz and Glenn, whose evening look included a clip-on bow tie and an enormous pair of eyeglasses with rhinestones lining the black frames. At the table, he'd pulled out a chair for me.

He smiled, and out came those eye crinkles. The tension from earlier had dissolved. "You get points for that."

"For letting you steal my cocktail?"

"For Nora Ephron. My mom loves her movies."

"*I* love her movies," I said, wondering what it meant that I ranked with his mom. Did that put me out of the running for sexual interest?

He leaned forward to pick up my drink, brushing my shoulder with his. He had on the linen suit I'd hosed him down in, sophisticated and casually sexy, and his cologne made me light-headed, worse than the tequila. The candles on the table coaxed green-gold glints from his eyes as he watched me over the rim of my drink.

"I already said you were perfect." He set down the glass, his lips damp and red. "You don't need to add to the list."

Breathe, Dale. "That's against ordinance in some cities, you know." I took refuge in what I hoped passed as wit. "Drinking out of other peoples' glasses."

He settled back in his chair, keeping his arm draped over the ladder back of mine. "Personal rule," he said, his voice husky.

"Never pay for your own alcohol?"

He glanced around the group, but no one watched us. Regan and Des were sharing a story of filming the previous *Visitors* movie that had Pete and Madz in stiches, while Glenn and Taiye conferred over desserts for the table, the server nodding and offering input.

"My dad was an alcoholic," Kay said. "And my mom drank, or used to. So I don't plan to cave to genetics and develop an alcohol dependency."

Without thinking, I took his hand and brought it to my cheek. "So you steal drinks."

He lifted one shoulder in a shrug. "I don't keep alcohol in my house. I can only drink when I'm out, and when other people make it or order for me. And then I can only have one." His crooked smile made the warm, tight ball in my chest turn in circles, like an animal making its bed. "But I can sip from other peoples' drinks. If I don't mind their germs."

My eyes prickled in an alarming way. Suddenly his habit was less annoying. None of his internet profiles had mentioned his father or his relationship with alcohol. He wasn't a man who wore his vulnerabilities openly, yet once again he let me peek behind the curtain.

He trusted me. My heart squeezed.

"If you're sober, then you can keep track for me. I don't know if we've had one or two or three."

The drinks, like the food, kept appearing, and I kept moving them towards my mouth to keep from talking too much, asking too many questions, or commenting on the weather. When was the last time I'd been this fluttery on a date?

My twenty-second birthday, just out of college, when Ritche took me to the supper club for prime rib. He wore a tie, and I knew he'd slipped a velvet ring box in the pocket of his sport coat.

Nope, Ritchie didn't get to be on this date with me. I focused on Kay, on the growing scruff along his jaw, that skin the rich color of desert soil.

"I don't suppose you dance. That would make *you* perfect." I poked at the ice in my drink, embarrassed I'd let that slip. I didn't need to tell him he was checking all my boxes. It had to be obvious in the way I leaned toward him, falling into his gravitational pull.

He tilted his head. "I haven't danced since my mom made me take ballroom lessons with her when I was in college."

My heart melted at the thought of a young Kay, embarrassed but determined, showing up for his single mother. That loyalty in his character only made him more attractive.

He was *too* perfect. It had to be a trap. There had to be a sucker punch coming, like the one that had ended my marriage.

The drummer began an easy rumba rhythm, a languorous shake of the rattle and the steady click of the claves. I floated out of my chair, hoping I looked as graceful as Regan had at lunch, and held out my hand. "Time for a refresher."

I'd taken lessons a few years ago, one of the many hobbies I'd tried out to keep me from sitting home alone in front of the TV while Ritchie climbed the corporate ladder. Adam's mom had signed up with me, and we'd hashed out many a parenting struggle while learning to swing, cha-cha, and foxtrot over the floor.

It was very different to step into closed position with Kay. He cupped my left shoulder blade, a light pressure, and I raised my right hand. Our elbows brushed as he curled his fingers around mine. The key to rumba was eye contact, like most dances, like sex. *Not here, Dale. Just dancing.* I held his gaze with a challenge.

The guitar climbed in a flight of plaintive chords, and Kay counted softly under his breath, preparing me. Then he stepped forward, and I knew from the first slide of his hips that I would have to work to follow him. Match him.

One thing I'd learned from my marriage was how to follow. But Kay kept an easy box step, guiding me with his shoulders and a firm, easy grip that poured heat over my skin. My body followed his as naturally as if we'd rehearsed together a thousand times. We fit perfectly—a profound surprise and an obvious truth.

"Oh, very good, Dale." Taiye twirled Regan onto the floor and paused to correct my posture. "Relax your shoulders. Soft here." He poked my back. "And drop your knee to swing your hips. Get that Cuban twist. That's it, girl!" Then he swept Regan into a set of flashier steps, and I was glad no one would be watching Kay and me.

The world narrowed to his eyes, his body, his hands on me, the sensual swing of the music, the heat lingering in the desert evening, soft as silk on the skin. The air carried the sting of mesquite mingled with the fireweed and amaranth blooming in the lot next door. The chatter and laughter of the people around us receded to a quiet hum.

More drinks and more dancing followed, then a leap of flames and cheering as the server lit the platter of bananas foster and dashed in extra rum. My buzz didn't quell in the back of the car as Madz drove us to the Desert Bloom. I hummed like a nest of wasps as I stood in the dim hallway outside my room, peering up at Kay. My head didn't quite feel attached; in fact, every part of me felt light and indistinct, like I was a rough sketch of myself.

His face wove above me in the shadows. There had been reasons to steer clear of him, many reasons, hard and sharp as Pecos diamonds. They lay buried too deep to unearth. I was wrapped in a warm net of enchantment cast by Kay, and I didn't want it to end.

"Um. Do you want to see my Pablita Velarde paintings?"

His eyes flared, and he traced a finger from my temple to my jaw. "Yes," he whispered. "Yes, I absolutely do."

***

I woke, and for a minute I didn't know where I was.

That had happened only twice in my life. The first time, on my honeymoon, I woke up staring at the side of a snow-covered Crested Butte. I'd wanted to honeymoon at an all-inclusive resort somewhere south of the United States; Ritchie wanted to go skiing in Colorado.

The second world-tilting moment was opening my eyes to the dull beige wall of my bedroom in the apartment I found when Ritchie and I separated. I'd look around for a full puzzled minute until I remembered I didn't have a home anymore. The man I'd built a home with didn't want me, and since his parents had sold us his childhood home, I couldn't very well kick him out.

This was different. I felt like I was home. Safe. Comfortable. More content than I could recall being in years. Ah, Bernie's. There were the Pablita Velarde prints with their vivid shapes, bright orange and turquoise.

"Whoa." There was Kay, in my bed.

"Hi." He gave me a sleepy smile.

He looked rumpled and disarmingly adorable. Not the Hollywood powerhouse who dressed like a tourist but still projected an air of authority wherever he went. Not the man in charge having a power lunch. Not even my hot date of the night before. This was the man underneath it all, warm, solid, defenses down. A tight pressure knotted my chest.

"How long have you been watching me sleep?" I asked.

"Only long enough to be mildly creepy."

He rubbed a hand up my back and slid his fingers into my hair. I patted my hip and chest. Panties. Oversize cotton T-shirt that I usually slept in. The product had been brushed out of my hair and only the normal amount of morning goo clung to my eyelashes; I'd been functional enough last night to wash my face. I'd invited him to see the Pablita Velarde paintings. Had I let him see anything else?

The curtain fluttered at the window and bright sun gushed inside. I rolled to my side and threw an elbow over my face. "Light. Bright."

Sleepy, sexy Timothy Kay in my bed was too much to take in. The robin's egg-blue walls glowed with golden light. He smelled like sweat, bergamot, and agave. He propped himself on an elbow to watch me, and I peeked open an eye. He was wearing pants, but no shirt. I couldn't resist touching his chest. Firm, very warm, and smooth, the dark hairs soft as silk. I pressed my palm flat against the muscle.

His heartbeat was steady, but not slow.

Kay. In my bed. *Proceed carefully.*

"So. Ahem. About last night."

His naughty smile made my toes curl. "Trust me, Dale. If I put the moves on you, you'd remember."

I opened my other eye. "I like that confidence." I groaned and rubbed my throbbing forehead. "Three drinks shouldn't hit me this hard. Since you drank one of them."

I hadn't been thinking clearly, obviously, if I threw on my usual pajamas when I had invited Kay into my bed. Why hadn't I chosen something sexy? Did I *have* any sexy lingerie?

No. No, I didn't. And when the moment of truth arrived, and I had Kay alone in my bedroom, I'd panicked and dove for the unsexy shirt, retreating into my routine, to safer ground. Not yet ready to cross that oh, so shaky bridge.

He traced the faded Greek letters of my college music sorority, brushing my breast beneath. A tingling heat flared between my legs. He hadn't pressed or offered a word of disappointment. He had simply stretched out on my bed, held out an arm, and I crawled in.

He kept his gaze on my chest, the uneven rise and fall. He knew I was inching, step by slow, careful step, and he let me.

"So this is the Pablita Velarde room," he said.

For some reason I couldn't comprehend, this man was attracted to me. I felt the proof of it against my hip as I turned to look into his eyes.

"You know how to rumba," I said. "*And* samba."

"Thanks to Taiye for the tips. You're not too bad at the waltz."

He lifted a handful of my hair and let it fall through his fingers. I loved how he seemed fascinated by my hair. It wasn't anything astonishing, plain, dark brown locks, but his caress made my scalp tingle.

"You could use a little practice, though." The corners of his eyes crinkled. "With me."

Yes. And yes. That I remembered, swirling across the courtyard outside the Adobe Rose in Kay's arms like we were in a movie,

Strictly Ballroom or *La La Land*.

I tried sniffing my breath, wondering how bad it was, but Kay didn't care. He kissed me, his tongue sliding in my mouth, and my body turned molten. The throbbing in my head spread everywhere.

The fantasy narrative continued into the morning light, then. But it *was* a fantasy. Falling for Kay was very different from falling with him. One happened at a safe, impossible distance. The other—here he was, the reality of him invading my senses.

I'd lost myself to a man before, wanted him so much that I'd hidden and held back parts of myself to keep him.

Now, I finally had the chance to find myself, and I didn't want to throw it away.

I came up for air, and he stroked my back in a way that was soothing and arousing at the same time, as if he sensed that I wasn't ready. I lay in his arms a minute, not wanting to leave, yet too wary to take the next steps. My phone buzzed with a text. I used it as an excuse to scramble out of bed. Why was I not grabbing on to this man with both hands and my teeth?

I didn't have the answer to that question. I scooped up my phone, aware that in all his times with me, he'd never let his phone come between us, and he was way more important than I was.

The text was from Taiye. *Breakfast at 9. Go clean up.*

"Taiye is part machine," I said aloud. "He danced all night, he drank more than we did, and now he made us breakfast."

"He's younger than we are," Kay said, stretching his arms. I paused to admire the flex of muscle and delicious skin.

I pulled down my T-shirt so it covered my butt. "How old are you?" The internet bio didn't say.

"Thirty-six." He stretched his arms behind his head. "Thirty-seven in April. Aries," he added.

I shook off a twinge of—I wasn't sure what it was. Another fear that I wasn't right for him. "I'll be forty next month," I said.

He nodded. "Libra. I could tell."

"You could not." I went to my closet, where I'd only half

unpacked my bag. I didn't put the least stock in zodiac signs or astrology or anything that said we were ruled by forces outside ourselves.

"Social, shares well, likes gentleness and the outdoors, hates unfairness and cruelty."

I opened my mouth and stared at him. "Not all Libras are like me."

"Libra and Aries are very compatible." He linked his hands behind his head. "My mom's friend Naomi does readings. She told me when I was sixteen that when I fell in love it would be with a Libra."

"And did you?" I faced my closet, thoughts racing. He was thirty-six. Not so much younger than me, but that made me a cougar. And he lived in Hollywood, a place that worshipped youthful beauty. Thirty-six was a mature age for a man. He would have had life experiences. He would have fallen in love.

"I'll let you know," he said softly.

This man was going to wreck me. I was trying to talk myself into incredible sex that I knew would burn me to the ground and leave ashes, ruining me once and for all for other men, and he had to go and mention the L word. Another minefield.

Best run and hide from this discussion. I rummaged through my closet for my wide-legged capris, the most comfortable pants I had, and a loose blouse that I hoped would hide any bloating.

"Need help?" he called as I opened the door to the hall.

"You'd better get dressed or we'll eat all the breakfast before you get there."

The thrum of running water drifted from the bathroom, followed by a feminine squeal, then a giggle, then a low masculine chuckle.

I stepped back into my room. "Bathroom's occupied."

Kay rolled out of bed, rising to his full, glorious height. "Come use mine."

"You'll be using yours."

He raised his eyebrows wickedly. "I share."

Despite the offer, I showered alone, quickly, then brushed my hair while Kay cleaned up. I felt self-conscious entering the kitchen with him. I hadn't felt any reservations dancing in his arms last night, leaning close to him at dinner as he whispered in my ear, taking every opportunity to touch him. Yet in the bold light of day, with the full loaded ice cream sundae in front of me, complete with whipped cream and cherry on top, I couldn't bring myself to pick up the spoon.

It was too rich for me. Too *much*. It was too good for me, and I didn't deserve it.

How long had I had that voice in my head saying *you can't have this, so stop asking*?

I went to the counter and occupied myself with squeezing orange juice. I knew when that voice had arrived.

Regan entered with Pete right behind her, no more than a half inch of space between them. Pete had the look of a kid who had ridden the best roller coaster at the park and wanted to get back in line immediately. Regan wore a small, satisfied smile much different from her gloomy sadness yesterday. In a pair of cut-off jean shorts and faded T-shirt, her hair pulled up in a high messy bun, she could have passed for a regular person, save for the unmistakable slant of her cheekbones, famous lips, and glowing emerald eyes.

Kay eyeballed the espresso machine. "How does this produce my coffee?"

I snorted back a laugh and moved toward him, opening the cabinet with the coffee tins. "I'll make it."

He didn't step aside, instead letting my body brush his. "Feed me good coffee and I'm yours forever."

He said this in front of the entire room. Taiye, aproned at the stove, paused with lifted eyebrows in the middle of breaking an egg over the softly boiling water. Cristina, browning tortillas and stirring the cast iron skillet at the same time, stifled a giggle.

Regan slid into a chair at the dining table and leaned back against Pete's chest as he leapt into the chair beside her. Golden morning light poured through the glass doors and high windows. The plants I'd stashed along high shelves and above cabinets unfurled in the sun, as warm to the core as I felt. All my trees stood in their fresh holes, taking root. I looked around, staggered by a rush of pure contentment. After my divorce, I hadn't ever expected to experience that feeling again.

"So," I felt obliged to say. "We usually serve guests in the dining room?" It was currently empty, though I saw a placemat out. The writer must have eaten his breakfast and removed to the screened-in porch, where he seemed to spend most of his days on his tablet or his phone, not so much on his computer.

"I helped in the yard yesterday," Regan said. "I'm practically on the payroll."

Taiye placed a bright yellow mimosa in a champagne flute before her and she blew him a kiss. Pete laid a possessive hand over her shoulder, fingers nearly brushing the top of her breast. She didn't shrug him off.

"Nothing against Georgia O'Keeffe, but I like the light here," Kay said.

I handed him his mug of coffee, and he slid his fingers over mine. Pleasure curled through my belly. He took a seat at the table, then pulled out a chair for me.

"Cristina, let me help." I pulled plates from the cabinet and opened a drawer for napkins. She winked at me as she piled warmed tortillas in a wicker basket lined with a towel.

"You and Mr. Golightly having a good time together?" she whispered.

Another twinge of unease bit at me. I was forgetting to use his alias as Bernie had instructed. Glenn wasn't here; Madz had driven them and Des back to the Artesia Hotel sometime early this morning. The NDA I'd signed meant I couldn't share anything I knew about the movie, which wasn't much. But here I sat, having a lively breakfast with the director and his lead actress. Once again, I'd been invited to the popular table, allowed inside the enchanted circle.

It was a forbidden peek behind the scenes, but not the scenes of the movie. A peek into Kay's real life. The person he was when he woke up and showered and had breakfast and his all-important coffee. The person he was when he wasn't behind a camera or a screen.

Timothy Kay in real life had to be forbidden. At least for me.

I pasted a smile on my face and tried to be nonchalant about breakfasting with movie stars while Taiye served mimosas and he and Cristina sat down to breakfast. Taiye praised Kay for his samba and Pete teased Taiye about his disappointment that Des turned out to have beautiful wife he'd met in Kenya and brought home to Canada, and who was currently expecting their first child.

I tried to pretend I was fine, perfectly normal, when Kay's arm brushed against mine, or draped his wrist over the back of my chair and dangled his fingers against my shoulder, or met my eye as he cracked a joke and stroked the nape of my neck. I was a trembling bird ready to inch onto his finger.

Could I do this? Have a fling with this man, a casual, short-term, film-set fling, a holiday excursion before I had to return to my real life and continue putting together the pieces.

Nothing about being with Kay was going to be casual, not for me. I'd already been blown to smithereens once and was still picking up the pieces. Only a fool would put herself through that twice.

I didn't hear my cell phone until the ringtone escalated above the volume of chat. My heart dropped into my stomach and the rest of the room faded away when I saw the number, the plus sign and then a country code. The connection crackled and fizzed as one would expect from a call coming from the other side of the world.

I curled the phone in suddenly freezing fingers. "Maya?"

"Mom. I can't..." I could barely understand her through the heaving sobs. "I can't stay here another minute. Dad's being so horrible. I want to come home." Her wail set off sirens in my head, as had been the case since she was a baby. "Can I just come home, please?"

Chapter Eleven

The kitchen was silent when I ended the call. Kay's eyes held concern, and his outline backlit with the morning sun that had a moment ago been so innocent.

I took a moment to gather air into my lungs. "I have to fly to Switzerland. I have to bring Maya home."

He straightened. "What happened?"

"I don't know, but I've never heard her this worked up. I have to go get her. Excuse me." I looked around the table, ashamed I'd ruined the fun. "I have to book a flight, and my computer's in my room."

"Bring it out here." Kay took his phone out of his pocket.

"What?"

He pressed a button and held the phone to his ear with one hand, gesturing around the table with the other. "Two of us here have flown internationally quite recently. Maybe three?" He looked at Regan, who nodded, wide-eyed. "We'll help. Hey, Glenn?" He turned to the phone. "We need a flight from Switzerland to New Mexico. As soon as possible."

Something familiar and unknown bubbled in my chest. Panic, uncertainty, and surprise that Kay leapt in so confidently. This was my mess, my problem to solve.

"Who's Maya?" Regan whispered to Pete.

"Her daughter." Pete, Taiye, Cristina, and Kay all spoke at the same time.

"Whoa. Dale has a daughter? How old?" Regan sounded like she had a right to this information and was outraged that she had been denied it.

"Seventeen. I'll take care of it," I said weakly to Kay as chatter around the table took off. "I don't want to bother you. Or Glenn." The panic in my chest turned and twisted like a snake.

Regan sat up. "Oh yeah, there's the mom thing. Won't ask for help. Single parent?"

"Divorced," everyone else, including me, said at the same time.

Regan nodded. "Bring your computer out here. We'll get this done."

I fetched my laptop and brought it to the table while Cristina cleared plates and dishes to make a small workstation. Kay, Regan, and Taiye scrolled through their phones while Pete washed dishes at the sink.

"To Switzerland." I sank in my chair, reminding myself of the credit card I'd set aside for this purpose. "You said *from* Switzerland, but I need to go *to* Switzerland to pick her up."

His thumb flicked over his screen. "Glenn says the next flights anywhere near Switzerland are out of Seattle tomorrow or LA the next day. And they have massive layovers. You wouldn't get there until two, three days from now."

My mind raced in circles. I didn't know where my passport was, though I'd packed it. "That's too long."

"But there are flights out of Geneva all day," Taiye said, looking at his own phone.

I took a bracing swig of Kay's coffee. He didn't blink. "But that means she'll be traveling alone. I mean, she's seventeen. I'm sure she could do it. I trust her. It's just—"

"Other people you don't trust," Regan guessed.

I nodded miserably. "And it's not just because we watched *Taken*."

"Pierre Morel. Started as a cameraman," Kay said. "I wonder if— no, he's filming in the United Arab Emirates." He looked at Regan.

"Who do we know who might be in or around Europe right now?"

She leaned her elbows on the table. "Satya Verinsky?"

"The Hollywood producer?" Pete looked up from the dishwashing. "*The* Satya Verinsky?"

"I think Satya's in Thailand," Kay said. "I could call Seth."

Regan smoothed her hair. "Eve, my manager, is in Monaco. Let me give her a call." She paused. "Or, um, maybe you should call her," she said to Kay.

"I can't ask anyone to give up their vacation," I protested. Panic still twisted in my chest, but an odd, tight feeling grew around it. Everyone in this kitchen was on my side. Helping me. I didn't have to solve this all on my own. I had a team.

"She's at a film festival, I think?" Regan said. "Or some premiere. She's due back soon. She could swing by Geneva and meet your daughter there." She shrugged. "Can't hurt to ask."

Ask some powerful Hollywood type to take time out of their fantastically busy schedule to escort my daughter? The very idea was insane. And hadn't Regan said she'd recently broken up with her manager, romantically if not professionally? I wasn't sure that was a wise ask.

My flight search proved Glenn right. All the flights to Europe from anywhere within five hundred miles of Artesia were full. I'd have to drive to Seattle to get on a plane today or get to LA for a ridiculously early flight tomorrow. While Maya waited, frantic and miserable.

Regan stepped onto the porch to make her call. I heard "daughter" and "Switzerland" and "something going on with her and Timothy." A pause, while I strained every muscle in my head trying to listen. "No, for real. I think it's serious," Regan said. "Anyway, her name is Maya, and…"

Pete ran water to rinse, drowning out the rest of the conversation. Regan stepped through the open door to the porch and Kay put a hand on my arm as if to brace me.

"Eve can do it," Regan reported. "Her client is wrapping

interviews right now. She can fly to Geneva after and meet Maya there."

"Glenn found seats on a flight leaving Geneva tonight," Kay said, examining his phone. "Stops in London and Dallas, arriving in Albuquerque. She could be here by noon tomorrow."

"Okay, Albuquerque. That's about four hours away, right? I can pick her up there." I had gas in the Jeep.

"Madz can take you," Kay said. "Or we can have someone bring her here. Artesia has a municipal airport, doesn't it? I know a guy in Albuquerque who's a private pilot." He tapped his phone again. "I'll see what I can do."

My mind spun with how fast all this was happening, and what was possible when you were super rich and knew people everywhere. Part of me felt frantic that I wasn't in full control, and part of me was euphoric. My desperate daughter, stranded half a world away, could be in my arms this time tomorrow.

"What's Eve's last name?" I asked Regan while typing new info into my flight search.

"Adesina, and you'll have to go first class. Eve does *not* fly coach."

"I'll pay the difference," Kay said at once.

"I got it," I said coolly, and kept my poker face while I booked a first-class ticket for Maya. What a story this would make later. It was worth any amount to make sure my daughter got home, if that's where she wanted to be. I seethed with the need to call Ritchie and chew him out, but Maya was the priority here. I wanted her side of the story first.

After the flight site confirmed my credit card would be charged a year's worth of rent, I opened a new tab and searched Eve Adesina. The images stunned me, quadrupling my guilt. Regan's manager was gorgeous and had the effortlessly glamorous celebrity look nailed.

"I can't believe I'm asking a complete stranger to fly home with my daughter," I said. "But also, Maya is going to be so excited to be traveling with a Hollywood powerhouse who looks like Beyoncé with a bronde balayage."

"A what what?" Pete asked.

"Hair, honey, and trust me, you like it," Taiye said. "Now, I know our Maya is a tiny little thing, but where are we going to put her?"

I blanked. I couldn't afford a hotel room for a week or more, and I couldn't ask Bernie to put up my daughter for free, but I didn't want to leave without finishing my landscaping project.

I didn't want to leave Kay.

"She can have my room," Pete said off-handedly.

Regan whipped her head around. "You're moving out?"

"I have an apartment outside town. I only crash here sometimes." He put the last plate in the drying rack and winked at her. "I'm sure I can find someplace to sleep."

Regan curled a lock of wavy black hair around a finger and made a small humming noise.

"Thanks," I said, my voice quivering. "I'll make sure it's okay with Bernie. And it's only until I finish her yard."

"And then what?" Kay looked relaxed, but I could tell he was alert.

I stared at my computer screen. "Back to Hastings, I guess." To the town with the job I no longer wanted, the apartment that had never felt like a home, the house I'd spent twenty years of my life in, and the husband who had divorced me.

This—Bernie's bed and breakfast in this tiny town in New Mexico—was the first place I'd felt sheltered. Felt safe.

And now it held Kay.

THANK YOU MOM. Maya's text buzzed through, followed by heart-eye, crying, and hugging emojis.

I'll video call in a minute, I texted back, then closed my computer. "I've got some calls to make," I said to Kay.

He nodded. "Me too. Meet you here later?"

The panic withdrew into a coiled snake, leaving the warm mushy thing to flip-flop in my chest. He was planning his day to include me.

"I'll be here," I said. "Playing in the dirt."

He leaned forward and brushed a kiss across my forehead. It was a sweet, chaste kiss, and I still wanted to grab his face and suck his tongue into my mouth.

"Don't work too hard and finish your project too quickly," he said.

I touched my lips, lost. He'd seen me freak out, he'd called in his troops, and he'd solved my problem in the span of half an hour, keeping his cool the whole time. This was not a man I had to guard myself around for fear he couldn't deal with my emotions. He stayed steady while I flipped out.

Maybe I could trust he was steady about other things, too.

Madz came to collect Kay, and I took my computer to my room, that strange flutter lingering in my chest. In less than a day, Maya would be here and mom duties would resume. The fantasy escape would end.

I had one more night with Kay.

***

On my computer screen Maya sat curled up on her bed in the ski lodge, packed luggage staggered around her like a barricade, her eyes rimmed red.

"Let me guess," I said. "You told your dad Adam's starting his physical transition, and your dad freaked out because he's worried something's going to go wrong."

She sniffled. "That's part of it. I don't get why he's so weird about medical stuff."

I knew, but I wasn't here to explain Ritchie. "What else happened?"

She hugged her pillow. "It's just everything. They made me go skiing when I wanted to go to the museum. Dad picked this awful French restaurant because he thought Lisa would like it, and the food was terrible. Then Lisa I guess felt bad that they were ignoring me and asked me where I was applying to colleges, and I told her I hadn't figured out yet what I want to do, I can't even decide on an internship, and he started his whole lecture on responsibility, blah blah blah."

"And?" I probed gently. Maya was sensitive, but she was used to her dad pushing her. All through her childhood, I'd been the overprotective, sheltering one while he was the tiger mom, demanding achievement and perfection. We'd made him a shirt with a tiger logo for one Father's Day as a joke. But there was something else going on here.

Maya rubbed the corner of her mulberry silk baby blanket, the one she'd had since birth. It was her favorite, and my chest hurt to think she'd brought it with her, the impulse of the child needing security pressing against the wish of the young woman for adventure and independence.

"And then Lisa asked me if there was any guy in my life." Maya kept her eyes down, her dark bangs hiding part of her face. "And I said I was too young to think about it now, but I told her Adam and I made a pact that if we weren't married by thirty, we'd marry each other, and ohmigod you should have seen Dad's face."

I wasn't sure what my face was doing at the moment. *You're too young to be thinking of marriage!* I wanted to shriek, which I guessed was exactly what Ritchie had done.

She blew her bangs out of her face. "I'll give him credit. He waited till this morning to barge into my room and lecture me. I'm too young to think about commitment, which I already *said*, and if I can't commit to a major how can I think I could commit to a person, and Adam and I are being foolish to make such promises when we're both so young and have our whole lives before us, blah blah blah." Her face crumpled. "But then he went off on how I'm so irresponsible that I can't even decide on an internship, and I'm throwing away my future by waiting because it will look to colleges like I'm not serious, and he's had to work hard for everything he earned, and I just look to you guys to provide everything. You know, the usual, but with an extra heaping of scorn."

She choked back a sob, the sound tearing at my heart. "And that's when I lost it and went off on him for being so hard on us and how nothing we do is ever good enough for him, and you know how he loves it when I talk back. All hell broke loose." She wiped her face. "And when I thought of four more weeks of him pushing and sniping and dropping his hints and letting Lisa choose everything that I hate, I ... I just couldn't do it, Mom."

"It's okay, Mymy." My heart ached that part of this rift was because of her standing up for me. Ritchie would see it as taking sides, and he would just grow angrier. "I've got someone coming to get you."

A pounding came from her bedroom door. "I want to talk to your mother." Ritchie sounded angry. "This is insane. Maya. You can't leave over one little fight."

"Why not?" Maya yelled back, her voice screeching through the computer connection. "You left Mom, and you guys weren't even fighting."

I rubbed my forehead. "I'll call your dad. Then I'll call you back when I know about your ride. Glenn—that's Timothy Kay's assistant—they've arranged a driver to take you to the airport and you'll meet Eve in the airport lounge."

Apparently concierges all over the world existed to serve the whims of rich people, and Glenn knew a number of them. I was glad that Maya would have an escort of a bonded, security trained employee so I wouldn't have to worry about who would approach her on public transportation. I'd checked crime rates in Switzerland, and they were less than one-tenth the rate in the US, but still.

Maya wiped her face. "I'm so glad I don't have to fly alone, Mom. I mean, I know I'm already causing everyone so much trouble—"

"It's not trouble, Meiying Rose, for you to say what you need."

She nodded, her eyes huge. When I used her Chinese name, she knew I was dead serious.

Ritchie banged on the door. "Come on, Maya. We can talk about this."

"Cuz our talks always end so well," Maya yelled back, and the pounding desisted.

Why don't you call Adam with your flight info," I suggested. "And your grandparents too. I'm flying you here so I can finish my project in Artesia, but they'll all want to see you once we're home."

She raised her eyebrows. "A project, huh? I want to hear about your thing with this Timothy Kay guy. You get this tone in your voice when you talk about him—"

"Go make sure you didn't leave your shampoo in the shower," I said, employing the mom tone.

"I didn't—oh, whoops, yes I did." Maya ended our call.

I went outside with my phone and grabbed the scuffle hoe. I would attack the puncture vine and tumbleweed trying to take root in Bernie's backyard so I wouldn't attack Ritchie.

"This is stupid, Dale." His voice echoed over speakerphone. "You can't fly her home just because she got mad at me."

It was odd to hear his voice coming from another country. Once he'd been the most familiar thing in my life, the most significant presence. The hardest thing about our separation had been learning to reorient myself with that part of my foundation gone.

It was also somewhat startling to realize I'd gotten used to not living with Ritchie's continual corrections, criticisms, and complaints.

"I'm flying her back because she wants to come home. I'm not making her finish this trip if she's miserable."

"I was just trying to give her some good advice! She's throwing away her future every minute she waits to decide about college."

"What if she doesn't want college, Ritchie? Are you going to tell her what she needs or are you going to help her figure out how to get what she wants?" I stabbed at a spreading puncture vine, hewing around its root. The day was hot already, and sweat gathered beneath my bandana.

Ritchie huffed into the phone. "You don't even know what it's been like, with her moping around and complaining about everything we do, when we thought we were doing her a favor and bringing her our honeymoon. Now she gets to run to you, and you get to be the good guy."

I took a calming breath as I swung at a sinewy stem. For Ritchie, everything was a competition, and he had to win.

"I am not going to get in the way of your relationship with Maya. I told you that in the divorce hearings."

"I'm not paying to change her return flight," he exploded. "The cancellation fees—"

"Her flight's already booked. And I have a driver coming to pick her up. You don't even have to take her to the airport."

A moment passed. "You need to teach her to stay and face her problems. She can't just run to you whenever someone says or does something she doesn't like. She's got to learn to stand on her own two feet, Dale."

"I agree with you, but given that she's seventeen, we still have some time. I think you'll all feel better if she just comes back here. You and Lisa get time together, Maya gets time to settle down and make decisions about her future."

And I would have to cut short my time with Kay, but I was used to not getting what I wanted.

I knew he saw my point, perhaps wanted the same thing, but couldn't admit I was right. "I've already made all these bookings, and I get stuck with her return ticket."

The buzz of a notification cut through his complaint, and I glanced at my phone screen. "Get credit for Maya's ticket and take Lisa somewhere for your one-year anniversary." I pulled up a massive rootball of puncture weed with a savage satisfaction. "The car is coming for her at five. Please help her get loaded and wish her safe travels, and try to resist telling her once more how she is supposed to feel."

He snorted. "I'll have Lisa—"

"Deal with your daughter, Ritchie. Face to face. At least tell her goodbye."

He hung up the phone.

I was bagging tumbleweed for the municipal compost site when another number I didn't recognize appeared on my phone. *Kay,* I thought, my heart lifting before I realized they'd all gotten different, international-capable cell phones for their trip.

"Dale?" It was Lisa. "They're not talking. What am I supposed to do?"

"I'll talk to Maya." I squeezed my forehead, which felt hot and tight. "Ritchie will complain a while and want you to tell him he's right and he's justified in being angry with her. Whatever you do, don't try to make him see her side of things, or he'll think you're making him the bad guy. He has to come around on his own."

I stuffed tumbleweed into the bag, wondering how I had become the marriage counselor for my ex and his new wife. But I liked Lisa. Ritche had met her at a financial conference on the East Coast when she was interning in college. He'd fallen hard. I learned later that she'd told him she wouldn't get involved with a married man, so he'd asked me for a separation. She still told him no, he went ahead with divorce, and she married him. I sometimes wondered if Lisa had fallen as hard for him, or if she were running away from something else.

"Okay." Lisa paused. "It's just, he's being a little…He likes to have things his way, doesn't he?"

I tugged the bag shut. "Story of my life, Lisa," I said. *And now yours,* I almost added.

I told her Maya's flight plan, and after we hung up, I started covering my drip irrigation pipe and picking at the tangle of emotion in my chest. Guilt. Exasperation. Hurt, still. And, largest of all, relief. I didn't have to arrange my life around Ritchie's moods and tempers anymore. That was someone else's job now.

I could please myself. It was still hard to believe, but I was getting better.

When Kay stepped onto the porch that evening, I knew it before I turned around. Something beyond my understanding tapped my shoulder and made me look up.

He held up a carry-out bag. "I hope you're not sick of burritos. We stopped by Caraveo's."

I stood for a moment and took him in. Today's T-shirt sported a Death Valley National Park logo with a buzzard and a skeleton in a lounge chair. His thickening scruff and rumpled shorts said he was making no effort to play up his remarkably well-formed face or body. He was like no one else I'd met in my life, and yet he made perfect sense.

As if I'd been waiting for him, and he was finally here.

I knocked the last of the dirt off my scuffle hoe. "You know, if you feed me, I'm going to follow you home," I said, gathering up my tools.

He watched me move toward him. "I sure hope so."

Anahita was back on duty, and she joined us in the kitchen to share updates. Her time at the observatory had been fruitful, and she had programmed the telescope to capture the images she wanted over her next slot of assigned time. It sounded complicated to me, and she was thrilled. She seemed impressed that we had another celebrity guest—though I didn't know where Regan was at the moment, or Pete—but she was more interested that Maya was coming.

"Of course we'll find a place for her," she said instantly. "I can't imagine Bernie will object."

"She said it was fine." I tried and failed to take a delicate bite out of my enormous taco.

I wondered what Kay thought of all this. He'd hinted that he booked the B&B to get away from crowds, and now the Desert Bloom was filling to the ceiling. But he didn't seem concerned as he devoured his carne asada and started polishing off the pico.

Anahita went off to snuggle with her tablet and her piles of new data, and I sat with Kay at the island in the kitchen, watching the sunset streak red and ochre across the sky. I tried to fit this moment into what I knew of my life. My daughter was getting pampered in a first-class airport lounge in London, drinking all the sparkling water she could handle and texting me snaps of Eve Adesina, Regan's manager, with different filters.

The fantasy I'd mapped onto Bernie's backyard seemed suddenly achievable. Like I could pull this off, water feature and all.

I sat in Bernie's beautiful kitchen with Kay, who somehow belonged in this moment with me, with the golden light bronzing his face and the crinkles around his eyes.

"I don't get how you're single," I said, popping the last of my burrito into my mouth.

He lounged in his chair. "I'm really picky."

"And you flirt with older women."

"I like older women. Always have. I asked Naomi, my mom's astrologer friend, to prom."

"Did she go?" I grabbed the rest of the pico before he could eat it all. He leaned over and dipped a chip in the bowl anyway.

"Yep." He licked his fingers. "We had a great time. She taught me how to dance."

In the cool quiet of the evening, as anticipation wafted in the air between us like candle smoke, I was ready to let my defenses be razed. One night, and one night only.

"Have you tried the jacuzzi in your room yet?" I reached forward to take his plate.

He turned his head and his breath wafted across my cheek. "I'm afraid to swim alone."

"Do you need some supervision? A lifeguard?"

It was a subtle shift in his face, eyelids lowering, his mouth quirking up at one corner, and yet everything about his look blazed with sensuality. "Are you finally going to bring truffles for my pillow?"

My heart raced, my entire body lighting with energy. Eagerness, and terror. I didn't know what I was getting into, but my instincts said it was going to be scorching. I just hoped for scorching in good ways.

"What flavor do you prefer?"

There was no mistaking his come-hither look. "All of them," he said.

Chapter Twelve

Kay followed me upstairs as if worried I might bolt if he led the way. I waited at the top, and he reached around me to unlock the door. His arm brushed my hip, and my breasts grew full and heavy. If I were twenty and this was my dorm room, I would have pulled him to the bed with no preliminaries.

But I was a grown woman who didn't do hookups. I didn't know this script.

He put the key in the red glass dish beside the door, and I checked on my plants. I'd done the same thing this morning, and there was no change.

"They like it here." I noted new growth on the coleus.

"Me, too." He tinkered with the telescope and I watched, enthralled by his interest in the equipment.

"Full harvest moon tonight," he said as I climbed the stairs to the jacuzzi loft.

"No wonder we were all in high spirits last night." I sorted through the basket of bath condiments, the pair of bath robes and bath towels. A shimmer of anticipation ran through me as I lit the soy candles.

"We'll see Jupiter rising before astronomical twilight."

"What's that?" I hadn't brought an overnight bag. It seemed too calculated to go to my room to pack, plus that gave me an escape later.

If I wanted one.

He hadn't tried to escape me last night.

I opened a jar of bath salts as Kay surfaced in the loft. "There are three stages of twilight. Civil twilight, when the sun is just below the horizon. Nautical twilight, when you can still see the horizon and take a navigational reading of the stars." He leaned against the shelf holding the algoanema, which brushed a red-veined leaf against his arm. "And astronomical twilight, when it's fully dark. There's a terrific night sky out here."

"I love that you're a starry night nerd." I started the water, testing its warmth. "You and Anahita should talk."

"She's way too advanced for me. Besides, I feel like there's a certain point of study where all the romance drains away."

I glanced at him over my shoulder. "You don't really believe in zodiac signs. Planetary influences, all that stuff?"

"I think it's an interesting theory. That we can be influenced by forces we don't even think about." He moved closer. "Jupiter, for instance. The ruler, sign of good fortune. Brings wisdom, prosperity, but can also—" He touched my hair, rubbing it between his fingers—"cause reckless behavior."

"So if you do something reckless tonight, you can blame it on Jupiter."

"And so can you."

He kissed me and thought melted away. So did my clothes. I'd changed out of my grubby jeans for dinner and the clingy fabric of my blouse slid off like rain as he ran his hands up my rib cage and over my arms, thumbs skimming my breasts. My nipples tightened to an ache as he stared at my chest.

I flinched, suddenly shy. I didn't have a Hollywood shape. But his face was reverent as he studied my body, then he urged me close and kissed me again, his hands sweeping over the exposed skin of my back. His T-shirt was worn yet still too rough for my sensitive skin. I slid my hands beneath the hem of his shirt, dragging my palms over his ribs and the hard plane of his chest, along the long, muscled length of his arms. As his shirt flew aside, I leaned forward to capture his mouth again and my nipples swirled through the soft black hair on his chest, an exquisite sensation. The tight bud between my legs radiated heat.

It felt so *good* to be turned on, to be touched as if I were newly fired ceramic, a work of art.

He moved his hands to my breasts, fitting his palms, kneading. Sensation raced across my chest, through my heart. I shamelessly pressed into him, and his arousal pressed back. He wanted me. Madness inspired by the moon.

"Dale." His voice was rough, ragged.

"Mmm?"

"You." He ran his lips along my neck to my ear, breathing me in. "Dale, Dale, Dale."

I was lost. So lost. He'd conjured me out of myself, and something wild was going to follow.

He hooked his thumbs in the waistband of my pants and pulled them off. "That's better."

I laughed. "Timothy Kay." I was having a harder time with the button on his shorts, the swell of his erection pulling the fabric tight. "I worried I'm going to hurt you."

"He doesn't mind it a bit rough." His mouth stayed fastened to mine as he freed the button. "But not too rough. Like, gentle rough."

"My specialty." I caught my breath as he shucked off his shorts and boxers and the velvety length sprang free. Every inch of him was beautiful.

We kissed while the tub filled and the scents of sandalwood and juniper swirled around us. He tasted like smoke and chili, primal. The water swirled higher as we mapped each other's bodies, learning textures and curves, the places where a finger-light touch made his heart thump against my breast.

He gripped my hair, nudging my head back for a deeper, hungrier kiss, and I shivered.

"Cold?" he murmured. "We shouldn't waste this water."

"No, indeed." I waited until he turned to the tub to peel off my panties and add them to my stack of clothes, then slid beneath the water to my neck, reveling in the silky sensations sliding around and between my legs, teasing my breasts.

"Perfect temperature." He stretched out on the bench seat, leaning into the curve of the corner, laying his arms along the tiled rim. The sea god Neptune, lounging in his natural element. I reached across him for the jar of salts, still nestled in its basket, and as casually as could be he pulled my nipple into his mouth. I froze, floating above him, caught in the tide of greedy arousal.

He moved to my other nipple, rolling it between his lips. I floated nearer, straddling his hips, bracing my knees against the smooth acrylic. His cock bucked at the contact with my inner thigh, and he sucked my nipple between his teeth.

"I was going to draw this out." He was slick and firm, and I desperately wanted him inside me. "Was going—to tease you...make it last. But I don't think *I* can last."

He pulled an accordion of condom packets from his shorts, and I smothered a giggle. "Surely you know your own size."

"I do, but Glenn wouldn't risk letting someone snap a picture of me buying condoms in the drugstore. Madz had to pick them up them, and he got the combo pack."

I squirmed with embarrassment, drawing back as he slipped one on. "So your whole entourage knows about your sex life."

He tossed away the empty packet. "I think Madz will be disappointed if we don't use them all."

He curled his fingers around my hips, tugging me back to him. The intensity in his dark gaze, locked with mine, seared every inch of my skin. He craved this as much as I did.

"But then it's all over." I eased myself down. He was big. Firm.

"Oh, Dale. We won't be done for a long time. This is just letting off steam."

"Like the valve on a pressure cooker." I held my breath. Pete had been skilled, but I'd been too self-conscious to enjoy it. Pete was fixing the plumbing. Ritchie and I in our good years had had a well-established routine that did the trick for both of us. But Kay was a wild new thrill and I already feared I'd never be able to get enough of him. He fit exactly right.

"Sure." He closed his eyes and bit his lip. "A quick vent so I don't explode."

"Mmm-hmm. For safety purposes." He sucked in air as I took him fully inside of me, deep and hard. A pulse of joy rippled all the way to my womb.

"Jesus. Dale."

"Fits," I said raggedly.

"Oh God, yes." He screwed his eyes shut, mouth working as if he was finding a way to cling to control. I didn't want his control. I wanted madness. I drew myself along his length and then eased down again, this time firm and sure, and he groaned with pleasure.

"*Fuck.* You're so tight."

The expletive, from reserved Kay, excited me. I found the angle that worked and rode him with abandon, relishing his way his hands spasmed around my ass, the way he grew harder and strained toward me, his body straining for climax.

"Dale—I'll try to—hold—"

I loved that he couldn't form words. But I loved that he tried. Ritchie had been nonverbal during sex, and sometimes expressionless as well, as if his mind were elsewhere. Kay was with me. His eyes flew open, reading my face, but I couldn't bear the intensity of his gaze. Instead I looked down at our joined bodies, watching my body embrace his.

"I'm coming," I gasped.

"Already?"

"Oh yes." I was almost there. I threw back my head and plunged against him, cried out in triumph as the wave crested and broke, then sank against him, letting the pleasure rocket through me in a shower of sparks. "Oh, *God.*"

He took up the rhythm, and I whimpered as my orgasm intensified, the pleasure burning brighter yet. It punched me fast and hard, and I felt weightless. I clung to his shoulders and moved with him until I felt him surge and his climax beat in time with mine. I savored the pleasure until the beats faded, and then I opened my eyes to a surprising sting. *God, Dale. Don't cry.*

His expression was so tender that I flinched. "You're incredible."

"No, *you* are." Carefully I eased away, the slide of skin almost too much. My whole body felt dazed with satisfaction. He lifted himself out to strip off the condom, and when he eased back into the water, I laid a hand on his chest. Curled beside him, I felt the pulse inside me match his heartbeat.

I didn't know what came next. Would he want me to go? Were we done here?

He pressed his lips to my forehead, wrapped an arm around me. "How soon can we do that again?"

I laughed, giddy with relief. There was more, at least for tonight. "Aren't you going to be out of steam for a while?"

"I guess we'll see."

I shut off the water, then keyed the control panel on the tub. The jets whirred to life and the colored lights blinked on. I found the remote for the overhead lights and turned them low. We drifted in an amniotic haze, enjoying the candlelight and gentle purr of the whirlpool, watching the full moon rise with a bright star beside it.

"Jupiter," Kay said, his nude length stretched along mine. "Sign of expansion. Philosophy, humor, expansiveness."

"And that other bright one? What star is that?"

"Saturn." His voice vibrated his chest beneath my cheek. "The disciplinarian. Represents—let me think. Time, structure, limits, restraint, fear, old age, loss."

"Hmm." That list felt disturbingly close to the concerns that had been plaguing my mind lately. "I think I'd rather be influenced by Jupiter."

Ritchie hadn't liked to cuddle after sex, not after the first year. I waited for a sign that Kay wanted me to pull away, that he was done for the night. But he merely flexed his arm to draw me close and tipped my head onto his shoulder. The sexual pull was still there, simmering, but tiny tendrils of something else reached out, newborn, seeking.

"Naomi—that's my mom's friend, the one who does astrology and tarot—she would say something about how every element has a benign and a dangerous aspect, or sometimes the same force can both harm and hurt, or—there's something about balance and nothing good or bad in essence, only in effect."

"Kind of like relationships," I said.

"You would know better than I."

"Surely you've dated," I murmured. "Fell in and out of love?" His defenses couldn't be so strong that no one had managed to burrow through his shell.

Kay doesn't do relationships. Glenn couldn't have been clearer.

Well, I wasn't out for a relationship. I was out for one night stolen from reality before my daughter came home. I was still crawling out from the land of heartbreak after my divorce. Why would I want to turn around and go straight back in?

"Tell me how you met your husband." Kay ran his fingers up my arm and traced my shoulder blades. "How did you know he was the one?"

I snorted. "Ritche and I weren't a grand passion. I met him in college, and all my girlfriends had boyfriends, or girlfriends, and it was nice that I finally had someone too. He was fun and everyone liked him, and my brother Kevin met his wife in college, so I guess I had the idea that was what you did. You got your degree, you got married, you found a house and all the rest." I bit my life. "Really romantic, I know."

Kay sketched his fingers over my skin as if he were learning me. Memorizing. "Where's your brother?"

"Seattle. I could have driven up there to get a flight. Or flew Maya in there." Maya was on her way. I looked around to distract myself. A serving tray with a bottle of red wine and two stemmed glasses stood on the bench in the corner. Had Anahita put it there, or had Kay planned ahead? I pulled the bottle toward me. "Want a glass? Or are you just going to drink mine?"

"I'll take a splash."

I poured us both a mouthful, not eager to repeat the morning's hangover. Wine in the jacuzzi was luxury living. So was Kay's body next to mine, brushing against my skin as I settled in next to him. My whole body smoldered like a candle, replete with pleasure and yet aware that I could have him again, and wanted to.

"Yet you married him," Kay said, continuing the inquisition. "So there was something there."

"You know how when you've been with someone a while, and there's really nothing to complain about, so you figure, might as well get married?"

Kay offered a wry smile over the rim of his glass. "Not really."

"Well, that's what we did. It was the finance class, actually," I said. "I took this business finance class my sophomore year, and Ritchie had it too. He already knew he wanted to be an investment banker, make the big bucks on Wall Street. I had a lot of interests and didn't know how to turn any of them into a career, until, it turned out, I was really good at the finance class. So my advisor tracked me into an accounting degree, and I figured that was a smart idea, steady work, I'd be able to find a job anywhere. Ritchie and I both got offers at local banks right out of college, and when his dad got offered early retirement, they offered to give their house to Ritchie. But, they said, he couldn't live there with a girlfriend. He'd have to be married." I shrugged. "So we did."

"Dream wedding?" Kay watched my face.

I laughed. "For his mom, yeah. She wanted him married in the church they attended, reception at their country club. I think she even made the arrangements for the honeymoon. My family didn't mind; they flew in and stayed in a hotel. We had a lot of fun. Then we went on a week-long cruise, came home and started our jobs, and moved into his house, living the Midwestern middle-class dream." I slurped my wine, suddenly self-conscious. The life that to me had been chosen, pleasant, all I thought I could ask for, must sound so dowdy and boring to him. I squirmed. Looking back, I'd never really wanted much.

I'd never taken a real risk.

"It sounds like Ritchie got his way a lot," Kay remarked.

"Well, he was an only kid. His mother had a really hard time conceiving him, so he was this miracle, late-in-life baby. Then he was sick so much as a child—he had leukemia, they thought he wouldn't survive, but he did, another miracle. Ruth likes to say that angels helped her raise Ritchie."

I felt a sweet sense of loss at the thought of Ruth. She was making an effort to keep in touch and be friendly; I knew it helped that Ritchie and I hadn't fought bitterly or parted on bad terms. But her priority, always, was Ritchie. Maya and I were going to slide off her radar, slowly but surely.

"So what made you decide to adopt?" Kay asked.

I poured myself another splash of wine. My breasts brushed his arm as I turned, and awareness flared through me. "You really want the whole life story?"

"Start to finish. You're not really giving me enough visuals," he said. "I've got the storyboard, but we'll have to go back and block out some of the major plot twists."

I laughed. "My life is not interesting enough for a movie."

He held out his glass for a tiny pour. "Maya's seventeen, you said? How young was she when you got her? I'm told international adoptions take a long time."

I shook my head and swallowed my mouthful of wine. "It wasn't international. My friend Jiayi, one of my best friends in high school, was in med school at NYU and got pregnant. The father skipped out and wouldn't help her. Her parents live in a very traditional village in China, and they couldn't handle the shame of their daughter having a baby without marriage. Ritchie couldn't have kids because of the chemo treatments for his leukemia, and we'd talked about adopting. I flew to New York for Maya's birth—Ritchie stayed home to work, he said we'd need the money—and Jiayi had the baby, we signed the papers, and I brought my daughter home."

"Did you want more kids?" Kay asked.

His attention was making me nervous. I slid lower in the water. "I thought I did. But it turned out Ritchie didn't like sharing attention. I think he was the best dad he could be, but..." I shrugged. "Maya was enough for him. And me."

"You're not bitter?" He took a sip of my wine, returned the glass. "You really don't bad-mouth him. At all."

"He's not a bad person. He's a hard worker, he's really smart, and he's protective of the people he loves. We had a good life together, for a long time." I stared into my wine glass, the rich red liquid catching the candlelight. "I don't think I would have ever left him, even though I wanted more," I said softly. "It took him to set us both free."

"I'd be bitter." Kay set his glass on the bench. "If I loved someone, built my whole life around them, and they cut me loose— I'd be bitter."

The candles tossed shadows along the lean curve of his cheekbones and temple, the strong slash of his nose. "I don't think you're capable of bitterness. Yes, some of Ritchie's quirks annoy me, but I think when you love someone, you forgive them. You accept who they are."

"Maybe that's why I'm single." He looked away, watching the stars emerge in the distant sky, a net of silver light. "Too demanding."

His guards were still in place. I might have clambered over them for the moment, but who was to say how many more barriers lay ahead.

I touched his arm. He was worth the wait. He was worth any effort.

"Your dad?" I guessed. "It still hurts you."

"It shouldn't. I should give him that power."

"But you're not bitter about your mom. You've never resented what she couldn't give you."

He combed his fingers through my hair, wet at the tips. "Oh, I resented like hell when I was a kid, especially when I got taunted by classmates. I beat them up, when I could catch them, but they picked on me for the limp too. I hated anyone who had a dad. Anyone who had money. Anyone who was good at sports, or good with girls, or had the fancy car."

I rubbed my cheek against his knuckle. "You're not like that now."

He curled his fingertips into my scalp as I brushed my lips over his skin. "My mom got sick while I was in film school. Breast cancer. She had chemo, radiation, several rounds of it. I missed a lot of school, leaving to help her. It put things in perspective."

That explained why he flunked out of several film schools. Not because he was a poor student—because he was supporting his mom. My heart squeezed against the tight band suddenly pressing against my chest.

"And now you're a hotshot director, and whenever you go back, all the girls want to date you, and all the guys want to be you."

He leaned back against the side of the tub. "They're impressed by the life. Not by me."

He'd said something like that before. "For the record, I like *you*."

He moved his hand so his thumb rested in the dip between my collarbones, where my pulse beat under the delicate skin. "How much?" he whispered.

"Lots."

He curled his finger around my shoulder, urging me closer. "Show me."

The kiss was sweeter this time, deeper, less urgent now that our bodies had been joined, but more intense now that boundary had been crossed. I dissolved into his arms, sinking into the rising heat. Then the heat was too much, and I broke away, panting.

"Hot," I gasped. "I need to climb out for a minute."

I hauled myself onto the side of the tub, water pouring from my skin, embarrassed as his eyes roamed over every curve.

"Hey, there's that telescope," I said weakly. "Don't you want to go look at Jupiter?"

"I like the view here."

He leaned forward to lick my breast, swirling a nipple into his mouth, and I whimpered as heat arrowed through my body. He mouthed and sucked, and I thought I really might cry from sheer pleasure. I tugged at his shoulder.

"I want you," I whispered.

"And I want you." He moved down my rib cage, skimming his mouth around my navel, then lower. "Lean back," he coaxed, gently pushing my legs apart.

"What? You can't—that's not—that's too much." I gasped. "It's so—intimate." It was one thing for his part to go into mine. But for his *mouth*—I quivered at the thought.

"I want to kiss you," he said, his voice a silky purr. "Will you let me?"

I leaned back on my elbows, squeezing my eyes shut. "Okay."

"Is that a yes?" He breathed between my legs, and I trembled at the moist heat.

"Yes," I squeaked.

He flicked his tongue out, gently tracing my most delicate parts. My head fell back, and I gasped with pleasure, chest heaving. "Yes?" he purred, enjoying my reaction. "Wait, maybe I didn't do it right." He licked again, right where I most craved contact, a delicious silky caress.

"Oh, God, yes," I moaned.

After that I had no words. He lapped, delicate at first, then with soft pressure, and then as I trembled on the brink, he nibbled. I shook and came apart, my whole body fracturing.

"You like that." He wore the cockiest smile. He knew exactly what he'd done to me, how much I enjoyed it.

"I don't think I can move." I felt boneless, a puddle of pure bliss.

"Let me help." He rose from the tub and scooped me into his

arms, lifting me as easily as a bag of fertilizer. I grabbed the towels as he carried me down the stairs, then dropped me onto the bed.

"There. Right where you belong."

"That's a little—" The words escaped on a gasp as he crawled over me, his body long and dripping water. "You're wet." I grabbed the towel and blotted his chest.

He shook his head, spraying droplets. "No, you're wet." He pressed between my legs. He was hot and hard and bigger than I remembered.

I wrapped the towel over his back, rubbing the long, smooth cords of muscle. "Everybody's wet," I whispered.

He reached into the bedside drawer and withdrew another packet of condoms. Hazily I wondered just how many Madz had bought. I lifted a knee so he was at the perfect angle to sink into me. I wanted to capture this moment in my memory: Kay framed above me, his face softly bronzed from candlelight and the dim glow of the lamps about the room. The stars wheeling beyond the glass, the bright gleam of the planets, the immense smiling moon. That moon had to be the reason I felt so far out of my usual self. I was in another country with him, some vast unexplored land of beauty and warmth and deep, deep delight. I touched his cheek.

"I think you better finish what you started here," I whispered.

He had himself sheathed before I could miss his heat. "I'm a standard size, by the way. And I prefer lambskin. For when you go shopping for condoms for us."

"I'll try to remember that." I drew him back into my arms. "I'm a little distracted at the moment."

He pulled me close and joined our bodies in one long, smooth, glorious stroke. I hummed with pleasure and wrapped my legs around him.

He paused, his head buried in my shoulder, nose in my hair. I nudged him with my hips. "There's more, right?"

"You feel so good. I'm not going to last this time, either."

I nipped his earlobe, chuckling. "We can always try again later.

Keep practicing until we get it right."

"Oh, you're right." He shifted and started a steady rhythm that was going to put me over the edge in no time. That mad, passionate moon. "You're *all* right."

He was right for me, too. It was the way our bodies fit, cementing the connection we'd formed with words. The way he was gentle and strong at the same time, in control of himself, utterly attuned to me. The way he burned through my defenses like a wildfire fueled by strong winds. Like everything else with him, my orgasm came strong and fast and shook me like a quake, and when I cried out in pleasure, he let himself go and followed me over the cliff, our bodies pulsing in tandem, on the same wavelength of bliss.

I floated in the afterglow while he dispensed with the condom. Then he lifted the coverlet and pulled it over both of us. I curled into his warmth with a sigh of contentment.

"Where'd you put my truffles?" he murmured into my hair as he reached up to turn off the lamp.

"Ha. Other nightstand. Way over on the other side of the bed."

"We'll get it later." He tucked his arm around me, rested his head on my pillow. I couldn't recall the last time I'd shared a pillow with anyone.

It was with Maya, when she was sick as a kid and would climb into bed with me. But my daughter was safe and on her way home. I was nestled in Kay's arms, and he was settling in to sleep. I'd never felt more filled to the brim.

"Good night," I whispered.

"It was a good night." He pressed a kiss to my temple. "I hope there are more."

He might have said something else into my hair, but I was already sliding into sleep.

Chapter Thirteen

I sat straight up in bed, the thought driving me to full consciousness. "Maya."

"Ergh." Kay rolled over and flung an arm across his face.

Fresh morning light poured into the Red Bluff Room. The cottonwood tree and the rooftops of Artesia burst with color. My body had come to fresh life after years of dormancy. Maya was coming home today, and Kay was stretched out in bed next to me. Naked.

The world was a beautiful place.

"Eek. There's a man in my bed. Again."

Kay muttered something beneath his arm. It sounded like "minute."

I slid down beside him and pressed my body against his, hooking my knee over his thigh. "Do I need to fetch your coffee?"

He curved his fingers around my shoulder. "Not you. You stay right here. Someone else bring coffee."

"So this is how Hollywood stars live." I ran my hand over his chest and across his stomach. "They get to lie in bed with naked women while people bring them coffee. And breakfast." My stomach growled.

"I wish that were my life. Every day." He lifted his forearm to peek at me.

"It's alive," I said. "It moves *and* speaks."

"It needs coffee." He groaned and rolled to his side to face me. I slid my hand along his smooth flank and down his thigh, and his cock bobbed to life.

"Or," he said, his eyes flaring, "maybe I need something else."

Brazenly I slid my hand along his arousal. It budged into my palm like a cat demanding pets. "What," I murmured, "could possibly be better than coffee?"

"I think that's a question worth exploring."

He slipped his hand between my legs, eyes locked with mine as his fingers gently stroked and probed. I was tender, a bit swollen, but the sparks of pleasure said I wasn't uninterested. "Four times within twelve hours? That has to be against some moral code."

He shifted and I cradled him in the curve of my body, welcoming his heat, his weight, his strength.

"I think it's a good bar to set," he said, brushing his lips over my cheeks, forehead, nose. "After this, we'll always say, remember that first night when we did it four times? We can't stop now."

He spoke like there would be more of this, more nights and more mornings. Like he had our film-shoot fling all mapped out.

We could talk about that later. Right now a different need ruled. "It would be like giving up," I agreed, tracing my fingers along the back of his neck.

I craved this. Him. It was like once I was told I could have the truffles, I couldn't stop eating them. Whether or not they were good for me.

But he was good. Very, very good. I closed my eyes as he worked his way in, gently. He waited until I looked at him.

"I'm here," I said.

"Good." He tucked his hands under my shoulders and shifted me into position, then rocked into me with deep, leisurely strokes.

"We don't have all morning," I teased. "We have to meet Maya at the airport."

His mouth twitched. "She lands at 10:30. Madz will bring the car at 10. That means we can stay right here until, oh, 9:55."

A tiny moan escaped me as heat swirled and grew. I slid hands over his nicely shaped ass and pressed him closer. "That doesn't leave time for coffee."

"Who needs coffee?" He pulled nearly all the way out until just his tip teased between my thighs, then plunged all the way in, deep, firm, deliciously slow. I shuddered.

"You do. It was in your operating instructions. When Glenn registered you." It seemed so long ago now that Ana and I had been joking about the Golightly character about to descend on us. He'd burrowed under my skin with dangerous swiftness. Just two weeks ago I hadn't known who he was. Now he was in my bed, connected more intimately than I'd ever known.

"I found something I like better than coffee." He teased me again, drawing out slowly, waiting. I wiggled my hips up toward him, aching, desperate.

"I do too," I panted. "Give it to me. Now."

"Give you what?" He nipped my ear.

"You." I snapped my teeth at him and stroked the base of his penis. His balls were taut and high. "This. Your big, hard, hot—"

He swelled, and his eyes grew hot and focused as he drove into me. "Vixen."

He dropped his head against my shoulder, and I whispered the foulest, filthiest language I knew into his ear. He groaned as he moved harder, faster, and my need whirled up to meet his as I clamped arms and legs around him and held on tight as the pleasure exploded.

As he shuddered in his own release, I cooed in his ear. "That's right. Very nice. Good boy."

After our breath slowed and he rolled off me and I contemplated how soon I'd have to rise and clean myself, he lifted his head. "Did you call me a good boy?"

I slid my fingers over the scruff of his beard. "You were good," I said seriously. "Very, very good."

"What's my reward?"

"Coffee." I slid out of bed and headed for the bathroom, so

replete with pleasure that I didn't even care that he had a full view of my backside.

"And then more of that," he called.

"Oh, no. Five times is against the law. It's actually on the books in New Mexico."

"That's a terrible law."

I sifted through the closet for a fresh bath towel. They smelled softly of juniper. "It's meant to prevent people from staying in bed all day and not doing their work to support the economy," I replied. "And to prevent people from stranding their daughters at airports."

"We have half an hour." He looked at his phone. "Glenn says they're on time. Left Albuquerque right on schedule."

My heart lifted in a loop-de-loop that pulled tight and hard. Maya would be here soon. And my time with Kay would be over.

"Long enough to eat and have coffee." I tried to sound teasing, light, though my throat ached all of a sudden. "I'm using all your hot water."

"Oh, no you're not."

He joined me in the shower and insisted on soaping and shampooing me, then washed me down with the spray nozzle. I purred as his hands slid over my slick body and his tongue licked water from my skin. He insisted on directing the spray on my most delicate parts—made tender from his handling—and then I took the nozzle and did the same to him. We stepped out of the shower laughing, droplets flying, and he kissed me.

"No more." I pushed him away playfully. "I have no more orgasms in me until..." I tried to find words for how satisfied I was.

"Until I'm in you again," he said smugly, rubbing the towel over his hair. "Do you know what we're having for breakfast?"

Cristina had made us a southwestern omelet, and she smiled as we strolled into the sunny kitchen. Anahita, in a hijab that matched the sea green tones of her shalwar kameez, winked and started coffee. Once again it didn't seem fair that I got to be served like a guest, but Kay didn't behave like a guest, settling at the kitchen table as if he were part of the household. I sat next to him, thrilled to be near him, and self-conscious at the same time. Whatever Kay and I were, we weren't a couple. It wasn't wise to make assumptions.

Madz strolled in ten minutes ahead of time and gave Ana a wide, flirtatious smile as she steamed half-and-half for a breve. "Glenn found a room at the hotel for Eve?" Kay asked.

"We did, but Eve doesn't want it. She's headed back to LA tonight."

"She's not going to stay at all?" Regan breezed into the kitchen, slipped into a seat at the table, and cut herself an enormous piece of omelet. She wore faded jeans that hugged her shape, a battered grey T-shirt, and a flannel shirt that belonged to Pete.

"I'm going to the airport with you," she added. "But Petey can't. He has to report to his job, poor baby."

She puckered her lips as Pete entered and gave her kiss. I tried to keep from staring. Pete had informed me, clearly and in advance, that he wasn't the boyfriend type, but he'd glued himself to Regan's side.

I wished I had that confidence, but one delirious night, for me, did not a couple make. Besides, with Maya arriving, my sabbatical was ending.

A black hole opened in my chest. I would get Maya but lose Kay.

I couldn't carry on a reckless, no-strings affair with my daughter watching. And at some point, if Kay really was storyboarding a film-shoot fling for us, I would have to tell him that.

"Maybe I'll tell the foreman I'm sick," Pete said. "I've never ridden in a limo."

"A what?" I said.

It was true. A black stretch limo hugged the curb outside the Desert Bloom. Neighbors loitered on the sidewalk, pretending to walk their dogs and clustering into small groups, talking.

"Way to be subtle," I said aloud.

"Eve gets a limo," Regan said. Without waiting for Madz, she dipped into the car with the ease of long practice, which I suppose she had.

Kay held the car door for me. It was more than mere courtesy. There was a challenge in his gaze—or an invitation? *This is my life*, he seemed to be saying.

I was never going to fit in that life, even if he invited me to. But this limo was taking us to the plane that held my daughter, so I took a deep breath and ducked in.

The seats were soft black leather, the windows tinted, and the minibar sparkled with crystal glasses. Kay sank into the seat beside me, stretching out his legs. He reached for my hand, as if sensing my nerves.

I couldn't remember the last time a guy had held my hand. I suspected it was my high school boyfriend, a fellow from the math league team. Ritchie didn't like public displays of affection, at least with me. Kay stroked his finger over my knuckles, and while Regan chattered, a deep sense of contentment washed through me.

How strange.

The Artesia airport wasn't far, with two runways and a small terminal that resembled a sandwich cookie. I managed to keep myself from running toward the small, sharp-nosed silver jet as it landed and slowed. After an interminable amount of time, the door lifted and steps let down, and a tall woman stepped out wearing a blazer and suede boots that looked straight off the fall fashion runway. As she strode toward us, the wind pressed her silk shirt and trousers against a gorgeously curved figure, and the wind rioted through her blond-tipped hair. She scanned all of us, then headed for Regan, arms wide, and folded her into a warm hug.

"This guy," she said immediately in a voice with a luscious accent. She pulled back and studied Regan's face. "The cowboy. He good to you?"

Regan nodded like a schoolgirl with a crush. "He is. Wait, how do you know about him?"

"You've been offline the past few days, luv, but the rest of the world hasn't." She turned to study me, slid her big brown eyes to

Kay, then came back to me. "And you. I have been *dying* to meet you." She held out her hand, gleaming with a French-tipped manicure.

"Uh oh." Her skin was softer than silk, luscious. "What did Maya say?"

"It's more like the pictures. *Who,* we all want to know, is making poker-faced Timothy Kay show so much expression? In public?"

What pictures, I was about to ask, but I was preoccupied by the open door of the plane, still empty. Beside me, Kay exchanged an air kiss on both cheeks with Eve. Like Regan, she was so beautiful it was hard not to stare, but at the same time, she was completely human.

"What is Maya *doing* in there?" I wanted to know.

"Maya? What an absolute doll. The pilot offered to show her his instruments." She raised her eyebrows.

"His what?" Maya had never been interested in flying.

Maya appeared on the steps, carrying her shoulder bag, in a bulky coat and her hair pulled back in a braid wound around her head. She looked pale and tired and thin and happy. Behind her, carrying her enormous black cloth suitcase as well as a hard-sided silver bag that must be Eve's, came the pilot. He looked like a graduate from a K-pop boy band, cheekbones dominating his face, hair rakishly gelled, a sultry set to those dark eyes. I understood why Maya had lingered.

I started toward her. "Baby girl." She was going to scold me later for that, but it popped out.

"Mama." She fell into my arms, and I pulled her in tightly, struck anew with astonishment that I was holding a young woman. For me, she was still the infant I'd cradled in the hospital, the toddler I'd chased all over Hastings, the schoolgirl peering through too-long bangs as she recited letters in the spelling bee, the limber pre-teen picking herself up off the gymnastics mat and running at the vaulting horse one more time.

Her hair smelled like coconut. Her shoulder blades poked through the wool pea coat. "Did your father not feed you?"

"We've been walking a lot. Mom, this is Eve, who has been so awesome, I can't even."

Eve embraced me too. "I'm in love with your daughter. The minute she wants a screen test, bring her straight to me."

"Eve," Kay said, "she gets to be home for five minutes before you recruit her."

Eve narrowed her heavily lined eyes at him. Her makeup was still flawless after an overnight flight. "When are you sending me Regan's contract for *Visitors 3*?"

A muscle clenched in Kay's cheek. "When I know there will be a *Visitors 3*," he said. "Ernie, you're coming with us for lunch?"

"Anyplace in this town serve noodles?" Ernie, the pilot, flashed a grin. "I'm about done with tortillas."

"I want a Niçoise salad." Eve flipped hair off one shoulder. "That's what I eat now. All the time."

"Cream puff," Maya said. "I had them with, literally, every meal I ate in Germany. I could eat cream puffs all day."

"I'm making you cream puffs every day to fatten you up," I promised, guiding her toward the limo where Madz was loading suitcases into the trunk. "Oh, I forgot. Maya, this is Timothy Kay. He's, ah, directing a movie in Artesia. Can you believe it?"

"My mom and a hot Hollywood director." Maya widened her eyes. "Dad is *freaking* out. Will he be at our Thanksgiving dinner? Because Lisa already asked. I hope you know she expects you to host it, Mom."

I couldn't sort out the wave of emotion that swept me. Rage, perhaps, that I was still expected to be the domestic provider, the one who planned and made and hosted and cleaned up after the holiday meals. Ready acceptance at being the nurturer, and tangled wistfulness for Lisa's innocence, at her eagerness to be on good terms with me.

But because I was only human, a touch of triumph that my ex was jealous. An in-demand director who didn't do relationships was not going to fit himself into my Midwestern life and come eat my grandma's pumpkin pie at Thanksgiving, but it was nice that Ritchie thought a Hollywood A-lister might actually be interested in me.

"Meiying Rose, where are your manners? This is Regan Forrester. She's acting in Kay's movie."

"I know. We love *Long Wet American Summer*. We've watched it, literally, a thousand times. Please tell me you have a bigger role in *Visitors 2*, because the first movie absolutely did not give you enough to do."

Regan beamed and hugged Maya. I bet Maya wished someone would take a picture she could post and brag about chumming with Hollywood stars. They were still people, I knew. They simply had jobs in creating illusions, but it was that talent for making magic that made me wary about what was real.

Kay cleared his throat. "The sequel's going to be different in a lot of ways." When Eve raised those very expressive and perfectly shaped eyebrows, the muscle in his jaw moved again. "I have a bit more creative license on this one."

"Because *The Visitors* landed major box office, because of my girl." Eve looped an arm around Regan, who glowed with the praise. The clear affection between them said that, even if the romantic relationship didn't work out, there were no lingering hurts or resentments on either side.

Unlike me and Ritchie. A little hiccup passed through my heart as I registered Maya's words. I'd never seen Regan's movie that she mentioned. She was talking about Adam. She and her best friend were her *we*.

Kay climbed into the car first and I followed with Maya behind me. I enjoyed the expression on her face as she looked around. "This is nicer than the limo Lisa had for her wedding."

"Eve, can't you stay tonight?" Regan asked as the two women found their seats.

"Ernie's flying us to LA tonight," Eve began.

"If the flight plan is approved," Ernie reminded her. He leaned forward to sort through the mini bar.

"Because Jason Devine suddenly wants to tour with this musical he's been in, and I need to talk some sense into him. Film roles, Jason. And champagne, Ernie. We deserve it."

There was, in fact, a bottle of champagne chilling in an ice bucket. I wondered if the limo came stocked with one. Since the glasses were next to me, I passed them around.

"Give me that. I've seen you open a champagne bottle." Kay leaned toward his friend. His shoulder pressed against me, and I caught my breath. One would think I'd be satiated, that desire wouldn't flare instantly at the mere scent of him. That assumption was wrong.

"Jason Devine?" Maya's eyes were enormous. "I've heard that divorce is going to be messy. I can't believe Melissa Waterstone dumped him for that tennis guy. She dumped Jason Devine."

"I hadn't heard this." Kay held this thumb over the cork and twisted the bottle, slow and steady. The cork fell gently into his hand and the bottle released a soft sigh. Much like my body when Kay's hands were on me. I felt heated.

"Honestly, Kay, do you not go online? The story is everywhere." Eve held out her glass for Kay to fill. "And so are pictures of my girl and her cowboy. Which, honestly, great move, *ti chouchou*. You have clearly moved on from Kevin the Rat Bastard."

Regan combed her fingers through her hair, looking unconcerned, but I felt a pinch of worry. Was Pete a ploy? I'd pointed her in his direction. Champagne stung my mouth. I wanted to ask more about these pictures, as there didn't seem to be any paparazzi in Artesia. Was someone watching Regan's life?

Was someone watching Kay's? With me in it?

"You can't ask Maya to sign an NDA," I said. "For one thing, she's a minor."

Eve shrugged and swirled her glass. "So it's on you, Mama, not to spill any movie secrets."

Maya's eyes widened further. "Mom, do you *know* any movie secrets?" She took the hand holding my glass of champagne and sniffed, wrinkling her nose at the bubbles.

"No, I don't know any movie secrets, and you can have one sip. A *small one.*"

Eve held up her glass, inspecting the color. "Swirl and sniff," she told Maya, "and hold a mouthful on your tongue for a minute. Then swallow."

I followed Maya's example and was astonished at the scents that hit my nose, the flavors that spread over my tongue. I'd gone forty years of my life not knowing how to savor champagne. What else had I been missing?

"Lemon," I said in surprise.

Maya wrinkled her nose. "Chalky."

"I brought sparkling water for the nondrinkers." Kay pulled two bottles of San Pellegrino out of the mini fridge, flicked the cap off one, and passed it to Maya. She thanked him with a shy smile.

The champagne must have rushed straight to my head, because my brain felt fizzy. I wanted to giggle with giddiness. Maya was home, safe, sitting next to me. Kay had thought ahead and made an effort to include her. We rolled along in a black stretch limo, drinking champagne and chatting about Hollywood gossip. I'd stepped out of a life with its desk job and loan payments and the same tired old ideas for dinner and stepped into a world of luxury and glamor.

It was a brief bubble, like those popping in my champagne. At some point it would burst, and we'd all go our separate ways, the world settling back to its usual order. I knew that.

I watched Kay drink, how his throat moved, and imagined brushing my lips down his neck. I wanted him so intensely that my fingertips tingled.

I didn't want the bubble to burst yet.

Chapter Fourteen

Maya wandered out to the front yard later that afternoon. After lunch, Kay left to meet Des and his entourage at the hotel to finalize the shooting schedule and Regan took Eve and Ernie off on some errand of their own. Maya and I returned to the Desert Bloom so she could rest and I could work. Napped but still heavy-eyed, phone in the back pocket of her shorts, she sat on the porch swing for a while, her hair braided and tucked beneath a sunhat, a light long-sleeved shirt thrown over her tank top so her fair skin didn't burn.

"What's this one?" She came down the steps and knelt beside me, touching the small sapling.

"Strawberry tree. They get to be a nice height, but not so high it will hide the house, and pink flowers will go well with Bernie's color scheme." I patted a small mound of mulch around the base. "It's not a native, but it does well in this climate zone, and once established it won't need a lot of water."

Maya held the bole of the little tree while I drove in a stake. "I love how much you love this, Mom. We always had the best yard."

She was right. Ritche's mother hadn't been able to look me in the eye for a year after I pulled up her scraggly arbor vitae and overcrowded hostas, but when she saw my replacement, the paths, the ornamental trees, the beds that bloomed in different seasons, she stopped complaining. My summer jobs in high school had been working for a greenhouse. I'd always loved pottering around with plants.

When Ritchie started traveling more and Maya had her activities, , I took evening landscaping classes to fill the gaps. But that was still puttering.

"I think I've bitten off more than I can chew here," I admitted. "I might have gotten a little too ambitious with my designs."

I blamed Kay. Vacationing from my real life, on holiday in Artesia, I'd let my fantasies grow. If they got too wild, they might pull me down and choke me, like vines.

"If you don't know, you learn. Isn't that what you always tell me?" Maya looked around at my handiwork. "Are you going to quit the bank?"

I wiped a drip of sweat off my temple, then wrapped a piece of cloth around the bole of the young tree and loosely tied the hemp cord to the stake. My heart thumped at the thought of leaving the bank. *Freedom.* Throwing off yet another piece of the me I had always been.

Who was waiting beneath? "I'm thinking about it."

"I got offered the internship with the children's program at the art museum," Maya said as I tied off the rope. "And the one at the agricultural learning center. And the spot in the symphony orchestra." Maya played the horn. She also danced ballet, did beautiful calligraphy, and had no idea what she wanted to pursue for a career, which is why I had suggested a gap year.

I kept my voice neutral. "Sounds like all of those would keep you close to Hastings."

"It's what I want, Mom."

I wanted to argue. I wanted her to experience more of the world than I had. To go further.

Be braver.

When she was young, I could override what she wanted with what was good for her. No, she couldn't have the cupcake until she had eaten her vegetables. No, she couldn't watch the TV show until she had been outside to play. Now I just had to cross my fingers and hope she would want the thing that was good for her.

Was I doing that? Sticking with the thing I thought was good for me—or the thing someone else thought was good for me—instead of going after what I wanted?

I sat on my heels and stared at my new tree. I'd gone after what I wanted, spending the night with Kay.

And the morning. He hadn't shown me the door and called for the next in line. He'd held my hand, casually, meaningfully.

I didn't know what that meant for him. For me, it made my heart quake with fear. And longing for more things I couldn't, wouldn't be allowed to have.

"How's Adam?"

She scuffed her bare toe at a clump of dirt as I walked around checking on my trees. "He called me a dork for cutting my trip short. He thinks I should have at least stuck it out for queer Berlin."

"Are you sorry you cut your trip short?" I examined the leaf of the fig tree, a healthy color.

She heaved a deep sigh. "No. There was no way I could put up with Dad nagging and Lisa hovering for one more minute. I'm glad you let me come here and didn't make me go to Nan and Pop or stay in Hastings with Gram and Gramps." She crossed her arms and lifted her brows, so much a replica of my college roommate that I nearly laughed. "I want to know what's going on with you and Mr. Kay."

"You don't have to call him that." I ran a hand along a branch of my desert willow. She read me so well, and always had. "It's none of your business, and I'm not done with you yet, young lady." I softened my voice. "I think your dad just wants the best for you, but he's got really strong ideas about what that best is."

She pursed her lips. "Is that why you always let him get his way? Because you thought what he wanted was best?"

"No." My shoulders sagged at her tilted head, firm look. "Yes. I gave in to your father to keep the peace."

"Well, I'm not going to take a crummy internship or choose a snobby college or do a job I hate because it pays money. I want to do something I love and be with someone I love. Like, *love* love."

Love. I stood frozen in fear. Love was so powerful. Destructive.

"I loved your father." It was a feeble protest.

"Yeah, but this thing with you and Mr. Kay? You *like* him, Mom."

"It is not appropriate for me to discuss my romantic life with you."

I tried out a scowl, and she simply laughed. "Sure hope you're having one anyway. I mean, if you're into tall dark and broody—"

"Let me distract you by saying that I actually agree with your father. You've got some big decisions to make, and the deadlines are coming soon."

She feigned a fierce face. "Are you going to tell me what to do too?"

"You have to give us a bit of a break, Mymy. Ten minutes ago I was changing your diapers. Five minutes ago I was crying when you graduated from kindergarten. And now you're thinking about college." I drew her into my arms, uncaring that I was sweaty. She nestled her chin against my shoulder and slipped her arms around me with a little sigh. She felt thin and nearly weightless, like a wild creature that might break from my grasp at any moment.

I sniffled, my throat thick, thinking about all the possibilities that awaited her. She could do anything she wanted. "Did you really make a fallback marriage pact with Adam?"

She giggled and readjusted the sunhat I'd knocked askew with my hug. "To be fair, it was the prom after-party, and we'd had a lot of pomegranate ginger spritzers."

Maya had never been in love. She'd never even had crushes. I'd always wondered about her untouchability, since at her age I had intense crushes. I had to be cautious. "What happens if you fall in love with him and he falls in love with someone else?"

She shrugged. "Like you and Dad? Yet look at you, still standing, and with a new bae and everything. Definite upgrade, if I get to say that."

I blinked. I might be finding my feet now, but in the first months when Ritchie asked for a separation, I hadn't been standing. I hadn't even been crawling. I'd been lying on my belly in the dirt, sobbing.

Exactly why I didn't want to grow tendrils for Kay and end up in the exact same place.

We walked around the house to the sunny backyard, where the cedar planks of the porch warmed in the sun, where the hole Pete was digging for my water feature sat gaping open, the stones piled beside it. I checked the mulch around the osage orange.

"Timothy Kay is not my bae. I definitely do not get to say *that*."

She gazed with me into the gully. I had yet to contour and plant down the steep sides, dig the grid in the gulch that would capture rainfall and keep all of it from washing away toward the Pecos. But I could see the vision in my mind.

"Well, why the heck not?" Maya demanded. "Are you losing your eyesight?"

"Show some respect for your elders." I looked up into the cottonwood where I'd first seen Kay. I wondered what he was thinking of me in the midst of his meetings the way my mind kept returning to him. The pull was undeniable, and it was strong.

"He's only here for a few weeks, Mymy. Even if I started something with him, it wouldn't last."

"Don't you always tell me to go for it? Why wouldn't you do the same?"

I stared at her, but I couldn't think of a good reason why my own advice shouldn't apply to me. This girl. She'd been teaching me how to grow as a person from the moment the birthing nurse placed her in my arms, and she was teaching me now.

What if I stopped bracing myself from falling for Kay? What if I just let myself fall? All in, relishing every moment. Trusting that I'd be able to pick myself up again at the end of it. Move on, rebuild, design myself all over again.

Because I was worried that the hurt of another ending wasn't going to just stunt my growth. It was going to kill me.

"You know what time it is?" Maya pulled her phone from her

back pocket.

I dusted my gloves. "Happy hour?"

She clapped a rhythm I knew all too well. "Any single ladies in the house?" she called out, running for the porch.

"Baby, my hips don't move like that anymore."

She whirled and pointed at me. "Those hips don't lie, and you're gonna prove it."

Her stern face melted me. Dancing in the kitchen had long been our way of releasing the stress of a long day. When a client made unreasonable demands or lost all their files just before tax season, when classmates teased, when she bombed her first SAT, we danced. When my new apartment was so tragically bare and my new life so painfully broken and lonely, and I wanted to put my head on my knees and weep, we danced through my tears and hers. Before I'd finished putting my tools away, Beyoncé was blasting through Maya's portable speaker.

And we danced.

We weren't thirty seconds into the song before the patio doors slid open. Regan charged onto the porch wearing a pair of cutoff jean shorts and a flowered sleeveless shirt with the tails unbuttoned and tied in a knot, Daisy-Duke style.

"Cried all the tears for eight stupid years," she bellowed and struck a pose.

Maya grinned and fell into a flanking position, letting Regan take the lead. It astonished me that Maya wasn't at all starstruck, but then, she'd grown up with Madame Rinaldo, who was the symphony soloist, community stage star, theatre professor at Hastings, and the only classically trained opera singer to be found in Nebraska outside Omaha. Mimi was a good friend of mine and helped every community fundraiser or school auction, but she was an unapologetic diva. Next to her, Eve Adesina with her limos and first-class flights was decidedly chill.

"Is that a remix lyric?" I asked.

"That's how long I was with Kevin." Regan tossed her hands up in the air and rotated her hips. "Oh, oh oh."

Eve strolled onto the porch wearing a long loose skirt with a slit up the thigh and a halter top that clung to every curve. Her martini glass cradled a toothpick with three huge olives.

"Drink on my lips, girl on my hips." She joined in, slinking her shoulders without sloshing her drink.

I made my best effort to follow Regan and Maya's moves, but I wasn't trying to be them. I wasn't trying to be anyone else, not anymore. I wanted, at last, to be *me.*

I gave myself over to the music, the effort, the steady, pulsing beat. Something rose up in me, something old, familiar, essential. She'd been away a long time, that free, wild girl deep inside of me who believed she could do anything. But she was back. It was exhilarating.

Eve whistled and clapped as the song ended with Regan holding up her left hand, pointing at her finger with a small pout. "I wish I had that on video," Eve sang.

"Next it's Shakira or Rihanna, 'Please Don't Stop the Music,'" Maya announced, checking her phone display.

"Girl, no shade on your playlist, but these songs were made before you were born," Eve said.

Maya pointed at me. "It's her fault."

My heart beat in my ears and my body thrummed. I felt *freed.* "I feel like the music shouldn't stop."

Regan threw up her hands and swung her head, flinging her hair. "Shakira, Shakira."

We danced, and the light turned golden. We danced, and my potted plants bobbed and waved to the beat of our steps. We threw off the regular shrug of time and made a festival day, one of those liminal times when troubles drew back and new things, tinged with magic, were possible.

We were shaking our hips all over the porch and howling, Eve included, when Kay and Pete came onto the porch from the kitchen. The expression on Kay's face was one I wanted to capture on film and carry with me into old, old age.

His pupils dilated and the air crackled around him. He stopped, crossing his hands over his chest, leaning back on his heels, shoulders bunched as if he were forcing himself to wait. The man was a master at self-control. But even as I twirled and danced with the girls, I felt his eyes riveted on me.

Not us. Me.

Shakira demanded that we let the she-wolf out so she could breathe, and I, panting, considered it.

Maya giggled and scooped up her phone when the song ended, looking for the next tune. The air on the porch sizzled. I stood trying to catch my breath, aware of Regan enjoying Pete's slack-jawed stare, Eve watching Pete watch Regan, but my eyes and mind were filled with Kay. He strolled toward me, his stride loose and easy, and my breath swooped away.

"Want some air?" he asked in that husky voice that lit me up.

I wanted *him*.

He'd hinted there could be another night for us. And my daughter had given me permission. I wouldn't be setting a terrible example if I had an affair with a hot Hollywood director while she was under the same roof.

What did *he* want, though? The man who didn't do relationships, had never been in love?

He took my hand, fingers threading through mine, and heat flowed through me like sap. Everything else shifted to make way.

"Tell me about your day," I said, feeling suddenly shy as we stepped off the porch.

The dust was warm and quiet, filled with insects and shuffling wings. He blew out air and ran a hand through his hair.

"They started hauling in the trailers today, and catering is getting set up tomorrow. Alex, my make-up head, shows up Sunday, along with the rest of the cast and crew, and Monday we start filming."

It sounded like Monday was the end of something. "Will I get to meet Chris Stevens?" That was the male lead, Regan's co-star. He seemed like a very vanilla guy, no gossip or scandal about him, and I only knew that because I had caved and looked online for every piece of info about Timothy Kay, and his movies, that I could find.

"If you come visit me on location, yes."

I caught my breath. "Is that an invitation?"

He turned and studied my face, his thick eyebrows drawing together. "Do you need one?"

I had no idea what he was offering. I had no idea how affairs like this worked. How *he* worked.

I'd have to figure him out on my own. Just like he was figuring out me.

I nodded. "Embossed, on heavy paper, with a firm date for RSVP. I…want things to be clear." Especially considering I was a divorcee with a kid, a member of the non-Hollywood world, the kind of person who had to sign an NDA.

He turned his body toward me, brushing his lips through my hair as he looked up into the canopy of the cottonwood above us. "Dale Rose," he said.

"Wrighton."

"Dale." He looked into my eyes. "I hereby grant you an invitation into anything to do with me or my life."

I fought back tears and pretended it was dust. His rawness, his honesty, his complete lack of hesitation made my teeth hurt. I was clinging to the cliff for dear life, my fingers white with terror, calculating all the ways I could fall and hurt myself. Yet he'd done nothing to indicate he wouldn't catch me.

At least until Monday, when his real life began and his Artesia holiday ended.

"You are…awfully trusting," I said, my voice catching.

He examined every line of my face, the curve of brow and temple, my eyelashes, cheekbone, jaw. Lips. "I know what I want."

"That makes one of us," I blurted.

He moved closer, pressing his chest to mine. "You have *some* idea," he said, his voice a low growl.

"Okay, that." I choked back a laugh. "No question there." But all the rest. How could I set down guardrails when I was in wide open territory, terrifyingly new?

And how could he just roll out the red carpet for me? This was a man who showed calculation, thoughtfulness, reserve in every other part of his life. I saw the barriers he put up with other people, even with Glenn and Madz, who were close to him. Why was he letting down the gates for *me*?

"I like being exclusive." I immediately blushed. That sounded like I was trying to hook him into something long-term. Something with promises and expectations. "I mean, like, one at a time."

He nodded. "Me, too."

"We barely know each other," I whispered. But did we need to, if it was just an affair? Weren't we supposed to enjoy ourselves as long as it lasted?

Except, as great as the sex was, I wanted more from him. I loved the way he talked to me last night. Talked to me now. Cupped his hands on my elbows and rested his chin on the top of my head, looking up into the cottonwood. I wanted to curl against him and purr.

"If I were to have any pet, it would be a snake," he said. "I hate the scent of vanilla. As a kid I had a collection of Wonder Women comics, some still in the sleeve, and a complete set of *Jurassic Park* action figures that I bought with my own money. When my mom got sick I sold all of them to pay for her treatments—all but one, which I take with me everywhere. It's my talisman, and I am not ashamed."

"The T-rex," I guessed.

"Dr. Ian Malcolm."

I clapped a hand to my mouth. "You're a *nerd*."

He nodded with an expression of studied solemnity. "And now you know. Time to run for the hills."

I pressed my nose to his shoulder. He smelled of sweat and creosote. "Wonder Woman?"

"I have a weakness for ass-kicking brunettes who are a little bit magical and use their powers for justice," he said.

I shoved away a tinge of regret, of longing. "I'm not magical."

"Look at that." He nodded toward the porch, where Regan was showing Maya how to two-step. Pete moved around them, touching Regan's shoulders and elbow, explaining framing and speed and the line of dance to my daughter, while Eve scrolled through the playlist. My heart melted at the sound of Maya's laugh. I realized now how forced her smiles had been on the pictures she posted of her European trip. She'd been miserable and trying to fake enthusiasm. Here, tonight, she was relaxed, flushed with pleasure, letting down her guard.

"You did that," Kay said. "Eve isn't on her phone making calls. I've never seen Regan Forrester laugh and be silly. At every other bed and breakfast around the world, people are sitting in their rooms behind their screens. Which is okay if they are watching my movies. But here, at this one—dance party."

"That's not my doing," I said, though I wished it were.

Anahita poked her head into the kitchen and was immediately drawn into the group, paired with Eve while Pete explained the basics of the two-step all over again. Maya twirled and giggled, and Ana's smile glowed. She was taking a tiny nibble of the forbidden, and she loved it. Taiye appeared in the kitchen as well, apron tied around his waist, juggling utensils in the air while he prepped dinner.

"You're making magic in this backyard," Kay went on. "Creating something out of nothing. It's beautiful. Moreover, you've made Glenn trust you. And Glenn doesn't trust anybody, at least when it comes to me."

"You're the one who makes magic," I said. "I mean, with your movies." I also meant, he was transforming me. There hadn't been the faintest whiff of magic in my life until Timothy Kay appeared under this cottonwood tree and stole my breath, and my margarita.

He wrapped his arms around me and I leaned against his chest, feeling the low vibration of his voice, the steady drum of his heart. A bone-deep contentment soaked through me. I wanted to etch this moment into my mind and carry it with me everywhere. It would be my talisman, my shield against all hurt.

"You didn't RSVP to my invitation," he whispered into my hair.

A painful gulp of air moved through my chest. "Let's begin with something specific."

"Do you want to visit me on set?"

"Yes."

"Good. Glenn is getting you clearance." He pressed a kiss to the side of my face, in front of my ear. It was like lighting the fuse on a firework, a slow buzz that I knew would build to something greater. "Do you want to come to my room tonight?"

"I—I do. Want to, yes. But if Maya wants to talk, I should stay with her."

I was still throwing up obstacles. Why? What did I stand to lose in a short-term fling with Kay that I hadn't already lost before, and, as Maya had pointed out, recovered from?

A sense of belonging. It hit me as we sat around the Bernie's hardwood dining table, the pendant LED lights in their hand-woven lampshades casting a warm glow over dishes full of vatapá, a creamy stew with shrimp and coconut milk, and empadãos, chicken and vegetables tucked into a deliciously flaky crust. Taiye outdid himself with dessert, and he beamed delight as he produced a platter full of small round balls bristling with shaved chocolate.

"Brigadeiro," he announced grandly. "Brazilian truffles. A treat for our beautiful guests." He presented the platter to Eve, Regan, and Maya in turn, giving them each equal attention. Maya glowed as she nibbled one, even though she wasn't fond of chocolate.

"I like your truffles better," Kay whispered, and the tips of my ears went hot.

I'd belonged before in a house, at a table, people I loved gathered around me. Perhaps not meals this glamorous, true, with mouth-watering food and laughter flowing along with champagne. I wanted to tuck this into my pocket and keep it for always, this treasured time at the Desert Bloom. There was a special beauty, the penumbra of loss surrounding the moment of happiness, which couldn't last. Like the faintest note of bitter cocoa in the brigadeiro, balancing the sweet.

Maya excused herself for bed in the middle of Eve's anecdotes about the time a naked Jason Devine called her to come pick him up at midnight at Zuma Beach, where he had lost his swim trunks in some incident he refused to explain. It was late, and the lack of sleep from the night before was catching up with me, so I excused myself to look for her.

I'd freshened up Pete's room for her and her luggage sat beside the small table, but Maya herself was in my room, slanted across the bed in her Magic Linen pajamas, sound asleep. I leaned against the door and soaked her in, the curve of her face pillowed in one arm, the soft rise and fall of her breath. It amazed and humbled me, how I could see all the stages of her life gathered into those features. The baby whose dumpling cheeks would push her eyes into narrow slits when she laughed. The tiny nose and stubborn chin of the toddler. The soft in-betweenness of her school-age years, before her cheekbones surfaced and her mouth grew big enough to hold her teeth. This young woman, the seventeen-year-old with her curtain of hair and flash of a smile and lyrical curve of jaw, might be my favorite Maya yet.

I knew who was approaching before I looked up. Guests weren't supposed to be in the staff wing, but Kay bent the rules from the start, coming in the back door instead of the front.

He stood for a while, watching me gaze at my sleeping daughter. "I feel like I'm witnessing the most powerful force on the planet. A mother's love for her child."

"She's done that since she was a baby," I said, my throat tight. "Slept crosswise. I'd find her in the morning curled like a pea in the corner of her crib. Even now, if you share a bed, I guarantee that at some point in the night she will flip ninety degrees and kick you in the kidneys."

He tucked away a smile. "You'd better come upstairs to my king-size bed, then. For your own safety."

I stared into his eyes, the green around his iris, those eye crinkles that I wanted to kiss. "What are we doing here, Kay?"

He ran his fingers through my hair and leaned over and breathed in, like he was inhaling me.

"You're solid ground," he said, his voice deep and quiet. "You're a piece of the real world, good, clean earth. You anchor me."

I blinked back sudden, stupid tears. "That's a good answer."

He worked his fingers through mine and tugged gently. He led, and I followed.

I silently gathered my hairbrush and toothpaste, located my one pair of PJs that wasn't ten years old, and followed him up to the Red Bluff Room. The full moon shone beside its companion planets, shedding an otherworldly glow into the room. I swore I could hear my plants quietly respirating. Further away came the distinct rattle of the Navajo refinery, extracting oil from deep within the earth and releasing benzene into the air. There was no place safe from the dangers of the world.

There was only what we did with the time we had.

I went to the telescope and peered through it. "Whoa. Are those the rings of Saturn? They're so clear."

Kay came up behind me and put his hands on my hips. I felt enfolded and cherished at the same time. His touch calmed me.

"I've never seen anything sexier," he said, his voice a low rumble, "than you dancing on the porch."

"Pfft." I turned in his arms. "You see sexier things every time you look through your camera lens."

He inched his fingers around my waist, his eyes shadowed. "You're not going to run?"

"Not yet." I nuzzled my nose into his scruff. Soft, like a pelt.

Who had run from this guy before? I couldn't imagine the circumstances. Hetero women must storm him in herds, trampling undergrowth in their eagerness.

"You know what I forgot?" I bit his chin, gently. "Your truffles."

"Guess you'll have to make it up to me." He walked us toward the bed, his arousal pressing into the delicate skin above my thigh.

I laughed and pressed my hands to his cheek, taking a moment to breathe him in, savoring the moment of free fall. The sheer exhilaration of feeling this way. The liberation of throwing my cautions to the wind, letting them land where they may.

"I'll do my best," I promised, and I did.

Chapter Fifteen

I was dating a vampire.

On one hand, I was dating, so that was nice. I woke up every morning to Kay's warm chest snugged against my shoulder blades, his arm slung over my waist. We wasted too much water playing with the spray nozzle in the shower and ate breakfast on the porch or in the kitchen with Maya if she was awake. Then Madz came to pick him up, Glenn popping in to say hello to me in between prepping Kay for the day's schedule, and with a quick kiss on my cheek—we kissed in public now, in front of people—he was gone.

I spent my days making dramatic changes in Bernie's yard, the scope of the project growing daily. There wasn't an end in sight, and wary, bitter Dale asked if loopy, high-on-daily-sex Dale thought it was wise to make sure she wouldn't be done for at least six more weeks, the exact amount of time in Kay's shooting schedule.

Loopy Dale wasn't taking questions. Kay would return after dinner and sometimes well after dark, finding me in the sitting room with the girls, flipping through a magazine or gardening book while Ana tracked starlight and Maya binge-watched dramadies about young adults with supernatural powers adjusting to the ups and downs of adult life.

He'd chat with us a few minutes—I appreciated that he took the time to talk to Maya, who still called him Mr. Kay behind his back, too in awe of him to say much to his face—and then he would lead me upstairs and my life would take on its own supernatural dimension, the incredible things this man did to me, and made me feel.

I'd fall asleep in his arms with stars showering in my head, dream the most vivid dreams of my life, and wake up to a silver-gold sun and the smell of him all around me. His morning kiss would rouse an ache that left me with a slow buzz of arousal that lasted all day, until my vampire lover returned and the flames consumed me once more.

Regan came back to the B&B some nights when she had a short filming day, but those weren't often. She was the co-star after all, at the hero's side for most of the action, plus she had a side plot of her own, though she couldn't tell me what it was. Anahita kept me company in the evenings, Taiye in the mornings. Pete showed up when Regan did.

For once, I didn't have a vision, a blueprint, a handbook, or rules. I was in open water, surrounded by sharks. Every morning, when Kay left, I thought this might be the end, and I prepared for him to be finished with me. Every night, when he led me upstairs, his hand around mine felt firmer, heavier. Like a commitment. His body against mine was a seal, a promise.

I threw myself into Bernie's yard, into more impossible dreams.

I was in for a hard, hard landing. I knew that, and yet I couldn't stop myself any more than a sunflower could keep from turning toward the light.

Maya surprised me with an announcement one afternoon while we sat on the front porch, sipping strawberry agua fresca.

I was watching where the afternoon light fell to determine where I wanted to plant my Mexican feather grass and false indigo. We were both barefoot, taking turns pushing the swing, and I was enjoying this moment of being in rhythm with her, so different from the hectic lives we'd led during the school year.

"I think I want to go into the medical field," Maya said out of the blue. "And if I do, I think I want to be a doctor. But maybe I should try it out first, right?"

"Hastings College has pre-med programs," I said, instantly

planning. "You'd probably want to major in biology or biochemistry, at least. I imagine you'll qualify for all sorts of scholarships, and you might have an in since your dad and I are alumni. That is, if you're still planning on staying around Hastings." I hadn't quite given up hope that at some point she'd want to see more of the world.

"There's that," Maya said. She never argued; her strategy was always *yes, but also*. "But also, there's a six-week CNA program offered through the Eastern New Mexico campus in Roswell. I just got off the phone with them, and they think they could fit me in. Classes start next week."

My heart skipped a beat. The Maya who hadn't been to Europe yet would have run all this past me, looked over my shoulder while I did some more research, and then held my eyes as I coached her through the call. The Maya who'd been to England, France, and Switzerland had called the school, found out the details, and come up with a plan.

"That could work," I said slowly. I was nearly done planting and just had the greenhouses to frame out and the water feature to build, for which I needed Pete. At least four more weeks of work. Kay was scheduled to be in Artesia four more weeks, shooting on location before they packed up and headed to a studio in Albuquerque.

Bernie had assured me I could stay as long as I wanted, and she was thrilled that Maya was here. She insisted I wasn't freeloading but rather adding life to the place and giving her staff a break. Only Bernie would cheerfully extend her invitation when I was tearing apart her yard, sleeping with one of her guests, and letting my daughter stay in one of her rooms for free.

There were other paying guests now that the construction guy was gone, tourists who trooped in and out. The writer was still around somewhere, and Ana said he'd finally paid his bill. But the Desert Bloom was far less lively with Kay gone all day, Regan gone most days, and Maya out exploring the town, volunteering time at the local history museum. Eve stayed one night and left the next morning, eyes hidden behind dark sunglasses, with Madz driving her and Ernie to the Artesia airport. She told me to call her when I was in LA, which I thought was very kind of her to offer, though I couldn't imagine when I would ever be in LA.

Unless I were visiting Kay, who also lived there. But I didn't think that's where this thing with him was headed. I didn't have fantasies that he would ask me to move to LA with him. We both understood what we had, this delirious and dizzying affair, came with firm borders and an expiration date.

That thought hurt, like a taproot pushing deep in my chest, and I blocked it out. "It's fine if you want to be a nurse," I said. "Nurses are superheroes too."

"No, it would definitely be doctor." Maya twirled the bamboo straw in her drink. "Dad is just so traumatized by all his treatments when he was a kid. I want to treat sick kids better. Plus, Adam's been telling me all about his therapy and the surgeries he wants, and I just love talking about how the human body works."

"You'd make a great doctor. Remember that time with the shrub rake, and you bandaged my ankle?" Maya still hadn't made up with her dad, and I wasn't going to push. I finished my drink and let the cool liquid slide down my throat.

"How are you going to get to Roswell for classes?"

She gave me an innocent look. "I thought I could borrow the Jeep?"

I choked on an ice cube as the Toyota Rav pulled up before the house. Glenn stepped out in a navy suit with white stripes, tight white tank top, clip-on tie, and their favorite sneakers. They'd tipped their short hair with bright blue color.

"Want to visit an alien colony this afternoon?" Glenn called. "I can get you on set today. Sorry, Maya, not you, just your mom. The studio is being very tight-assed about this production. They're freaking out over the pictures."

"What pictures?" I lurched from the swing, gaining my feet.

Glenn gave me a hard, level look. I had the clear sense that

Glenn's approval was conditional, and they'd throw me under a bus in a second if it protected Kay or his movie.

"Kay hasn't told you? They're shitty snaps, very amateur."

Cool liquid sloshed in my belly. People kept talking about pictures. Maya nudged my elbow. "You need to change, Mom."

"Why? Is there a dress code on set?" My heart skipped at the thought of seeing Kay, watching him work, viewing him in his natural element. It skipped some more at the thought that I might embarrass him. Glenn seemed more glammed up than usual and Madz wore a collarless black button-down beneath his black leather coat.

"It's a lot of sitting, and a lot of being silent," Glenn said. "So dress for that."

Maya made me dress down in a pair of faded jeans, so well-worn the denim was like silk and hugged my curves like a lover. She paired this with a patterned green blouse and a handmade beadwork scarf that I bought at the Taos Pueblo. While I slipped on my hemp moccasins, Maya tied the scarf in my hair, and I hesitated only a second before snatching up the green tourmaline necklace that Bernie had presented me as a divorce gift. I wouldn't admit to believing in the healing properties of stones any more than I believed in the influence of astrological bodies, but if this stone did half of what Bernie described, I wanted it on my side.

"I suppose I shouldn't expect you home tonight," Maya said with a mischievous smile as she walked with me onto the porch.

"Maya Rose. I will be home by curfew, as will you."

"Good luck with that." She winked. "Can I have the keys to the Jeep? There's a cute stationery store downtown, and I need school supplies. Anahita said she'd come with me."

I had no choice but to hand over the keys, and Maya laughed at my muttered warnings. "Enjoy yourself, Mom. You look great. You deserve this."

I slid into the front seat of the hired car, pulling my cork handbag onto my lap. Why did I need my daughter telling me it was okay to enjoy this time with Kay? Why was I having such a hard time giving myself permission?

"What about these pictures of Regan?" I asked as Glenn climbed into the back seat, phone out as they texted.

"They've been floating around for a while. Eve saw them when she was in Monaco. I don't know who's taking them, but I want their head. They're mostly snaps of her and Pete, really grainy and not very flattering. They make her look like she's slumming."

I winced. That had to be the worst part of being a celebrity: the public's unassailable belief that they had a right to know about your private life. I wondered how Regan endured it.

"Speaking of snaps." Glenn handed a camera over the backseat. "Here's how you can help. Our still photographer sprained her wrist, please don't ask me how, and Kay likes pictures of productions. We have the cameras capturing behind-the-scenes video, but you know Kay, he's an old-fashioned kind of guy. And stills are great for features, extras, promo, that sort of thing. So grab whatever catches your eye."

I took the camera with reverence. "A Sony Alpha 7? There's a damage waiver, right? I can't afford to pay for this if I drop it."

Glenn laughed. "I knew I could trust you with her."

"I'm not a photographer. The most I do is take pictures of ideas for gardens." I slipped the strap of the camera around my neck and cradled it against my chest. I'd enjoyed photography in high school, had in fact worked for the school's literary journal, and kept up the hobby when Maya was little. But then she grew, and Ritche was around less as his job grew more demanding, and photography, like my gardening, was something else I put aside. Promising myself I'd come back to it, someday down the road when I had more time.

Now, I had time. Someday was here.

I curved my fingers around the black plastic case. Ever since I'd arrived in Artesia, pieces of my old self kept coming back to me, like a resurrection.

Then there was Kay, who was blazingly, blindingly new, and yet felt like the thing I'd been wanting and waiting for, yet convinced my hand would get slapped if I dare reach for it.

Madz drove us west through the town of Hope, which wasn't as big as my high school graduating class back in Springfield, and then further through the dry brown grasslands scattered with dark green shrubs of mesquite and manzanita. Beyond Hope the flat plains of the Pecos Basin fell away and the ground grew more humped, until the dark ridges of Lincoln National Forest and the shadowy, far-off mountains of the Mescalero Apache Reservation appeared on the horizon. Madz turned down a dirt road, passed through a booth with a security guard checking ID, and then drove slowly into the makeshift village that had sprouted up overnight.

Glenn handed me a lanyard with a plastic tag stamped with my name, headshot—who had taken a picture of me, and when?—and, in large letters, VISITOR. Madz parked in a double row of other cars and equipment trucks, and I looked around, staring. To the north were rows of trailers lined up liked rabbits in their hutches, some of them with folding chairs set up beneath awnings. Food trucks and other portable buildings lined a dusty track leading to what could have been a row of booths from a carnival or Renaissance Faire. Each canopy was crowded with tables, chairs, people, and stacks of equipment that looked, even from a distance, incredibly complex. There were tall stands holding arrays of lights, tall stands holding whirring fans, stands with large fabric screens the function of which I couldn't guess, a tall crane with its arm hanging at rest, and another food truck.

I followed Glenn through the crowd of people toward what seemed to be the center of action. Beneath one canopy, in front of a smaller fan, Regan stood in a grimy white lab coat, leather heels, hair loose and streaming, dried blood caked on the side of her face. Makeup, I reminded myself, nudging my heart to calm down. She drank from a metal water bottle while someone rubbed dirt onto the hem of her coat and another person dabbed powder onto her cheek. Without thinking, I lifted my camera and snapped.

Beneath another canopy sat the other star of the film, Chris Stevens. He wore a tight brown T-shirt and dusty cargo pants and had fake dirt smeared across his epically handsome face. He was the kind of handsome that seemed cut and shaped, the product of careful honing. His battered black combat boots were stretched out before him, and he ignored the makeup artist carefully patting powder into his hair, his nose in a thick book. I strained to look: Colson Whitehead's *Underground Railroad*. I raised the camera and clicked, my stomach fluttering. It felt illicit and surreal to be behind the scenes, watching the actors be transformed, watching the magic being carefully crafted.

Kay loomed at the center of it all, the pulse of this snaky network of cords and displays and props and hundreds of people. Stooping, he peered at a panel of crazy-expensive looking equipment, composed of screens, dials, buttons, and blinking lights. Des stood beside him, peering at the same thing. At least half a dozen people stood around watching them, holding clipboards, coffee cups, and more expensive-looking equipment.

Regan's blood-stained face filled the screen, wearing an expression of disbelief. Kay pointed something out to Des. Impulsively I raised my camera and snapped. I loved this job, and I would ask for this picture later, capturing the moment that I gained another insight into the real Timothy Kay.

He conferred with Des, gesturing to the landscape beyond the camera. He wore his Aviators ballcap backwards, thick hair springing below the brim, his beard growing shaggy. His T-shirt advertised the Violent Femmes and his shorts hung from his waist, as if he were shedding pounds. I watched the flex of his shoulder blades, his articulate hands, the flash of a smile as Des made a comment, and heat roared through me like a speeding locomotive, carrying a realization I didn't want to confront. I wanted to wrap my arms and legs around him and press my lips to the tender back of his neck, and then his throat, and then every other part of his body, yes. But I didn't want to think about what it meant, this urgency, this craving that went deep beneath the skin.

He lifted his head as if he sensed me, and his smile sent excitement pounding through me like waves crashing on the beach. I couldn't hear him over the blood pounding in my head.

"Finally," he said, moving toward me. "This day has improved one hundred percent."

He pulled me close, one hand on my arm, and dropped a kiss on my cheekbone. I flushed with pleasure. "Hi. I am your still photographer for the day."

He inhaled in that way he did, breathing me in, and my heart flopped like a hooked fish. Timothy Kay, Hollywood director, the brains of this operation, drawing support from me.

He closed his fingers around my wrist. "Can I keep you always? I'll fire the other one."

Des chuckled. "Union'll have something to say about that. What do you think of all this, Dale?"

"Big." Words failed me as I looked around. It was confused, chaotic, completely unromantic, and terribly exciting.

"Big mess." Kay ran a hand over his face. "Des, set up for the next close-up. Avery, prep Chris." The assistant director, a slim, undistinguished-looking man with a ponytail and wireless specs, nodded and slipped off toward the actor's tent. Kay turned to me.

"Maybe you can give Regan some moral support. She's in a slump today."

"What happened?"

"The internet is blowing up with some pictures of her and Pete. Don't know where they came from, or who's to blame, but they're grubby and the press isn't good." He blew out a stream of air. I wanted to press my fingers to the line between his brows, smooth the frown away.

"Glenn said something about it. You think I can help?"

"She likes you." He lifted the ends of my scarf, rubbing the fabric between his fingers. I quivered as if he were caressing my skin. "Almost as much as I like you. How does everyone like you? How do you do it?"

"Not everyone," I said with a laugh. I tried to think of an example and then stopped myself. Why would I give him examples? I *wanted* Kay to like me.

"If you can perk Regan up, it will save some footage and possibly my entire day," Kay said. "I don't have an inch to spare in the budget as it is."

"I'll see what I can do."

Regan's tense expression broke into a smile as I approached the canopy where the hair and makeup team were prepping her. "Dale. I'm glad you're here."

Regan had a multi-megawatt smile she could use at will, as I'd seen, but I was foolishly happy that her smile for me seemed genuine. I hadn't done a thing to win her confidence, yet she seemed ready to trust me.

"Kay said it's been a difficult day."

"Have you seen the pictures? Lola, show her the phone."

A slim girl with severe black bangs and enormous black-framed glasses stepped forward with Regan's phone. The pictures were terrible. Pete looked unkempt and hungover, his expression a foolish leer. In the photo of them kissing, blurry and faraway, only his hand on her ass was clear. A crass move, even for Pete. The worst was one where Regan seemed to be tripping over a bike rack. They were outside the Fat Straw, a place I'd recommended they could hang out without being gaped at, and someone caught Regan at an ungraceful moment, her face strained and surprised, while Pete's move to catch her arm looked more violent than chivalrous.

"Regan Forrester caught in clinch with seedy cowboy." the headline said. "Sexiest Woman Alive slumming?" Lola clicked through several sites showing the same pictures, while the clickbait captions grew worse.

"Ick," I said. "Who *does* that?"

"Anyone who can." Regan took another drink of water, mouth set in a grim line.

It made me queasy to think that she'd come to Artesia for refuge, to try to forget how quickly the world had forgiven and taken the side of a man who had attacked her in her own apartment, then did his best to smear her in interviews, putting her family, her relationships, her history in the worst possible light. I'd caved and crawled the Internet for news, and I wasn't proud of it. Now, when she'd met a guy who happily distracted her, who made her smile a sweet, silly smile, some rude photographer made him look coarse and her desperate.

"Fake news. The internet lies." I wasn't helping.

"They're right that any publicity is good publicity." Regan stared out at the grey, dusty landscape with the band of dark blue clouds piled on the horizon. "Kay will be happy for the buzz about his movie."

"Not at your expense," I said. "He's concerned for you."

"Thick skin." The artfully applied dirt and realistic wound against her glowing copper complexion made her look young and vulnerable. "Rolls right off me." Bright green lights glittered in her eyes.

I lifted the camera and snapped another picture, then immediately caught myself. "God, I'm so sorry. That was thoughtless—I didn't even ask."

She looked at me and forced a smile. "It's okay. It's in my contract. Ready?" she said to someone over my shoulder.

Avery, the A.D., nodded. "When you are." His soft accent hinted at Australia.

I followed, beating myself up for making things worse, but I'd given myself too much credit. Regan was a pro. Her entire demeanor changed as the A.D. called everyone to settle and snapped the clapper. I held my breath, determined not to make a sound.

Chris Stevens was a decent actor; he knew how to create an effect. He was watchable, but Regan was mesmerizing. She poured emotion into the smallest movement, a flicker of the eyes, a lilt of the head, a slight catch of breath. She beamed fear, vulnerability, and steely determination in the tremble of her dewy lips, the tightening of her heavily made-up eyes.

A slight movement from Kay's direction made me glance at him. He'd taken the camera from Des, had it strapped to him in a way that brought out the muscles of his back, the weight of it showing in the flex of his chest and arms. He crept toward Regan as if he, too, were mesmerized by her performance, as if he couldn't get close enough. Every part of his being was focused on the small screen filled with her face, so close the camera caught the breeze that stirred the tiny hairs at her temples. He stared, I stared, the camera stared, everybody stared at Regan, who held her expression longer than seemed humanly possible.

"Cut." Finally, at long last, Kay stepped back. "Great. Absolutely perfect, Regan."

The words sent a shiver down my back, of regret, perhaps envy. It was clear the camera adored Regan Forrester.

I still couldn't believe that Kay, staring all day and every day at that angelic face, didn't fall for her, too. But here in action, I could see his discipline, his efficiency, his ability to set aside distractions.

He'd moved on from Regan Forrester without blinking. It'd be even easier for him to move on from Dale Rose.

The thought made my hands shake. The next picture would be nothing but a blur.

"Okay, reset up for Chris's close-up," Kay called to everyone else standing around. "Des, I'll shoot this one too. I want you to see what I was talking about."

I stood by, feeling hyper self-conscious, in the way, and, despite my sudden agony, not about to leave. It was high time to stake some things out with Kay, and besides that, I'd never been on a movie set before. People swarmed the spot where Chris and Regan had been sitting, moving lights and the white screens and fans into different positions. Des tried to explain the various people and their roles to me, but it all sounded like made-up words—sparks, grip, best boy, gaffer. I snapped a picture of Kay, absorbed in his camera, and he looked up at me briefly and smiled.

This was his world, and he'd welcomed me in. I was getting a front-row seat to his skill, his interest, his passion—the thing that drove him—and I loved it.

There was that L word again. It floated dangerously close to the realization that had surged through me earlier and still hummed around in my veins.

I held my breath again as Chris and Regan played the scene over, the jaded soldier and the earnest lab tech discussing what to do with the alien nest. Regan turned it all on again, the steely determination, the dewy tremble. Des squatted in front of them with a second camera while Kay focused on Chris Stevens with the same complete absorption he'd shown filming Regan. I found myself being pulled into the scene, believing the urgency, the desperation. It amazed me that they could pretend so hard—make it *feel* real—when the lighting stands and power cords and a crew of at least twenty silent people were all right there, not to mention someone holding a boom microphone just above their heads.

"Cut," Kay said, and the actors rose to their feet. "That's good for eighty." He started unstrapping the camera. Three people ran up to hold it while he untangled himself.

"Eighty?" I said to Des.

"The scene number," Des said.

"How many *are* there?"

"Thirty-minute break," someone called. "Back here and on marks for scene ninety in thirty minutes, everyone."

Des rolled his shoulders. "I love US union rules. Power nap."

Kay brushed the back on my hand. A tingle shot from my fingertips to everywhere. "What do you want to see?" he asked.

I stared at him, not knowing how to phrase my response. I wanted to see all of it, everything to do with him. "Your trailer," popped out instead.

His eyes darkened, his eyelids tensing in a look I'd begun to recognize. "Come with me."

I followed him along the dirt track, the line of canopies, the food truck, and the portable buildings to where the RV trailers sat tucked nose to nose. One was set a bit apart, as if for privacy. He took my hand and held it to his back as he unlocked the door, and the tingling of my skin intensified.

"Introducing *mi casita*," he said, turning to pull me against him.

"So this is where you're staying." I touched his shoulder as he kissed the side of my neck, rubbing his cheek against my scarf.

"This is where I have a spare set of clothes. I'm staying at the Desert Bloom."

"For the next four weeks." I sifted through the curls growing at his nape. A skylight in the ceiling turned the air golden. "Then Albuquerque."

"That's the plan."

"Then I guess I'd better enjoy what I've got, while I've got it."

He stilled, his nose in my Taos scarf. "Things end in Albuquerque?"

I went for a laugh, light as I could make it. "That's also the plan, isn't it? I mean, I think we've been clear from the start. Neither of us is looking for long-term. You don't do that, and I'm not ready." I dug my fingers into my shoulders. I wished I could be ready. I wished I could simply let go and fall into the mighty wind rising around me, paraglide into the unknown.

That was my problem. I wanted to know where I was heading. I wanted blueprints, flashlight, and a backup plan.

"Any way I look at it, your life is in Los Angeles. Mine is in Hastings. I have Maya to look after, and you have your job."

He nuzzled his nose against my neck. "Los Angeles isn't that far from Hastings. Cars go there now. And planes."

But what was he offering? And where could this possibly go? My laugh sounded even more forced, unsteady. "Well, what were *you* thinking happens next?"

He didn't lift his head. "I don't know, either. I haven't thought ahead. I'm just responding to the fires in front of me."

I knew that. I *knew* he simply lived in the moment, present, aware, responsive. It was one of the things I loved about him.

Loved. Oh, God.

I tightened my arms around him. "Enjoy what we have while we have it."

I leaned into his kiss, wishing I could sidestep all the heavy things reaching out to entangle me. I didn't want the rest of our time to be desperate, stolen. Let it be playful. Fun. I needed that in my life.

"I've heard of something called the casting couch, but I'm not sure what it is," I whispered against his mouth.

"Let me introduce you." He lifted me into his arms and carried me toward the sofa, scattered with Kokopelli prints in bright colors. "What role are you auditioning for, Miss Rose?"

I slid my hand between his legs, fondling him through his shorts. He was ready for this, if nothing else.

"I want a big part. Big." I nibbled his earlobe, and he shivered. "Not just the pretty sidekick. I wanna drive the getaway car. And I wanna maybe shoot somebody."

He fell onto the couch and pulled me down with him. "Show me how much you want this part."

I pressed him onto the couch and had my wicked way with him, glad I'd worn the green satin lingerie set as I stripped him and slithered down between his legs, delighting in the hitch in his breath, his small groans. It wasn't long before he pulled me up and atop him, fisting a hand in my hair while I surged against him, a gentle collision, an inevitable meeting of tide and land. I came apart quickly, and so did something in my chest, something I'd kept tight and hard and locked for a long time.

He shuddered inside me, then lingered, his face in my neck. "How is it you make everything better?" he murmured near my ear.

It hit me again, that senseless, crashing wave, and I struggled not to cry. It wasn't simply release. It was knowledge, unavoidable, inescapable, that crept up my rib cage and curled around my heart, squeezing out the truth I'd tried to glance away from.

I was in love with Timothy Kay. This wasn't a thing, a fling, a rebound, or a holiday. Not for me.

I was in love. Deep, hard, and solid. It felt *wonderful.*

And I was completely unprepared for what that meant.

Chapter Sixteen

"Seedy cowboy." Pete snarled as he thumbed through the pictures on his phone. "Dimestore cowboy. Drugstore cowboy? I'm not an addict."

"Put it away. They don't mean anything. Just some rude people trying to make a buck." I reached across the small table and tugged at his wrist, trying to pry his hand off the phone.

"The whole world thinks Regan is slumming." He leaned back in his chair, glaring at the other tables as if daring people to judge him.

We sat on the sidewalk outside the brewpub where about half the tables were filled, other people finishing up their meals or lingering over their drinks. The night air was warm and sticky. The next day promised rain, which meant Kay was staying late at the shoot, making sure all the equipment was under cover.

I knew he'd fret about the budget, but a rain delay might mean he'd have an extra hour or two to spend with me.

Pete drummed his fingers on his phone, and I tapped his wrist again, trying to snap him out of it. "Do you care what the world thinks?"

He blew out air and sat forward. "Yes. No. Yes, because she'll care. She has to worry about her image so that she'll be offered the roles she wants."

"That's Eve's job, as her manager, to worry about Regan's image," I said. "What are you really worried about?"

He turned a shade frantic. I'd never seen Pete, cool, collected

Pete, frantic about anything. He was the definition of laidback.

He gripped my hand with tight fingers. "That she *is* slumming. And she thinks so too. We're just civilians, Dale. We're not in their class at all."

My heart thumped. I was in the same situation, whether I wanted to admit it or not.

But I'd known from the beginning what I was being roped into, as surely as that cowboy downing the calf in front of the Hotel Artesia. I signed an NDA, for crying out loud. I lived in a world of plant catalogues, and Kay lived in a world where he couldn't buy condoms for himself.

"What do you want to happen?" I asked Pete.

He lifted one side of his mouth, an attempt at the cocky rodeo rider I knew. "Why did you sleep with me, Dale?"

I flushed. Did we have to talk about this now? "Because I knew you weren't looking for a relationship. I needed to be touched, and you weren't going to demand anything more than that."

He nodded. "So you used me for sex."

"No." I smacked him with my free hand. "Well, yes. But I thought you felt the same way. You were exactly what I wanted at the time, and you were very cool about working with me after. No weirdness at all."

He held my eyes. "It's different with her," he said.

The raw look on his face tugged at me. Pete wasn't a guy to sit and contemplate his feelings. "How?"

"There's going to be weirdness."

I picked up my beer. "You want more."

He sat back, our hands parting as the server approached to take our empty plates. "Yep."

I didn't know how to answer that. His admission sank into me like a spear in the stomach.

I wanted more from Kay, too.

The Toyota pulled up to the curb a minute later, and Regan climbed out first. She wasn't a tall woman, yet somehow she looked all limbs and sleek hair, even though she was dressed down in faded jeans and a tight black tank top, dark hair pulled up into a messy bun. Pete came alive at the sight of her, as if he'd been plugged in.

"It feels cold," she said, sliding into the chair next to him. "Are you cold?"

Pete immediately peeled off his flannel and wrapped her in it. She smiled up at him, and they sat like that, his beefy arm around her shoulder, her radiant face turned up to his.

Whatever she was doing, Regan wasn't using Pete for sex. She was hooked.

"You're tired because your mean director is working you too hard," Pete said.

"We had to squeeze in extra shooting today in case we get rained out tomorrow." Kay folded his long frame into the chair beside mine. "Why did no one tell my location scout how windy it could get here? Or that September gets nearly as much rain as July?"

"It's going to be great for the catchment system," I said. "I'll get to test out the drip irrigation system we just finished installing today. Pull up a chair," I said as Glenn approached. "We weren't sure if you'd be able to join us."

"We can't," Glenn said. "I'm helping the producer come up with an alternate shoot schedule for tomorrow to see what we can do indoors, while my boss relaxes at the pub and has a beer."

Kay lifted his nose from my glass and licked his lips. "Mmm. Chocolate and coffee. What is this?"

"The Crude Oil stout, made right here," I said. "Pete's drinking the Roughneck Red."

"I want the pale ale with a bison patty melt," Regan announced. "And fries."

"I want to know who's responsible for the pictures." Glenn fixed a hard gaze on Pete.

He stiffened. "So do I."

Regan frowned. "I want to know why they make me look so dumpy. The ones of Dale are so much better."

My hand froze, reaching to take my beer away from Kay. "What pictures of me?"

Glenn shot a look at Kay. "You didn't tell her?"

Kay lifted an arm to the back of my chair, brushing his fingers over my shoulder blades. "This is the first I've talked to her all day, Glenn."

Suddenly the night was much too warm. "What pictures?"

Regan sat up, wide-eyed, clutching Pete's flannel around her. "Dale. You didn't know?"

Glenn tapped their phone and held the screen toward me. Kay curled his fingers around my shoulder as if bracing me against the impact.

It was actually a lovely shot. The light fell golden and graceful across my face as I stood on the sidewalk before the monument of Ellie Chisum. My hair floated in the slight breeze and the skirt of my dress outlined my thighs. Kay was in profile, sunglasses shoved back on his head, but there was no mistaking it was him. The photographer had captured me staring up at him as if he were the most astonishing, delightful, amazing thing I had ever seen in my life. I wore the same expression Regan had worn a minute ago for Pete.

The expression of a woman on the brink of falling in love.

"See what I mean? The light? The framing? You look good, Dale. Whereas I just look frumpy." Regan pouted.

Pete said something to her to the effect that she could never be frumpy, and she turned to him, giving me a minute to catch my breath. Kay watched me, his face guarded, that bland reserve in place, but the tight lines at the corner of his eyes gave away his concern.

"But this was weeks ago," I said. "Our first day together. Why now?"

"I saw this one weeks ago." Regan's eyes grew wide. "I told you, remember? Eve forwarded them to me."

"They showed up on some social profile we couldn't trace, but I didn't get my knickers in a twist because they didn't get picked up," Glenn said grimly. "But now Regan's opened the tap, and she and Kay are both targets, and I'll bet there's a ton of these going to be fed to the paps like fish at the killer whale exhibit. Any idea who was following you that day?"

"Besides Madz? No. I didn't think anyone recognized who Kay was."

I sat back, reeling. Even with all the attention on Regan, I hadn't seen this coming. I hadn't thought for a minute that I—or rather, Kay—might be a target of attention too.

"Timothy Kay flirts with local while setting up for shoot." Pete read the short caption aloud. "The director of the sci-fi blockbuster *The Visitors*, which smashed opening records last summer, is in Artesia, New Mexico, to start filming the sequel, which sources say is about…" He trailed off, murmuring the rest.

"They didn't say anything more than what the studio has already released," Kay pointed out. He sounded and looked relaxed, but I sensed the tension in his body. "And it's not a secret that we're filming here."

"The only secret is the mystery woman," Glenn confirmed. "The heat is going to be on, Dale." They looked at me with concern. "They're going to start digging through your life, talking to your friends, trying to find dirt, because that's what sells."

I forced myself to breathe. In through the nose, out through the mouth. "The only dirt on me is under my fingernails."

To my own ears I sounded whimpering, not glib, but Glenn nodded in satisfaction. "That's my girl. Don't let them get in your head. Kay, I'll send you the call sheets after I talk to Emeka. We'll have to send them out tonight."

Regan sighed. "Can I get a six o'clock for makeup? I'd love to sleep in."

They were back to movie business, as if my world hadn't just been upended. I focused on breathing. In, out. A picture. That had captured me gazing adoringly at Kay. Big deal. Plenty of women had done the same. My being star-struck with him was not remarkable. Or love-struck, either. I'd known the risks from the beginning.

I simply wasn't prepared for how it would feel to have those private moments on display, available for the whole world to look at.

"Who cares what the world thinks?" Pete sat forward and spoke softly, reminding me of the words I'd said to him. Words that had come so much more easily when it was him being judged, not me.

"Right," I said, lifting my beer. "Who cares?"

Kay wasn't fooled. He waited until we were quiet in bed that night, tucked into the Red Bluff Room, with a soy candle softly burning in one corner and the stars flung across the night sky, glittering fragments against an immense cloak of black.

"It stings, I know." He combed his fingers through my hair, over the curve of my ear. "You think you have something all your own, and then, bam. There it is. On screen for everyone to look at, like, or comment."

I drowsed under his touch, warm and safe, the threats of the world far away. All that mattered was what we shared here, between us. This was the real world.

I turned on my side to face him, grateful to be understood, and ran a hand over his bare chest, the hair soft beneath my palm. "You don't like it either, but you bear it."

"It comes with the job. The difference is I signed up for it. You didn't. Anyone around me—they don't ask for that."

"Is that what makes it hard?" I whispered. "Because I mean, on the street, in civilian life, a guy like you would not be single for five minutes."

He chuckled and rested a finger on the hollow below my ear. "You were listening. The girls I like don't want that life, in the camera lens 24/7. And the girls who want that life, I don't like. It's a Catch-22."

His voice was warm and deep in the quiet. I moved my fingers over his heart. It beat steadily, unhurried, strong and firm.

"What's the way out?"

He ran his fingers down the side of my neck. "I haven't found it yet. But I'm hoping there is one."

He stroked my collarbone, the gentle touch soothing and arousing at the same time. I rested my hand over his heart, enjoying the connection.

"At least you didn't break up with me," he whispered.

His finger resting between my collarbone suddenly felt heavy, pushing back my breath. I'd been drifting along in a kind of delirium, floating on the waves, pretending I didn't know I was in a wave pool and sooner or later the waves would stop.

My breath came shallow and fast. I didn't want to talk about this, even though the night, the shadows, made it easier to face the truth. "What's next for you after Albuquerque?"

"Finishing B roll, editing, sound, and fighting with production to keep the CGI from taking over." He moved his finger lower, tracing more delicate curves. "And you?"

My throat tightened. "After Maya finishes her coursework and I finish my job for Bernie, I guess we go back to Hastings. I have a decide if I'm going to keep my job, and Maya will be applying for schools, and I…"

Would be nursing a broken heart, all over again. Parting with Kay would be like losing a limb. I was sure of that.

While a broken heart was exactly what I'd been trying to avoid, all this time.

Kay brought his finger back up to curve around my breast. The air conditioning clicked on, stirring the pot of anthurium.

"Los Angeles and Nebraska aren't different solar systems."

What was he asking me? I couldn't read his face in the shadows. His heartbeat gave nothing away, as unhurried as ever.

He'd never been in love. He'd admitted that. He wasn't tossed and shaken with the feelings that stormed through me, the peaks of passion, the depths of fear. Whatever he felt, it was real, it was sincere—there was affection, attention, care. I felt it from him, deep and strong.

But whether it came with dedication and commitment—that we hadn't discussed. That belonged in a separate realm, too.

"Tell me what you want," I whispered.

He slid his hand down my chest, perhaps so he could feel my heartbeat. It was hard and erratic, gulping and racing with all the emotion flowing through me. I couldn't hide my feelings from him even if I wanted to.

Maybe this was why he was still single. Maybe, no matter how good it was, the ease and companionship and the connection that deepened each day, there was a limit to how close people were allowed to get to him. A woman who wanted him, really wanted to be with him—she wouldn't be content with being held at arm's length.

I wouldn't be content with being held at arm's length.

A few internet trolls commenting on how I wasn't good enough for Timothy Kay wouldn't be nearly as bad as staying with him, loving him, and knowing I had no claim on his heart.

"The picture thing rattles me," I said, my voice a whisper in the quiet. "I don't know how Regan can stand it. She told me she has a thick skin, but—I don't, Kay. My skin is really, really thin. I would never be able to live like that, examined, gossiped about, judged."

He held his palm above my heart, firm, solid, radiating warmth.

"I want you to stay," he said. "No matter what the pictures look like. Or what people say about them."

There were only a few weeks more of this. Of hiding away with him, making love with him, talking with him about movies and our families and our dreams for the future. Putting up with some rando posting pictures and making money off his access to Kay, however he'd gotten it, was a small price to pay for these moments.

"Okay. I'll stick it out," I said, moving to kiss him. "You're worth it."

I meant that, at the time.

Chapter Seventeen

In the pictures of me and Kay appearing in the media, I relived our romance. The way we smiled at each other, hands entwined, as we walked around Artesia. How we leaned toward one another across the breakfast table in the mornings. In the pictures of us dancing together at the Adobe Rose, I looked relaxed, happy, and carefree.

There was a snap of Kay on his morning run, something he didn't have time to do anymore. There was a snap of us on the couch before the TV, wrapped up in a kiss. That one rattled me—was someone lurking outside the house, peering at us through the curtains? Glenn scoured the internet for the day's crop of photos, vigilant for the slightest hint of libel. Glenn didn't accuse me, not outright, but I suspected once or twice that they were trying to decide whether I had leaked those pictures. I wanted to prove my innocence by turning in the culprit, but who had gotten close enough to take these shots? It had to be one of us, someone in the circle.

Des was simply curious when I showed him. "Nice framing there," he said of the picture of Pete and I teaching Regan to plant a tree. I had my hands full of soil while Regan stared curiously into the tender branches above us. "Bit of interest, too, with the blooming pots on the patio. Couldn't have set it up better myself."

Des hadn't been around in the early days. He hadn't been there to catch us at Abo School, holding hands as we stood outside the concrete block, our first kiss still tingling on our lips.

Was Cristina slipping somebody photos? She had a daughter to support and family back in Mexico. I gave her the day off with pay one morning and served the guests myself, ferrying heated dishes, bowls of fruit, and freshly squeezed orange juice into the Georgia O'Keeffe room. The family from Wisconsin thanked me, polished off their plates, and were out of the room in less than fifteen minutes. Maya sat with the writer, chatting about his book. They'd hit it off, but Maya was a favorite with everyone. Taiye had already declared he wanted to adopt her, she had a standing invitation to visit Anahita's family in Bahrain, and she was practicing her Spanish with Cristina's daughter.

Kay didn't eat at the table with the guests but stood at the kitchen island with me, spooning eggs into his mouth with diligent speed. It was a second day of rain, the last in the forecast, and he was waiting out the squall while enjoying a hearty plate of huevos rancheros that I had made and served him.

"How do you stand it?" I griped. "It's an invasion of privacy."

I kept one eye on the dining room and one on the way Kay's throat moved as he chugged orange juice. His scruff was on the verge of becoming a full beard. It was a superstition of his: he let his hair and beard grow while he shot the movie, and then he got a haircut and shaved the beard when editing was done.

"Because, like Samson, your power is in your hair?" I'd joked.

"More like, that's what I did with Seth's and my first movie. And then we won some awards, got picked up by a distributor, caught the eye of a studio, and I somehow decided the beard had done the trick. So of course I had to do it again."

I adored these tiny hints of superstition, how he remembered what his mom's friend read in his cards, how he knew what the planets meant in astrological terms. He wore his grandmother's ring—the one thing his father had given him—whenever he had a meeting with the studio heads, like he was summoning the power of the ancestors to watch over him.

He put his empty dishes in the sink, and something happened inside my chest, as if my heart had moved aside to make room for something else. It was like I'd been walking around with a hole in my life in the exact shape of him, and now that he was here, he filled it perfectly. I brushed a finger over his elbow, the soft skin and hair. I wanted to touch him all the time, even though every part of his body had been pressed around mine last night, and again this morning.

"I don't know how you can be so cool about it," I said. "People prying into your personal life." I was in agony over every new photograph. What did it say about me? What would people think? Glenn warned me not to read the comments—to never, ever read the comments—but the headlines said enough. How had this dumpy, unremarkable woman captivated the reclusive, powerful Timothy Kay? What could she possibly offer him?

"It's not actually my life." Kay rinsed his glass. "It's a story they're making up about my life. They have no idea how I feel about anything. It's a script. I'm in the business of telling stories about made-up people, so I kind of feel it's fair play if people make up stories about me."

"But it's your life," I said. "You're a real person."

"And I'm too busy living my real life to care." He brushed his thumb along my jaw and warmth coursed over my scalp and down my back, a delicious cascade. "What's between us is real, Dale. It doesn't matter what people say about it."

The picture on the gossip channels the next day showed us leaning toward each other right before the kiss, his hand on my face, mine reaching toward him. The morning sun lit the sky outside the windows, backlighting the cottonwood tree like a movie set. The person taking the shot had been standing in the door to the dining room.

At least I knew it hadn't been Cristina.

"Cute happy hetero couple," Taiye said when I showed him the latest news story. "You're like an advertisement for shampoo."

Taiye worked the morning shift. He'd have to be in league with someone to capture the shots of Kay and I kissing when he returned to the Desert Bloom at night.

Pete was as annoyed as I was the snap surfaced of us holding hands across the bar table outside the brew pub, him slouched in his chair, scowling, me leaning toward him, imploring. The headline teased at infidelity, asking if these two were carrying on a secret affair behind the backs of their famous lovers.

"Regan's going to be so pissed." Pete fumed as he shoveled dirt out of the hole for my water feature. I framed out the pipe we'd need to bury while he snapped open a measuring tape. "She'll believe me when I tell her it's bullshit, but she's going to think it's possible I could like you better than I like her. She already doesn't trust any man, thanks to that asshole ex-boyfriend of hers. He made her so insecure, she doesn't believe anyone could really, truly love her."

"You're kidding." I took out my notebook to check the measurements as he read them off. "She's the sexiest woman on the planet. Several magazines agree. I can't believe she's insecure."

"Because she hides it." Pete put down the shovel and reached for the roll of pond liner. "That's why things didn't work out with her and Eve, you know. She figured Eve was just taking pity on her because she was scared and lonely."

That explained Eve's attitude toward Regan: one part loverly, one part motherly, and two parts boss. I'd gotten the sense that Eve knew Regan inside and out and wasn't going to fight her nature. But she did love her, and that's why she would support her as she figured things out, even if it meant she moved on to someone else. That's why Eve would, without hesitation, do a favor for Regan like escort a stranger's daughter home from Europe so she wasn't traveling alone.

"Want me to talk to her?" I hopped down next to Pete and smoothed the liner over the bottom and sides of our hole. "Make sure she knows I'm not making a play for you."

"She'll probably believe you more than she'll believe me," Pete grumbled. "Hey, hand me that hose clamp and I'll set up the pump."

I had no other suspects. Anahita avoided interaction with men not of her immediate family; she wouldn't be tracking one down to take pictures. And Madz wasn't at the Desert Bloom often enough to have the opportunity to take half these shots.

Kay told me not to worry about the pictures, but I was on edge, looking over my shoulder every time I was with him. As filming intensified, our time together grew less, and now it was clouded by my self-consciousness, wondering how every exchange between us was going to come off online.

I wanted to stay in the fantasy bubble with Kay. But the bubble was shrinking, becoming too transparent, leaving a soapy taste in my mouth. Especially when the focus of the gossip articles moved from capturing the romance between us to digging up information on me.

People started calling the Desert Bloom. The people asking to talk to Regan, we were able to fend off easily. But then they started posing as legitimate journalists, wanting to do a feature on the Desert Bloom but asking personal questions about me. After I called Bernie to report falling for one fishing expedition, thoroughly disgusted with myself, she suggested sending all journalist requests to her. Her mom was recovering from surgery and Bernie was preparing to return to the Bloom.

"You know what we say in this business," Kay said that night, massaging my back to soothe away my sense of irritation and panic. "All publicity is good publicity."

"I don't think it's the same for the hospitality sector," I said. "Or financial services, for that matter."

He promised the interest would die down eventually. I hated complaining to him when he had enough to worry about with the film shoot; every problem, every decision, every technical glitch somehow devolved onto his shoulders. He didn't need to hear me complain that our stalker had caught my worst angle. I wanted our remaining time together to be an escape from everything else.

If there was one upside to appearing in the celebrity tabloids, it was that I heard from my friends and family more than ever.

Dale. Way to go. Snagging a hottie. Lisa texted from the beach in

Greece, sending me heart-eye emojis.

Why is this California magazine editor asking me about our childhood? my brother texted me from Seattle.

They called my boss at the credit union in Hastings and the mentor who'd guided me through my landscaping classes. Someone snapped a blurry picture of Adam letting himself into my apartment building. "Timothy Kay's new flame hires family friend to housesit while she's off jetsetting with A-listers," the caption read. The photo wasn't flattering at all; Adam was in a knit cap and a beat-up flannel, wisps of blonde hair covering his chin and upper lip. The snippet made it suggest I'd pulled someone off the street and gave them temporary housing, oblivious to any crimes they might commit on my property while I was off sunning myself in the New Mexico desert.

"Omigosh, he looks so different," Maya whispered over my shoulder. "I told you he hasn't been video calling me, right? He wants to wait till his beard is grown in."

That photo tore through my chest like grappling hooks. The press could tell what stories they liked about me. They had no idea. But to hit up my family and friends was going too far in search of a story. That wasn't just invasion of privacy; it was a hostile takeover.

"Oh, she was the nicest lady. She asked so many good questions." My mom called while I was bagging tumbleweed along the slope behind the Bloom. She'd happily spilled the beans on every aspect of my life to the reporter who called her.

"Mom!" I cried. "Did you not think to ask *me* whether I'd want you telling strangers about my life?"

"Well, she said she was from *Entertainment,* and you know your dad and I like that magazine. I thought you'd be pleased, honey! And maybe if you'd *told* me you were dating again, not to mention somebody famous…"

"Sorry, Mom. I should have warned you." I worked to steady my voice. I felt attacked, and I wasn't sure why. I didn't have any secrets, so why was I so upset?

Because this mystery photographer was spoiling what precious time I had left with Kay. That was one reason.

The other fell into place when Jiayi called.

I was out in the gully, inspecting how well my grid of earthworks had caught the recent rain and held it in place long enough to water my new plants. Jiayi had just finished up an emergency C-section.

"Okay, someone wants me to talk about Maya's adoption," she said. "But I really feel we should have this conversation together, don't you? And talk to Maya about it first."

Maya. "Oh, my God." I dropped my shovel and clenched my fingers around the phone. "Who called you?"

"I don't know—it was a California number, and he said it was for *Vanity Fair*. He kind of got upset when I said I couldn't talk to him right then," she added. "Said there was a lot of money riding on the article if he could get the scoop."

My heart raced, my head buzzing with panic. "Don't tell them anything. Don't even answer the phone if it's a California number."

"I have to take calls from California, Dale," Jiayi said with a laugh. "I'm doing that research collaboration with Stanford. What's going on?"

I told myself to breathe. I wanted to cry, and my voice nearly broke as I confessed all my worries to my friend. "I can handle them coming after me," I added after I'd poured out the whole story. "But I can't handle them coming after Maya."

But they were. I didn't realize how bad things had gotten until Ritchie sent me a furious text. *What the hell dale??1?*

I followed the link, and my heart stopped beating.

Maya looked beautiful and innocent. The photographer had captured her walking down Main Street Artesia with Anahita, both of them laughing, the end of Ana's hijab floating in the breeze, Maya's big bag swinging between them. There was a picture of her studying at the coffee shop, lip between her teeth as she took an online quiz on how to recognize signs of cognitive impairment. I sat across the table from her, browsing a magazine on composting.

"Insta-family for Terminal Bachelor Timothy Kay?" the headline screamed.

The media attention turned in an instant from obsessing about me and Kay to obsessing about Maya. There was Maya in my Jeep, Maya buying mochi donuts from Fat Straws, Maya stretched in the chaise on the back porch of the Desert Bloom, reading the latest novel by Celeste Ng. The camera lingered on her closely, lovingly. Kay was the clickbait, but Maya was the hook. The captions cooed about how fresh, how pure, how down-to-earth she was.

"I can't ignore this, Kay." I paced the Red Bluff Room that night, ignoring the telescope, the starry sky, the alluring promise of relaxation and bliss offered by the Jacuzzi in the loft. My plants stirred as if agitated by my stomping, the tension in the air. "I've tried. You've told me to let people make up their stories. But they're watching Maya now. That's not cool."

"It's not." His face was tense, sprouting new lines around his mouth, and his thick eyebrows were permanently together. He rubbed the creases at his forehead with a heavy sigh. He looked defeated, slumping in the red-upholstered recliner in the corner. He'd been slammed that day with a camera malfunction, the wind blowing in a direction that blurred his shots, and one of the grips had clocked out with a fever. If something viral went through the whole crew, Kay could kiss his budget goodbye.

My heart caught in my chest, stumbling as I watched him. Already he looked far away. I'd known the doomsday clock was ticking down for us, and I'd been greedy for all the time I could get.

But suddenly, time with Kay was a threat. The thought of parting with him no longer meant that I'd be torn in two and would have to start the process of nursing a broken heart all over again. Parting with Kay meant that the creep who'd been watching us would stop stalking my daughter.

"She's a minor," Kay went on. "There's usually some agreement among paparazzi not to target kids."

But Maya wasn't a young child. She was a blossoming young

woman, nearly an adult.

"I don't think this guy is a typical parasite. He waited to leak the pictures of us after he'd stirred up interest with Pete and Regan. And I don't get the interest in Maya." I ran my hands through my hair, tugging at my scalp as if the sensation could make my brain work better. "Why haven't we *seen* someone standing around snapping pictures of us? Or following Maya through the street, for crying out loud?"

"I can assign Madz to watch her if you think she needs a bodyguard," Kay said.

I sat down on the chair across from him, perched on the edge of the seat. Every nerve in my body vibrated. A small, unhappy voice in my head cried out that I didn't want to do this. But the rest of my head clanged like an air raid siren, calling for escape in any way possible.

"She doesn't need a bodyguard," I said quietly. "She just needs to not be associated with celebrities."

His eyebrows went up, and he lifted his head to look at me. "You want to send her back to Hastings?"

"Her course isn't done yet. I don't want to ruin that for her. She's made friends in the program."

"Then what do you mean?"

Intuitive as always, he read my face. I wasn't very good at lying, anyway.

"No," he said. "No. You're not breaking up with me over this."

I laughed, a stretched, brittle sound. "Do you see another option?"

"Yes." He reached over to me and pulled me onto his lap, wrapping his arms around me. "We stick it out. We don't care what they say. Don't run."

"You keep saying that," I whispered. "Who ran from you, Kay?"

He slid a hand into my hair, fingers rubbing my scalp, and as usual I curved into his touch like a cat. Outside the window, in the quiet dark, Jupiter swam his way through the night sky, with Mars rising behind him. Mars, the planet of force, drive, aggression, and courage.

"I met Gabriela while my mom was sick," he said. He watched my hair slide through his hands, his voice low and soft. I tilted my head and listened. Finally, I would know who had captured Kay's heart.

"She called herself a free spirit. She came to Vegas on a whim and worked as a cocktail waitress. She hung around through my mom's worst times, and she hung around through film school, and then she moved with me to LA when I was broke and no one, trying to get my foot through the door."

He turned his hand, letting a lock of my hair pool in his palm. "But the minute I got a break, won the awards, got a studio contract—the minute it looked like I might be going somewhere—she left. Said it looked like I had my future mapped out, and she wasn't the type to settle down."

"You said you'd never been in love." I didn't want to sound accusing, but part of me—okay, a lot of me—seared with jealousy for free-spirited Gabriela. She had known young Kay, vulnerable Kay, striving Kay, and had been there with him in his toughest times.

He shook his head. "I wasn't in love. And she wasn't in love with me. Obviously. I knew we weren't going to last. At some point I realized I didn't want to repeat the pattern of my parents, goading each other's wild behavior. But I never got why, after she put up with all the hard times, she didn't want to enjoy the good. She just cut me loose and took off." He stared at his hands. "Like my dad."

My stomach heaved like I was on a ship at sea. I cupped his face. "You are worth sticking by, Timothy Kay. I can't imagine how any sane woman would leave you of her own free will."

He wrapped his fingers around my wrist, looking into my eyes. "You're going to leave me," he said quietly.

How could I leave something I'd never really had? That was never mine to begin with?

"It won't be by choice," I said softly.

He clamped an arm around my back and stood. I yelped, wrapping my legs around his hips. He held me as if I were a bag of groceries.

"I'll fix that," he said, crossing the room. "I'll tie you to the bed." He dropped me on it and I bounced slightly, sliding across the organic cotton duvet.

He wasn't serious, but I couldn't sense how far the mood had shifted. My breath caught as he followed me down, his knee pressing into the bed by my hip, his chest a cage around me. I felt dominated, yet I also knew he'd never hurt me.

"I'll get free when you leave for work." I knew what his priority was. I wouldn't pretend otherwise. I had him in the corners and edges around his real life, his work, his projects, his passion.

"Nope. I'm not leaving." He ran a hand along my arm, stretching it toward the top of the bed, curling his fingers around my wrist. "And I'm not letting you up until you're in love with me."

My heart bounced against my ribs. I wasn't about to reveal my secret; it was mine alone.

"You can't *make* somebody love you," I challenged him.

He pulled the light blouse over my head, and his hips settled atop mine, radiating heat into the hollow between my thighs. He ran his lips and tongue along the top of my bra, my breasts bunched together by the lift of my arms. Then he hooked a finger in a fabric cup and tugged it down so his tongue could find my nipple.

"I'll make you say it." He nipped and sucked until I writhed. He dipped his hand inside my panties, and I moaned.

"Sex—and love—are different things." I panted, sucking in air as he shifted his weight slightly to tug my skirt, then my panties over my ankles. He kissed his way back up the inside of my leg and I let my knees fall apart, helplessly.

"I want your love," he said, his breath moving across the soft, quivering warmth of my tenderest places. "I want all of you, Dale." He dove in, lips and tongue and liquid heat, and I lifted myself shamelessly into his mouth, seeking the rush, the high, the wave flinging me toward release. It gathered, rearing behind my fear, my worries, and at last broke through my reserves, a surge that swept all before it. I cried out, my thighs tense and burning as the exquisite sensation focused and then exploded, flinging heat through every part of my body. Kay, devil that he was, clamping his hands around my hips and kept going, laving the flood into a higher surge, pushing at my pleasure until I thought it would drown me, until I feared the intensity would break me apart.

"You," I cried. "Mercy." I curled my fingers in his thick hair and pulled. "Come *here*."

He licked his lips and crawled up my body, eyes flickering as I reached between us to guide him home. "Love me yet?"

"I'll say anything you want," I wailed, "as long as you get inside of me *now*."

His eyes fluttered closed as he slid into me, long and deep and slow, and I cried out at the pleasure, the wave cresting again. Of course I loved him. I couldn't feel this connected to him, this abandoned—this entirely, completely myself—without absolute love and trust. I curled my arms around his shoulders and canted my hips to take all of him, deep and completely, and matched him as he fell into rhythm.

"Want me, Dale," he growled into my hair, a command, a plea.

"I do, I do." I was nearly sobbing as the raging storm sucked me in again.

"Need me," he said, thrusting, melding our bodies together.

I did, but I couldn't say it as his climax and shudder pushed me to the highest peak yet, a pleasure that juddered through me with palpable force. Stars swirled and floated against my eyelids. It went on and on, a wave I thought might never stop. Kay dropped his head to my shoulder, panting, and then he withdrew and curled his body around mine, his lips in my hair.

"Stay with me," he whispered.

"I will." I wrapped my arms around him, pressing my body against his as if I could shield him. Or draw out the poison, leaving nothing but contentment and peace.

I wanted to believe I could do it, stay with him until the end of things, so I said it again. "I will."

"Love me," I thought he muttered right before he dropped into sleep. I lifted his hand and kissed it, tears pressing from beneath my eyelids.

I didn't know how to tell him that I already did.

Chapter Eighteen

The end came the next day, when the video surfaced of Maya and Adam at their senior prom, lifted from their friends' social media feeds. They were dancing, laughing, whooping it up like the kids they were, Maya in show-stopping floor-length satin and Adam with matching cummerbund and tie.

It was Glenn who broke the news, as gently as they knew how. *Buckle up, girlfriend*, the text read. *Call me as soon as you can.*

I was outside in the yard and glad of it as I clicked through link after link, caught hook, line, and sinker.

"Timothy Kay's new stepdaughter-in-training dating trans man," the headline screamed.

"In Transition, Abandoned by Parents," started another story.

"'I'll stand by him no matter what,' broken-hearted girlfriend declares."

It was bad enough the reporters invented a love story straight from the soaps. I made the mistake of reading the comments.

I called Kay as soon as the first blinding rush of fear loosened enough that I could move. I knew my choice was inevitable, my path clear as I shakily pressed his name in my contacts. But when he answered instantly, I burst into tears.

"I can't do it anymore, Kay." It took a few tries to speak through the sobs. "I have to get Maya out of here."

I was panicking, my mind rushing everywhere. I could take her back to Hastings. No—the trolls already knew where we lived.

There'd been pictures of Adam entering my apartment building. I had to go to Hastings to get Adam, and then I had to take all three of us to a safe house. My brother's in Seattle. My parents in Illinois. Ritchie in—no, Ritchie wasn't a safe house. It would have to be Springfield. My mom would make up a guest room, Adam could sleep on the couch, and I'd find work, change my name…

I registered a long moment of silence on his end, decreasing background noise as he moved away.

"That's not the solution," he said gently.

He was so cool and calm. But he knew. *He'd seen this.* And he'd let Glenn be the one to tell me that every transphobe on the internet had been unleashed on my kids.

I hauled air into my lungs and wiped snot onto the cuff of my flannel shirt. "Tell me what is."

"Ignore it. You are not responsible for someone else's feelings."

"I'm responsible for her. I have to protect them. I don't see any other way."

"They're just trolls, Dale. You can't let them run your life."

"There are death threats. For Maya and Adam both."

A tick of silence. At least he wasn't rushing to tell me I was imagining things, or that I was overreacting.

"Trolls send death threats for everything they don't like," he said, still so quiet. "I've gotten death threats for killing off characters in movies."

I closed my eyes. I wore a hat, yet the sun pounded into my head. "There are worse things than death threats."

"Dale. What's worse than death threats?"

He wasn't mocking, but he didn't get it. I paced beneath the cottonwood tree, nerves screaming beneath my skin. Kay's experience with transphobia was when a woman he worked with at the studio had been deadnamed in the press by a rival doing a smear piece. But that woman was an adult and had resources, a legal team. Kay wasn't a parent, either. He'd didn't know what it felt like to fear hurt and loss for someone else more than you feared any injury to yourself.

My fingers felt like claws, taut and bloodless. "Go to the TMI article. Read what BuzzKill has to say."

Murmurs, calls, shouts, even a burst of laughter came from the background on his side. On mine, blood rushed through my ears.

"Christ," Kay muttered. "Glenn told you not to read the comments."

"And I'm sorry I did. But I can't unsee that. I can't pretend that maniac doesn't actually want to hurt my daughter like that." My voice broke, and I fought for control. "It's hard enough already, Kay. The hatred, the comments people feel entitled to make. Adam already has those people in his real life, and it's worse online. I am not going to amplify that for him, or for Maya."

"What do you want to do?" His voice sharpened.

"We're going to pack up and leave," I said. "Today."

"Dale—"

"She'll finish her course online. I'm sure she can work something out with her teachers. Or she can transfer. I've done enough on the yard, someone else can put in the last pieces. I have to get her out of here."

"That's not the problem." He sighed heavily. "You have to get her away from me."

My heart squeezed like a giant fist had punched into my chest and grabbed it. "You're not the problem either."

"But my association is. You said it last night."

Last night. I closed my eyes against the memory of how I'd slept in his arms all night, so safe and at peace.

"If you break up with me, the heat is off the kids. You said so yourself."

His voice was wooden, distant. He wasn't going to argue with me, demand I fight for him, for us. He was going to watch me cut and run, just like he'd had to watch his dad leave. And Gabriela.

"I don't know what else to do, Kay," I whispered. "Their safety comes first."

"I'll move to the set." He sounded businesslike. "Glenn will bring my things. They'll drop the news that we broke up. You can stay there. Have my room. Lie low for a day or two, and it will all blow over. There will be a new headline in twenty-four hours."

I pressed my head against the grainy bark of the cottonwood, feeling the hard knobs against my skin. "They won't come for her here?"

"You have to feed the machine to keep it running. Don't respond. Don't react. You and Maya both limit your exposure for a couple of days, don't read anything anybody says about any of us, and the trolls will sniff out new blood."

I flinched at that image. "I'll do whatever it takes. The very thought of someone—even *imagining* that about her—"

"It's their fantasy, Dale," he said softly. "It's a sick and violent fantasy, I agree. That person needs help. But it's a fantasy. Not real."

Just like our relationship. Fantasy. Not real.

I shook my head, scraping my forehead across the bark, as if I could make things make sense. My love for him was real. My hurt was real.

So were my fears, and they were more powerful than anything else at the moment.

"I'm going to miss you so much," I blurted.

"Nowhere near the way I'll miss you," he whispered. "Can you—at least tell me how you are? Now and then?"

I squeezed my eyes shut. He, the man who didn't do relationships, had asked me not to run. But he'd been waiting for me to cut him loose, just as I'd been listening to the clock tick down on our time together.

This was worse than the math league captain telling me he liked the girl captain of our rival team. This was worse than Ritchie telling me he didn't want to be married anymore.

"When it's safe, maybe," I said. "When I'm sure that—whenever the stalking stops. I'll—be in touch."

"See you around, Dale Wrighton."

I choked back a sob. "See you around, Timothy Kay."

I ended the call. Then I hugged my tree and cried.

***

I cleaned my face, tossed my flannel in the wash, and made a fresh batch of agua fresca for Maya. Being a mom meant I couldn't sit in my room and listen to maudlin music and cry; I had someone else to take care of. Right on time Maya breezed into the kitchen, tossed her bag and purse on the island, and took a long gulp from her glass. Then she saw my face and went completely still.

"Someone died."

"No." A short sound, distant neighbor to a laugh, strangled out of me. "No one died. I just wanted to see you."

Safe, in one piece, and so lovely. The current style for high-waisted baggy jeans and midriff-baring crop tops hadn't been attractive on anyone the first time it came around, during my girlhood, but Maya was slender and limber enough to pull off the look. She canted her butt onto a stool and took another long, noisy gulp.

"You broke up with Kay." She sighed. "Bummer. I like him."

"I like him too." My voice came out strangled. "But it was never going to work."

"Well, you tell yourself something enough times, you make it true, right?"

"What?" I stared as she swigged again from her glass. My own sat untouched. She'd probably break into it once she finished draining hers, and I'd let her. I'd do anything for this child. That's why we were here.

She shrugged, her dark hair rippling over her shoulders. Her upper lip shone with moisture. "That's what you always tell me."

"I—do. Huh." I tugged at the strap of my tank top, suddenly too tight. I said that, but it didn't apply here. I hadn't talked myself into falling in love with Kay, and I wouldn't be able to talk myself out of loving him. I simply had to face facts.

"Some things aren't a matter of perspective," I said. "They just *are.*"

Her phone pinged, and she slid it out of her pocket to look at it. I hated so much when people did that. "Adam's video calling. Can I?"

"Yes, of course. We need to talk to him."

She clicked on the call, then giggled. "Nice lumberjack style! Why are guys so in love with their facial hair? I don't get that."

"I want to see," I demanded.

"Show me Mother Rose," Adam ordered, and Maya turned her phone toward me.

Adam scowled up at me, his hair flattened by a thick knit cap. Blonde hair shadowed his upper lip and chin. His jaw looked broader, his nose thicker. My daughter had turned into a young woman before my eyes, and now Adam had gone from an awkward teen to a young man.

The thought of anyone even *thinking* about hurting either of them made me feel nauseous.

"You look good. Are you okay?" I asked him.

"Do you mean, have I seen the pictures that dropped today? Don't look," Adam warned me. "You aren't going to like them."

I wobbled to a stool and let it catch me. "Too late," I said. "You've—you've seen them? Are you sure you're okay?"

"Transphobe telling me I'm sinning against God and nature? Must be Tuesday. Or your neighbor in 1A," Adam said.

"Oh, honey. I never meant for this to happen. I thought my building would at least be safe."

Adam shrugged. "The lady next door, Mrs. Timm, she made me brownies this morning, since I helped her clean out her storage room downstairs."

"She's been wanting to do that for years," Maya piped up. "Anything good in there?"

"She had vinyl records from the 50s. I told her I'd sell them for her, get a good price. Speaking of gifts out of the blue." Adam held up a wristwatch, black and sleek. "Ritchie sent me a Victorinox Maverick. Said it was to help me time my injections. Is this a guilt gift because he yelled at Maya and made her leave Europe?"

Maya scoffed, and I tried to laugh. "No, this is him buying everyone expensive gifts to show Mymy he's still mad at her. You should see the purple jade earrings he bought Grandma Ruth. But he is worried your treatments will be rough, and he thinks a fancy Swiss watch will help you feel better."

"Well, it does. Almost makes me forget the size of the needle I have to put in my—"

"No needle talk, thanks? I can't handle it today," I cut him off.

"Hold on, gotta go, Mrs. Timm needs help bringing in groceries. Call you later."

I pressed my cool glass to the side of my cheek. "He's taking this way better than I am."

Maya nodded. "Those nerds are doing the work, aren't they? I mean, they went like way back to get those pictures."

Prom was less than six months ago, an eyeblink for me. "I'm so sorry this is happening to you. To you both."

She snorted, still glued to her phone. "Did you see the skinhead who's going to put me in a box and send me to straight camp? Bet it's in Texas. And then there's the incel who thinks I need *real* penetration." She huffed out air. "In your dreams, buddy."

My fingers froze around my glass, shaped into bird claws. "We're not supposed to read the comments."

"That's what I told Adam. But he reads them anyway, and then he works them into his fanfic."

She wasn't terrified. She wasn't crying. She wasn't collapsing into a quivering puddle of fear, like I had. "I want to put you in a box too," I said. "Keep you safe from all these assholes. And I can't."

"Duh, Mom." Eyes back to screen.

"Maya, they want to *hurt* you. That's a deal breaker for me."

"Do you mind if I? Thanks." She snagged my glass and downed a gulp. Then she wiped her lip and pushed the glass back to me.

"Remember that time I went into a tizzy and flew away from Europe because I was so mad over Dad bitching at me about college?"

I sipped from my glass and chose not to scold her for language. "I remember. I was there."

"You told me then running away wouldn't solve anything. My problems would still be here." She put down her phone.

Had I said that? It sounded like something a parent should say.

"So, what's going to solve our problem with internet trolls? Lash back at all the haters and tell them they're wrong and should stop judging? Waste our time and energy on them when this is how they get their kicks?"

"I have a feeling there's a box number three." I hid in my glass, wondering if it was too early to add vodka. Nothing about this hour felt happy.

She shrugged. "We live our best lives and don't care what anyone says."

I sat there as stunned as if my sweet, kind-hearted daughter had stood up and backhanded me. The late afternoon sun had that rich ombre color I'd learned to love, and it caressed the side of Maya's face, lighting her ear, her jaw, her oh so vulnerable neck. My daughter was a knockout, an inarguable beauty—one reason the online stalkers had picked up on her. I'd known every inch of this girl her entire life, and I'd never seen this brave, insouciant side of her before. Where had she gotten it from? Not me, that was for sure.

I cleared my throat. "That is a terrific option. I am one hundred percent behind you living your best life, my darling, perfect girl. But right now, I am worried for you and for Adam. Kay and I talked, and we think it's a good idea to take time to cool off. Maybe it's time to get away from here. You're almost done with your coursework, right? You could finish up remotely if you needed to?"

She put her phone on her leg and stared at me. "I knew it. You broke up with Mr. Kay because of me."

"No, sweetie. It was because of me." The truth slipped out before I could guard myself, as if I'd been desperate to confront it all this time. "The things I'm scared about have as much to do with me as they do with you. But it's also true that I can't handle you being a target. Or Adam."

"We've had a lot of practice, Mom."

I'd given up Kay to protect her, and here she sat, texting on her phone with Adam, her armor securely in place. My armor was nonexistent.

She put down her phone and stared at me, brow furrowed. "You said you'd stay till you finished Bernie's yard."

Another fantasy I'd thrown myself into. Another grand dream I couldn't see how to make work.

Maya swilled the rest of her drink and rapped the glass on the counter like we were doing shots. "You don't break your promises, Mom. And I'm not going to run and hide because of what people are saying about me. I tried that, and it was stupid. I'm finishing my course, then I'm going to start my internships, and all the haters can suck it. You should hear what some of the kids at school have said to Adam," she added, sliding off her stool. "This is nothing."

I opened my mouth and then closed it. She slipped her phone in her pocket, gave me a quick kiss on the cheek, grabbed her bag, and headed to her room. I sat there holding my glass, trying to absorb the evidence that my daughter was braver than I was.

I had always, always reckoned with what people thought of me. As the younger child, I lived to please my parents. My brother Kevin was good at everything, so I had to find a different way to distinguish myself. I'd lived to please my teachers in school, my extended family members on visits.

I'd married Ritchie because being married was what you did right out of college, and he was there, and we got along.

Then I'd spent my marriage trying to please him, because I thought that was what kept a marriage strong and healthy. Not until Ritchie cut me loose did I begin to think about what might please *me*.

Pulled up by the roots, I'd started to probe new ways to grow. I'd come to Artesia to help Bernie. I'd begun the overdue and essential task of figuring out what I wanted to do with my life.

Then Kay came along and reoriented everything. Suddenly, everything I wanted included him.

Then, at the first hint that some people might not like me—that as his girlfriend I was going to be watched, judged, commented on, and my daughter and everyone close to me would be judged, too—I'd crumbled.

I'd broken my promise to Kay. *Don't run*, he'd said. His one ask. Yet the minute I saw an out, I took it.

Who had been telling me I wasn't good enough to have what I really wanted, all this time?

That desperate, judgmental voice in my head, so scared I'd do something that would get me hurt. That's who.

Why had I so sincerely believed her?

I cornered Glenn an hour later when they came to pick up Kay's things. "Is he all right?"

Glenn looked scuffed and harried, face weary, string tie askew. "Did you ask him that?"

I hung my head, guilty. "I called. It went straight to voicemail." And how did that twist in my gut, that he might be avoiding me.

"He and Des went back to Carlsbad Caverns for an evening tour. I came to get his stuff."

"Packed and ready." I pulled Kay's hard-sided suitcase from behind the lectern with the registration book. It was still open to his page: *Mr. Golightly.*

"Wow, you didn't waste any time kicking him out."

"We're, um, taking a break. To let the story die down. Let attention move on from Maya and Adam."

Glenn nodded. "Yeah, the trolls need fresh meat." They weren't buying my weak excuse for a minute; I knew by their narrowed their eyes. "Some time is good. Kay needs that. Needs to focus on the job."

"Okay." I gulped. I'd asked Kay for time earlier, hadn't I? Now he needed some space. From me.

Glenn left without saying goodbye, and it was another punch to my shriveled gut to realize I wasn't just losing Kay but Glenn and Madz and Des and maybe Regan too.

I went out to the backyard, just coming to life, so much possible. Maya was right: I needed to keep my promise. Bernie was going to get her landscaping if I filled the gully with tears while doing it.

But I didn't see any way my other fantasy could come true.

Chapter Nineteen

Glenn released a public statement that Kay and I had split. It was amicable, and we'd both decided to pursue other projects. The headlines didn't stop, only changed in focus.

Hollywood's hottest director dumped by new love. The picture caught Kay in profile, coming out of Fat Straw, ball cap pulled over his unruly hair, his beard thicker than ever. Mirrored sunglasses shielded his eyes, but tense lines framed his mouth, and my stomach pinched. He looked driven and tired.

The pictures of me made me look like I should just kick myself to the curb. The one of me under my Jeep, changing the oil, made me look like I was trying to make auto mechanic porn, jeans tight around my hips, shirt pulled up to expose my belly.

In this new reporting, I was the villain. The consensus on social media was that I'd toyed with Kay's affections and then dumped him. I was flying off to Europe for a menage á trois with my ex-husband and his new wife, I'd fought with Kay because he wouldn't adopt Maya, I was having an affair with Pete behind Regan Forrester's back.

At least the only pictures of Maya were of her with me, though in every shot, I looked troubled and lonely.

Regan moved into her trailer, and Pete got grumpy having to visit her on set. He found me sweating in the backyard one afternoon and stood, arms crossed and glaring, while I mortared the trim around my water feature. It was my version of magical thinking: if I did this right for Bernie, the ache in my chest over Kay would eventually lessen.

"Kay's being an asshole on set. Driving everyone like cattle. You couldn't have kept banging him for a few more weeks?"

"And let Maya and her friend be targets? Nice priorities, Pete."

"Seriously?" Pete looked different from when I'd first met him: settled and solid, filled out, polished.

I'd felt the same way, for a hot minute.

He picked up a hammer and started pounding the frame of Bernie's new greenhouse together. "Dale. Keeping yourself from someone you love isn't going to keep your kid safe."

I decided not to address his choice of words. "It might if he's not famous."

He swung the hammer and spoke around the nail in his mouth. "Sure you're not just keeping yourself safe?"

Cristina couldn't believe I'd let Kay go. Taiye thought I screwed up. Even Anahita, lounging on the back porch with me with her hair uncovered, legs crossed in a comfortable pair of turquoise shalwar kameez, lectured me as she entered data from her charts. "I think it's this Western notion that passion makes everything magical and easy." She shook her head. "At least I know, when my parents arrange my marriage, we will have to build the love. It will not be easy."

I kept my nose glued to *Mother Earth News*. Ana had never been taken out at the knees by lust, had never slept the night in the penthouse in her lover's arms, his breath tangled in her hair.

I had no idea how to rebuild with Kay. If he even wanted to. Why would Timothy Kay, the man who didn't do relationships, want long-term with me? Each time I reached for the phone to call him, another picture surfaced, reminding me I hadn't yet pulled my own weeds.

Maya suggested she clear out to see what happened. She took her CNA test early, wrapped her class, and agreed to spend some time with my mom and dad in Springfield before her internship at the art museum began. I knew she'd be safe there, and she persuaded me that she was fine flying alone.

I thought briefly of Kay's friend Ernie, the pilot. A quick call, and—

No. I couldn't enjoy the benefits of knowing celebrities if I couldn't pay the price.

"Mom. I'm going to be *fine*. You worry too much," Maya said outside the security checkpoint as I hugged her for the third time.

"It's my job to worry. It was in the contract signed with Auntie Jiayi."

Maya was leaving. She'd been my shield, a reason not to commit to Kay. A reason our lives were different, too different to mesh. And now she was off to live her own, best life and be spoiled by my parents in a way they had never indulged Kevin or me when we were growing up.

"Are you Maya and Dale?" A young girl came from behind the books and snack counter and held up her phone with a shy, eager wince. "I'm so—this is—I can't believe it! Can I take a quick picture with you? I won't tag you if you don't want."

I froze in horror, my nightmare flashing before my eyes. This utter stranger would make one innocent post, put Maya in the spotlight, and the trolls would leap out from behind the fiddle leaf fig, tearing her apart.

Maya must have read my face. "Mom," she hissed out of the side of her mouth, "it's *one* picture. It will go on my socials. You can do this."

I couldn't. I couldn't stand here and smile for cameras. Be photographed as Timothy Kay's love interest, or the tramp who wrecked his life, or whatever they decided to call me. This was why I'd run. The threats, the scorn, the judgment.

The girl smiled, bumping her glasses up her nose with one knuckle. She looked sixteen and beamed at Maya adoringly. "Sorry to fangirl, just—I followed you, because it's Artesia, right? You're, like, local."

"You *have* to tag me," Maya sang, tugging me forward. "My mom's not online, if you can believe that."

"So you took the museum internship?" the salesgirl asked after pictures were snapped and both girls, facing each other, tapped busily at their phones.

"I think I want to do museum studies," the other girl said. "My experience is the UFO museum in Roswell, which, I mean, enough with the little green men already, but it's a start, right?"

"OMG, I totally wanted to do the museum from the minute I got here, but Mom wouldn't come with me."

Fangirl turned to me. "Sorry it didn't work out with Timothy Kay," she said. "I was totally Team Dale."

"Thanks," I said, trying to process the incongruity of being recognized, of having a total stranger know about my recent heartbreak, and seeing my daughter make a new insta-friend from someone who followed her on social media, but never would have known she existed if not for Timothy Kay.

"How much has your social media exploded?" I clung to Maya's side, though she was almost to the screening tube.

"I'm gaining, like, thousands of followers a day," she said. "It didn't slow even when you dumped him. It's okay, Mom. I'm not posting anything bad."

Thousands of people watching my daughter. Following her on social media. I was right to run from Kay. I was *right*. How could I protect her when she was such a target?

But all of a sudden, she was a young woman of influence. She was inspiring others with her story. She was finding new opportunities, new friends. What gave me the right to hold her back?

I'd planned to sit in the lobby and watch her plane take off, but I saw three phones raised in my direction, one person behind a ticket counter and two tourists wrestling with bags. I went out to the Jeep and stared at the airfield through tears. I sat long after her plane left, my heart crammed in my throat, cutting off air.

Maya was gone. Kay was gone. Filming had wrapped and the

production lot had shut down and everything moved to Albuquerque. He'd finish filming in the studio there, where the rest of the production crew had been building sets, designing costumes, and laying track for the cameras for months.

I could stay at the Desert Bloom, my safety net, my hidey hole, as long as I wanted.

But Kay had awakened a braver, wilder Dale, and I didn't want to try to stuff her back in her old carapace. Bernie was in the kitchen when I got back to the Desert Bloom, rummaging through cupboards. She'd let her hair go gray in her time away and there were new lines around her eyes and mouth. She looked utterly normal, sane, belonging in this picture. She took out a tin of coffee, opened, sniffed.

Kay's coffee. My throat grew tight and hot.

"Dale." She held out her arms. "My yard. You made me a sanctuary, heaven on earth. I love it." She folded me against her, soft, smelling of hand sanitizer and powder, my anchor, my angel, my guide. "I *knew* you had this in you," she said, and I burst into tears.

***

Over homemade loaded nachos and a pitcher of margaritas, we laid everything out in the open. I let Bernie go first, since moving her eighty-year-old mother into a memory care facility ranked higher on the tear-jerker scale. She walked me through the whole of my time with Kay, beginning with my hose assault under the cottonwood tree, through the surprising twist of Regan Forrester showing up at the Desert Bloom, Maya returning from Europe, our love affairs becoming fodder for gossip, and the way attention had shifted to Maya, prompting my freak out, meltdown, and pulling away.

"I get it," Bernie said. "You don't want your whole life on display. Some things should be private."

"Strangers in airports are taking my picture."

Bernie popped a cheese and pepper-laden nacho into her mouth. "It's different for these kids, though. They're used to crafting an image and presenting it the world. They compete to see who can get more followers, be an influencer."

I nodded, trying to swallow salsa around the lump in my throat. "Kay said he couldn't fall for the people who can play that game. Think about their image all the time."

"Well, then." Bernie topped off my margarita. "No wonder he fell hard for you."

"Bernie." I put down my chip. "A Hollywood director does not actually want *me*."

"Why the hell not?"

She pushed my glass toward me. "Listen, sister, you've always been good. You were a good girl, a good wife, and you're a good mom. You can't stand to make other people upset. You also can't stand to get hurt. But you are good enough for a guy like this. When are you going to stop twisting yourself around to be someone else and just be *you*?"

I gulped my margarita and choked.

"Do you know where I get that from? Grandma."

Bernie tilted her head a bit tipsily. "Grandma Dale who started the cosmetics line?"

"That was Dad's mom. I'm talking about Mom's mom, my *pokni*."

Bernie poked a chip into a mound of melted cheese. "The one who was Chickasaw?"

"So we think. But her parents didn't leave when the rest of the tribe was removed. I told you this, right? They buried their culture and passed for white so they could stay on their land and raise my grandmother."

Bernie opened her mouth for the loaded nacho chip. "You're obsessed with this story."

"Because of the lesson. That story taught me that you have to hide who you are to survive. If I start popping up in paparazzi shoots as this public figure, or I make waves, and everyone is looking at me, then someone can come and take everything I want away."

Bernie chewed and swallowed delicately, as if trying to accord this breakthrough proper reverence. "Well, then. Good thing you tossed it all away before someone else could get there."

I hiccupped. "Bern, you're supposed to be on my side."

My friend's look was gentle, wise. "No, you're right," she said. "You could get hurt. Better run for cover and stay there."

"Oh, Bernie." I put a hand to my mouth. "I'm an *idiot*."

She nodded. "You survived the photo shoot today, right? So maybe it's not always heavy fire. And if there's no drama to manufacture, maybe the buzz actually will die down. Two people happy in love, taking care of each other? You understand why there are exactly zero TV shows and movies on that topic."

I held my margarita glass to my chest like it was a wishing stone. "I never said the L word."

"Well, maybe you should say it. To him." She nudged my phone toward me.

Taking a deep breath, I pressed the name that was still first under my favorites. Timothy Kay was and would always be my favorite. My heart throbbed like an engine in my ear, so loudly that at first I couldn't place the voice that answered Kay's phone.

"What's up, Dale?"

"Glenn?" My heart shut off, total engine failure. "He's having you screen calls from me?"

"We had a malfunction on a camera crane and Kay is on a different phone bawling someone out. He's been a bit tense lately." Glenn sounded frazzled. "Hey, did I text you earlier? We got a lead on those pictures. They're all coming from one guy at *TMI,* and our tech nerds traced his source. Wanna guess?"

"Where? Who?" My fingertips went numb around the phone.

"The IP address is linked to the Desert Bloom. The call is coming from inside the house, Dale."

I couldn't breathe. "Then the asshole's been under our noses all this time."

"If you want to bring me his head, that would be really tasty. I have to go, Kay's off the phone and it looks like another shit storm's brewing. Call you back."

I stared at Bernie. "Someone here is taking those pictures. Did they hack your security cameras somehow?"

Bernie narrowed her eyes and licked her fingers. "I don't think it's that sophisticated. Come with me."

Bernie pulled open the door to the guest wing. I followed her down the breezeway, noting the plants due for watering. The cute couple from Lubbock were out on their ghost town tour, trying to locate all the places in the area that had once been thriving communities that disappeared. The honeymooners who wanted to stay in the same room as Regan Forrester had gotten the Red Bluff Room and were currently having dinner at the Adobe Rose. Kay had paid his whole tab, or rather Glenn did, and Bernie had no qualms about double booking.

She stopped before a door and rapped on it. Rapped again.

The writer opened the door in a torn T-shirt and pajama pants. He too had grown out a beard, but it wasn't attractive like Kay's. His thinning hair needed a trim, and his eyes were strained and watery as he stared at Bernie.

"Uh, what?"

"Hi, Jonathan." Bernie smiled widely, like a shark. "We met before I left. Bernadina Ajuntas. Can you tell me why you've been taking pictures of my guests and selling them to the internet to pay your bills?"

The writer's eyes grew as round as his glasses as he looked from Bernie to me.

"Oh, shit," he said.

Chapter Twenty

Twelve hours later, I was on my way to Albuquerque.

"I'll be back on the weekend to get the greenhouse finished," I told Bernie as I rolled my suitcase out of my room, prepared—hoping—for an overnight stay. "Pete and I should have it up in a day or two."

"Pete will still be in bed with that hot little Regan Forrester this weekend," Bernie said.

"Hell, yes," Pete said, dropping his duffel bag on the front porch.

"I have no idea how to do this," I said to Pete once we were on highway 285 headed north. I blew hair out of my face, my breath hot and frantic. "I mean, how does this even work?"

"Well," Pete drawled, stretching out his jeans-clad legs. "He has a part and you have a part, and when those parts fit together…"

"I'm serious." I decelerated as we neared the Welcome to Roswell sign with the crowd of cars stopped around it, tourists taking a picture. "You and Regan are making it through. How?"

"Rodeo skills," he said. "You tune out the noise of the crowd and just hang on for the full eight seconds. Tell me again the look on the writer's face when Bernie found him out."

"Like I was going to rip his head off and drink blood from his skull. Which I considered doing."

Pete didn't laugh. "Can I have the leftovers?"

Maya's cell number popped up on my console. "Nan and Pop want to know if you're there yet," she chirped.

"Is everybody watching my love life unfold?"

"Adam says you need a grand gesture. Like the end of *Crazy Rich Asians,* when Nick proposes to Rachel on the plane, then takes her to a rooftop party and everyone she knows in Singapore is there."

"I don't have a grand gesture." Just an apology. And a wild, wild hope.

The nerves slithering in my belly mounted as the Sandia Mountains grew in the distance, sandy humps topped with layers of velvety green. Coming from flat Nebraska, and before that flatter Illinois, vertical terrain never failed to excite me, and as we snaked our way through the gap, my ears popping at the rise and then fall in elevation, my stomach rolled and thrashed.

Pete directed me along the bypass, hugging the mountains as we skirted town.

My palms sweated on the steering wheel. "I didn't book a hotel. What if Kay turns me down flat?"

Pete looked over. "He's going to pretend he's hurt and unavailable for maybe ten seconds, and then he'll cave. Five seconds if you let your hair down. Zero if you take off your blouse and just go with the tank top."

I glanced down at my cleavage. "I'm practically naked in this tank top."

"That's what I said. Turn here."

The studio lot was enormous and the parking lot even bigger. I had plenty of time for my stomach to inch toward my strappy heeled sandals, the one concession I had made to trying to look chic. Why hadn't I worn my dress? With every clip of my cork heels through the acres of parking lot to the front courtyard, Pete trying and failing to limit himself to my stride, my courage ebbed.

I had no sign that Kay still wanted me. He hadn't reached out once since I'd cut him off. But I had to apologize, tell him how I felt, in person. This wasn't something I could do over the phone.

The lump in my throat kept me from saying my name properly to the girl behind the desk in the atrium. "Umm, we're here for *The*

Visitors? 2?"

She squinted at both of us, then held out one slim brown hand. "ID." Her fake nails were at least an inch long, gold sparkles at the tips. Why hadn't I taken an hour to get my nails done? Kay moved among the most beautiful women in the world; couldn't I at least make an effort?

Her eyes were kind as she tapped at her tablet and handed me my license. "He's on stage B," she said. "Or on the backlot."

She didn't ask who I was here to see. She knew already. My heart did laps in the bottom of my belly as I followed the signs to Stage B.

Pete ditched me the second we entered the huge cavern of the soundstage. There were stands of equipment and people everywhere, but Pete seemed to know his way around. Regan lounged amid a cluster of props, studying her phone, and Pete homed in on her like a bee to honey. The second she saw him, she leapt out of her seat and directly into his arms. He caught her, lips and bodies fusing, her legs locking around his hips, ankles crossed. My stomach slithered into my shoes. I wanted Kay to greet me like that.

He stood with Des and several others before a tall light while a lighting tech moved a screen back and forth, demonstrating something. I stood and stared at him for a minute. The very sight of him made my stomach settle. There was simply no one like him. He gave his crew the same concentration he'd focused on me, solid, intelligent, warm, and so deeply sensitive. He was a craftsman, a businessman, an artist, and a dreamer all in one. A man who brought fantasies to life.

If I couldn't have and hold him—if he wanted someone who'd never run—well, I'd learned from Ritchie how to survive a blow. But I wouldn't move on the way I had after Ritchie. I was never going to get over Timothy Kay.

He turned and saw me. The room went quiet, or maybe that was just my head. All I heard was the pulse in my ears. He didn't say a word to his group, just held his camera out for someone to take— Des tucked his arms around it—and then he walked toward me.

Was that good? I couldn't read his expression. That famous reserve, that poker face, was on full display.

A large cargo door in the wall stood open, filled with some massive prop on an enormous dolly, the sun and a warm autumn breeze filtering through. I backed toward it hoping the fresh air might clear my head.

Kay stopped a few inches away. Close enough that I could fist my fingers in his shirt and tug him toward me if I dared. Instead, I twined my fingers together.

"What are you doing here?" His voice was hoarse, like mine at the entry desk.

"I have something to tell you." Nothing like getting it out there right away.

He held still, but his gaze moved over every line and curve of my face. "And?"

My bubbling heart pushed the words up my throat and out. "I love you."

His shoulders twitched as if a current had passed through him. "You tell me this *now*? After you put me through hell—"

"Hell?" Was that what he thought of our time together?

"Of course, hell." He crossed his arms and glared at me. He was wearing a faded T-shirt with a vintage movie poster of Jaws on the front. His muscles had grown more defined, hauling heavy cameras around. "I fall for you, so hard—this is why people don't want to be in love, isn't it? To protect themselves. Keep their hearts from being shredded."

He loved me. All the air left my body. "You could have told me."

"You could have *noticed*. How much more obvious could I be?"

"It wasn't obvious to me." He *loved* me. Me, Dale Rose. "When did you know?"

He scowled. "The first time you yelled at me, I knew I was in trouble. You didn't notice I put my arms around you within two seconds of meeting you? I don't grope strange women, Dale."

"Yeah, but I had a garden hose." Sun pounded on the back of my neck. We'd never argued about anything, and here we were arguing about when we'd fallen for each other.

"That day at Abo school. I thought, when it went dark, I'd kiss you on the cheek so you'd know how I felt. But you were leaning in and you kissed me too."

"I knew none of this." I pushed on his chest, firm yet soft. "You are the most buttoned-up, unforthcoming—"

"Wasn't I showing you? Every time I touched you?"

He had been. But I'd been so busy hiding behind my barricades, telling myself it was just great sex.

"You don't exactly come with a dictionary, Kay. I'm still learning you."

He clamped his lips in a line to match his scowl. "Yeah. You learned a bunch of bullshit comes with my job, and there are a lot of people out there who get a thrill from watching other people, and while I make a lot of money off that, it also has its dark side." His eyes darkened, narrowed. "And you ran."

"I went for a walk. Cleared my head." I drew a breath, and his eyes flickered to my tank top.

"Bernie figured out who our stalker was," I said. "The writer. You met him. He was trying to write his novel and getting nowhere, but your alias tipped him off and he started following you—us— taking pictures. He said it was *research*."

Kay cocked his head, listening. "When Regan showed up, he knew he had a gold mine. Everything she did would sell. When the rag wanted more pictures, he fed them the ones of us. Then Maya showed up, and he got obsessed with her and started digging." I took a deep breath, harnessing that reflexive dart of fear. "He said he was sorry. He looked really embarrassed as he packed his things. And he paid what he owed Bernie. Apparently selling clickbait made him a lot more money than selling books."

"I'll have the studio go after him. Or Glenn. They were as upset we broke up as—"

I heard the rest even if he didn't say it out loud.

I twisted my fingers. "So, I need to know. What are the chances? How often do you get a weird stalker who develops an obsession and then goes digging? Is that going to happen a lot?"

"More often than you'll want it to." He was still scowling, but the brows were sliding apart, the clouds loosening. "But less than you think."

I searched his face, looking for the crack in his façade. How could I convince him I wouldn't run again? How could I persuade him to trust me?

How could I promise him I'd be gentle with his heart? He'd held on to it so tightly for so long. No wonder he wasn't going to bare himself so I could take a stab again.

My heart rapped inside my ribs.

"So if the chances for a rando psycho stalker are actually quite low, then the issue is not having privacy. And all of the commenters who are going to say I'm not good enough for you."

"And you believed them," he said bitterly.

"No, I believed it already, about myself," I said. "They were confirming what I knew."

The breeze riffled his hair and mine as we stared at each other.

"Do I get a say?" he asked.

I drew in a long breath, let it go. "That's why I'm here. For your say."

He lowered his chin. The green line around his eyes stood out vividly. "We stay boring," he said.

My heart raced up my throat, poised on my lips. He said *we*.

"I guess your mom could teach me the red carpet thing. She seems really good at it." He stepped toward me, and my mind blanked. "I know we haven't talked, and I don't know if your invitation still stands, and I didn't even ask what you wanted—"

I took a deep breath, trying to catch my flailing heart, hold it still for a moment.

"I got really scared because I didn't know what this was, and I like to have guidelines for things, but then I thought, why does it have to be anything? Why not just plant something and see if it grows, and—"

"And you can move to LA." It wasn't a question.

"Whoa, back up," I said, thoughts scrambling. I'd been mapping out ways to make long distance work. Alternate weekends. Maybe calling in his friend Ernie once in a while for private flights. If I lived in Artesia, I'd be closer than Nebraska, but—LA?

"I don't like going weeks without you," he said. "It sucks. And it makes me really crabby."

One arm still crossed over his chest, as if he wasn't ready to cave completely, he reached out and hooked a finger in the belt loop of my capri pants, coaxing me to him.

Kay, at the center of my life. My whirling thoughts stilled. That made sense.

I tried to laugh. It sounded breathless. "Yeah, I heard you've been a bit grouchy—"

"You can come on shoots me with me. Find work in LA or not. You can do whatever the hell you like, as long as you come home to me."

Home. A home with Kay. The ground shifted beneath me, tilting me toward him.

"That's…" I tried again, palms sweating. "You're several steps ahead of me." But I didn't resist the pull. I swayed toward him.

He hooked his hand on my waist and brushed his lips against my forehead. Heat shot through my body, fusing me to this spot, this moment in time. To him.

"Let me catch you up," he said. "You go with me. We need a base in LA for my work, but we don't have to keep my house. We can buy a new house. We can have houses anywhere you want, plural. A vineyard in France. A villa in Mexico. When you're ready, we'll get married—"

"Not in Vegas," I said weakly, pulled under, drowning in his assurance. The future falling open with amazing speed, a future that felt so incredibly right.

Because he was in it.

"Wherever you want." His lips moved to my temple, the top of my ear, and butterflies lifted and flew.

"Kay," I said, sliding my hands up his arms, discovering him all over again. "I'm still at square one. Which is, I know I want to be with you."

"Then I suppose it's too early to talk about kids—"

"Holy hell," I squeaked, and he kissed me.

I was dying for him. His big body firm against mine, heat pouring off him, the joy that soared through me as our mouths locked, our tongues twining.

He dipped into my mouth like he was drawing out a promise. I gave it, freely.

"I have to lock you down," he said when he let us come up for air. His voice was ragged, hoarse.

Unflappable Kay, flapped. I loved it. I tilted my chin, giving him access as he kissed down my jaw, below my ear, along my neck. Sparkles danced and fireworks went off every place his lips touched.

"Low jack," he added. "So you can't run again."

I dug my fingers into his arms and pressed my cheek to his. This man. This entirely surprising and perfect man. "You know what's wrong with you?"

His brows tightened instantly. "What?"

I sighed. "Absolutely nothing."

He laughed and lowered his head. We fell into an endless, whirling kiss, a song of passion and fire that made the world disappear.

Until once more Kay drew back, his lips hovering above mine, his eyes arrowing into the deepest part of me, looking for all my secrets. I was caught and held completely. No running. No fear. This—this circle of us—was complete.

"Des," he growled, "if you don't get that camera out of our faces, I'm going to smash it."

I gulped for air, looked around, and yes, we had an audience.

Most of the cast and crew, from the looks of it, gathered in the cargo door, watching us.

"Break's over, boss." Des called. "We have a schedule to meet. Budget. Does your guest have clearance?"

I laughed, realizing he was imitating Kay. "Hi, Des."

"Dale. Welcome back."

"Um. Hi, everyone." I waved from my sheltered space inside Kay's arms.

Glenn pushed past Des's big shoulder, crisp in their button-down shirt, trousers, suspenders, sneakers, now with a pair of black-framed glasses. "Dale. Thank the goddess you've come to your senses. The crew was about to mutiny and kill him."

"What?" Chris Stevens, the clean-cut lead, looked around in surprise. "No we weren't."

"Oh, we had a plan where to bury the pieces," Des said, clicking off his camera.

"But then we realized we'd be out of a job." Regan grinned from her own shelter, wrapped at Pete's side.

"You're all fired." Kay was smiling. *Smiling.* His cast and crew stared in amazement. It looked really good on him.

"Dale." Regan unwrapped herself from Pete and tugged me out of Kay's arms, pulling me into a hug that smelled of makeup and hairspray. "You are my favorite right now. You brought Pete. You're staying, right?"

"Yes." For once Kay's reserve had vanished. I saw clear into him, into the mind and heart of this man I completely loved and couldn't wait to know better.

"Yes," he said again, planting a kiss in my hair. "She's staying. For good."

Epilogue

Bernie had already decorated for the holidays, though it was early December. I shut the car door and stood on the curb, studying the gabled slope of the roof. The Desert Rose felt like home. Or one of them. I wandered through the yard to check on my plants while Madz unloaded suitcases.

"Don't try to sneak in the back way," Kay called, grabbing his camera case and roller bag. "They'll think you're a creeper and attack you with a garden hose."

"Ha ha. Look, my trees are taking really well, even the cherry. Bernie must be following instructions."

"To the letter." Bernie came out on the porch with a cocktail glass in hand. "Plus that drip irrigation system works like a charm. Absolutely no maintenance, which I love. Come on, we started happy hour."

"We?"

Two other women joined her on the porch, Lana and her best friend, Naomi. Kay's mom threw open her arms for an enormous, sandalwood-scented hug.

I hadn't expected Kay's mom to embrace me. I was divorced with a kid, and here was her son, who didn't do long-term relationships, bringing home a woman with so much baggage.

When I'd met her over Thanksgiving, she'd given me a fairly light interrogation, roped me into helping her baste turkey and mash potatoes, and by the time we'd polished off the apple pie and whipped cream, we were in love.

"We got in this morning, so happy hour started then." Naomi threw her arms around me too. Her many necklaces clacked and bracelets tinkled so loudly I almost missed her next words. "Let me do your charts before you choose your wedding day, okay?"

"Don't spoil any surprises, Nome." Kay hugged his mom, then Naomi, and nodded to Bernie. "We're in the Red Bluff Room?"

"I wouldn't dare put you anywhere else." Bernie waved us inside.

Kay pulled me into his arms as soon as he set the suitcase down. "Time for a quickie?"

I nestled in but couldn't help peeking over his shoulder to see if everything was in place. The telescope. The Diné weaving on the wall. The Maria Martinez bowl. Bernie hadn't changed a thing.

I spotted the polka dot on the nightstand and I gasped, pushing at his shoulders. "The plants. Rescue first. Sex later."

"That's a first," Kay said, palming my hip as I moved away. "I can't say I appreciate your priorities."

I winked at him, making a promise for later, and grabbed the watering can.

Anahita was waiting when I came down the stairs. She wore a brightly patterned hijab and matching silk shalwar kameez.

"Missed you." Her hug was warm and fragrant, but she winced at the sight of the watering can. "I'm sorry, I'm doing what you say, but they don't love me like they do you."

"Come with and catch me up on everything," I said as I started my rounds.

I'd been away a couple of months, but so much had happened. I'd been on the move, splitting my time between Hastings and Albuquerque, with side trips to Vegas to see Kay's mom. Kay had flown us to LA so I could see his house, and if I liked it, to start thinking about landscaping ideas.

I liked it. It was a lovely old-fashioned Hollywood bungalow, complete with pool. I'd already sketched out a catchment system as well as some garden designs. Kay had designated an old shed as my workshop and promised I didn't have to go to a single show, party, or publicity event I didn't want to attend.

So far, the media attention hadn't been a burden. I'd begun to think of it the way Kay did: letting people spin a story that helped them relate to him and his work. Besides, I liked enough of the people he worked with that parties weren't a burden. The wrap party when filming ended for *The Visitors 2* was a blast.

"So now it's wrapping up the B roll and starting the process of editing," Kay was telling Taiye when Ana and I entered the kitchen. Kay stood with one hip braced against the island, eating cassava cakes while Taiye fried balls of black-eyed pea dough for acarjé. "And then post-production, which will take about a year."

"I won't see the film until next year?" Taiye waved his spatula. "I'll be back in Bahia then."

"Well then, you can bring all your friends and make sure we open well internationally."

Kay's eyes darkened as I approached, and he brushed a kiss over my cheek. It never failed to surprise me how affectionate he was, at least with me. "Make us a margarita?" he suggested. "Your secret recipe."

Lana breezed in. "Your dad couldn't make it, Tim," she said. "He's at the sweat lodge up in Duck Valley this weekend."

One surprising and, I hoped, good thing had come from Kay's time in the celebrity papers, and mine along with him. His dad had emerged from the woodwork and gotten in touch. It turned out he'd been trying to get sober for years, and the only therapy that worked were regular sweat lodge sessions.

Kay dealt with the turmoil of his feelings by keeping a calm façade. I was learning to read him, though, and I could see that while he was wary of this man who had let him down so many times in the past, he still wanted to have a relationship with him.

"But he said he'll be in Seattle for New Year's," Lana added, refilling her glass from the pitcher.

"We'll be in Seattle for New Year's." I looked up from cutting lime. "Kay, we should arrange a visit. I haven't met your dad, and…"

A look flashed between mother and son. I put down my knife. "What's going on?"

Lana flicked another look at Kay. "Let's wait till everyone gets here," he said.

"I don't like not knowing what's going on," I said, determined not to pout.

I adored Kay's mom, but that secret communication reminded me of how much I still didn't know about him. Of how much my insecurities still dogged me. That I couldn't be a celebrity wife. That I couldn't handle this life. That I was going to mess up, or hurt him, or he would just get bored—

He looped a hand behind my neck and kissed me. "I'm plotting something," he said.

My stomach flipped over. I loved this man with everything in me. And if I was going to end up looking like a fool, so be it.

Still, Seattle was supposed to be when he met my family. We were scheduled to visit my parents in Springfield for a few days, then fly them with us to Seattle to see my brother Kevin and his family for Christmas.

I wanted to see the Space Needle, whales, and Pike Place Market, in that order. I wanted my average, middle-class family to meet my celebrity boyfriend and make it seem normal that I had fallen in love with a Hollywood powerhouse who, I was learning, had a lot of money.

"You gotta see Capitol Hill," Glenn chimed in, strolling into the kitchen. "Don't worry, the people you want to see are behind us. I brought my wife, Patti."

I stared at the young woman wearing a tailored wool pea coat with a fur ruff and sheer leggings with thigh-high boots. "We get to meet Mrs. Glenn? Wow. I didn't expect you to be so…"

She raised slender brows. "Vietnamese? If you're going to tell me to go back where I came from, it's Jersey."

I laughed and held out my hand. "Glamorous. I meant glamorous. Glenn never showed us pictures, though they talk about you all the time. Nice to meet you, Patti. Thanks for coming to my birthday party."

"Oh, we hug." Patti wrapped her wool and fur around me. "My Glennie likes girls. This is the first thing they said about you. 'I found a woman you would totally want for a threesome, but she is one hundred percent hetero, and Kay is going to fall flat on his face for her.'"

"How did you know?" Kay demanded, waving my margarita glass. "I mean, I had a feeling about her right away, but you couldn't."

"Well, number one, she's totally your type, boss. Plus, she was so unfazed by the fame thing." Glenn wrapped an arm around Patti. "Then the background check was squeaky clean and internet presence was zero. I knew you were a goner."

"Is that all it takes?" I asked. "I'm lucky you didn't pick somewhere else to film."

"We're here. Ahead of schedule, thanks to our awesome pilot." Maya sang out from the doorway. "We had to stop by the Fat Straw. Adam wanted to try a Love Potion."

She flew into my arms and I held her tight. Ernie entered with Madz, and Bernie made introductions.

"I told him to try the Pink Señorita," Madz said.

"Emerald Sunrise." Taiye gave Madz a fist bump. "Is this everyone?"

"Hi, Mom." Adam grinned as I pulled him in for a hug.

"Oh my gosh, let me look at you two." I'd been in Hastings three weeks ago, but Maya looked older. Her hair was a curtain of silk and her tunic was new, though I recognized the skinny black jeans as her favorite. "Adam, did you dress up for my party?"

"Too much?" He smoothed the frilled front of his shirt and adjusted the lapels of his dark blue suit. His light blond beard was filling in, and he'd trimmed his mustache.

"I love the bowtie," Glenn said, "but did you think about a skinny tie? And wing tips."

Adam's eyes widened. "For real?"

Maya hugged me again. "Oh, Regan sends her love. She says to tell you happy belated birthday, so sorry she had to miss, but she's in Vancouver filming. She'll pop down when we're in Seattle, though." She queued up a video on her phone and held it out. Regan made a duck face and blew kisses at the screen, temporarily lost the phone to Eve, who sent her own greetings, and ended with a promise to see us all soon.

"We're going to have a busy New Year's in Seattle." I couldn't be angry my vacation plans were vanishing. It would be fun to see Regan.

I looked around to show Pete the video, but he was turning away, the raw hurt on his face lancing me with guilt. His fling with Regan had ended when filming did. It felt unfair that mine with Kay was lasting.

I meant to make it last as long as I could. I was learning to live with the frequent travel, the cameras everywhere, the publicity that came with his job. But that was the outside world. The inside world that we created together—that was ours alone.

Kay set my glass on the counter and took my hand. His grasp was firm, his fingers cool from the ice. As we stepped outside, he slipped off his jacket and tucked it around my shoulders, leaving him in his twill pants and tight black T-shirt that clung to his chest. He walked us through the pathways Pete had finished, and I tried to reconcile two images in my mind: the bare dirt pile this yard had been when I first saw Kay beneath this cottonwood tree, and the lush place it was now.

Bernie's greenhouse sprouted with vegetables, my flowers bloomed as I'd planned, and in the slope to the gully and the wash below, my trees were putting down roots. This blank space had been transformed to something vibrant, nurturing, and full of life.

Just like me.

250

Kay paused beneath the tree. "I wanted it to be here," he murmured. "Where I first saw you."

"Wanted what?" I reached up and stroked a leaf, inspecting the tree. She was strong and healthy.

I turned to find Kay holding a small fabric-covered box. A ring box.

The breath stopped in my throat.

His eyes glowed, but he looked so serious. "I'm not going to make this fancy," he said. "It's a simple story. I never thought I'd fall in love. I thought maybe there was something wrong with me, that I couldn't feel that way about anyone. And then I came here, and I met this woman, and she was—" He broke off.

I swirled close, drawn by the intensity of his gaze. "Say it," I prompted. He *never* did this, made declarations. I wanted desperately to hear it.

He cleared his throat, Adam's apple bobbing. "Gorgeous," he said. "Knock-me-off-my-feet gorgeous, with these eyes that took my breath away. And this body." He surveyed the dress that clung to my breasts and hips, a bold flowered pattern. "I said it before. I knew I was in trouble as soon as you turned on that hose."

I grinned at the memory and reached for the box, but he held it, taking my hand instead.

"She was smart," he said. "And funny. She liked old movies. She drove this badass Jeep, and she knew her way around a toolshed. But she had the softest, kindest heart for anyone who came in her orbit. I'd never met anyone more—" He searched for the word. "*Real.*"

I swayed toward him, under a spell. I wanted to stay there forever.

"You woke me up," he said softly. "You made me see the world in ways I've never seen it before. I want that for always."

"Me too," I whispered. He held the box before me, and I hesitated. "What's in there, Kay?"

"The low jack." He looked worried. I'd never seen Kay worried about anything. "It means you can't run. Or, if you do, you have to clear your head and come back. Again."

I opened the box, barely able to see the ring through the blur of tears. "Are you sure?" I whispered. After all, I was the first person he'd ever felt this way about. Maybe he'd change his mind when he discovered what it took to make it through the long haul. The bumps and boulders.

"Are *you* sure?" He touched my shoulder, rubbing his hand in circles. "You're the one who's been through this before. You told me how much you were enjoying your independence, your freedom, and here I am trying to lock you down again." He bent his head to peer into my eyes. "Is this what you want, Dale?"

I held the ring between us. "Marriage? To you?" My eyes blurred again. "Yes. Definitely."

He kissed me. I slipped my arms around his shoulders, pinching the ring between my fingers. When the rush in my ears subsided, I heard applause.

I wiped my eyes and laughed as I turned to face the crowd of our friends on the porch. "Again? Are we always going to have an audience?"

He took my hand and slipped the ring on my finger. "I thought we could have the ceremony in Seattle when your family is there. I talked to everyone here." He nodded at our small crowd. "They're saving the date. Plus Seth is up there filming, with Des, so they could both stand up for me."

I dragged a hand over my cheek, glad that on a hunch, I'd worn the waterproof mascara. "This is what you were plotting? You were planning our wedding without asking me?"

Out came those crinkles around his eyes, that expression of mischief, of humor, that I so loved. "I thought that maybe, if everyone else committed, then you couldn't say no."

"Bridesmaid," Maya called, barreling off the porch toward me. She hugged me with one arm while she grabbed my hand and inspected the ring. "I called Auntie Jiayi. She said she'll take off a week and find someone else to be on call."

"I guess it is all planned." I laughed, though I felt breathless. This was happening very fast.

Bernie brought us inside and gathered us around the dining table. With my plants lining the space, the bright colors of the Georgia O'Keeffe room had never felt warmer or more festive. She tapped her fork to her glass to get our attention. "Thanks everyone for coming to celebrate Dale's fortieth birthday. A few months after the fact, but who cares? She's still forty."

"The new twenty," Taiye called, and I raised my glass to toast him.

Bernie beamed at us all. She loved having the Desert Rose filled to the brim, and ever since word got out about her celebrity guests, business had been good.

"And now it's an engagement party too," Bernie said. "We all know it probably took some thought, and Kay was the most worried of all of us, but—she said yes." Bernie raised her glass. "To Dale and her fiancé, Timothy Kay. Cheers."

My phone vibrated while I tipped back my margarita. Lisa's face popped up, requesting a video call.

"Did he pop the question yet?" Lisa demanded. "Maya said he was going to. Can I see the ring?"

I showed her, and Lisa gave a little gasp of dismay. "That's it? Nothing flashier?"

Ritchie's face joined hers on the screen. "I thought he was rich."

"They're lab grown diamonds, not mined." Kay slung an arm around my shoulder, joining me in my little tile in the corner of the screen. "I asked for blue because that's her favorite color." I don't think Ritchie had ever known that. "And the band is recycled silver. I know someone in Nevada who does a lot with recycled metals."

His demeanor was easy, but his arm was possessive. He was showing them I belonged to him. With him.

Lisa glanced down, I guessed looking at her own ring, convincing herself Ritchie's enormous princess-cut diamond reflected her worth to him. "Um, that sounds like something you'd love, Dale," she said politely. "Good for you."

"We can make it to the wedding," Ritchie said. "Maya told us the date. If you, um." He cleared his throat. "Actually want us to be there."

I looked at Kay. "Of course," he said.

I nodded, and something happened deep in my belly. The last little thread of worry—the last wall I'd been shoring up—shifted and melted away.

Kay accepted me wholly, with all my history, all my baggage, all my flaws. I didn't have to hide pieces of myself for fear they'd make him uncomfortable. And I sensed he was learning to be forthcoming with me, trusting that, together, we could find our own way through the thorns and brambles.

I didn't need a map. I just needed him beside me, holding my hand.

"Okay, tell me your colors so I can harmonize," Lisa said. "And, like, maybe a note about the style. And send pictures of your dress. And hair. And if you need to do any shopping—"

"We're about to have dinner," I said fondly as Lisa sped off on the mental path dearest to her heart. "Call you soon, okay?"

"I can't outshine the bride," Lisa was explaining to Ritchie as I hung up. "But, you know, you work with the overall feel of things—"

"Kind of a paltry ring," Ritchie grumbled as the call cut off.

I met Kay's eyes and smiled. Relieved, he smiled back, the crinkles deepening.

"I love my ring," I said, looking at its gentle gleam on my finger. It was lovely and understated, and most of all, it said I was cherished by this man. The man I loved. "It's perfect."

He drifted his fingers over my shoulder, his face sobering. "Nothing's perfect, Dale."

"You're perfect," I whispered. "For me."

"No more running?" He looked worried again.

I tipped my face up to his. I'd prove that my love was real and deep and lasting.

"Not so fast you can't keep up," I said, and sealed the promise with a kiss.

ABOUT THE AUTHOR

Misty is a fiction writer and medieval scholar. While her academic and creative nonfiction deal with monstrous women and motherhood, in her historical fiction and contemporary romances she likes to reward her ambitious, rule-breaking heroines with handsome heroes and happy endings.

She lives in Iowa with a handsome park ranger, two other budding authors, and a heavy collection of books.

Connect with Misty:
website: mistyurban.com
fb : /authormistyurban
IG:@authormistyurban
TT: @misty.urban.writes

www.BOROUGHSPUBLISHINGGROUP.com

If you enjoyed this book, please write a review. Our authors appreciate the feedback, and it helps future readers find books they love. We welcome your comments and invite you to send them to info@boroughspublishinggroup.com.

Follow us on Facebook, Twitter and Instagram, and be sure to sign up for our newsletter for surprises and new releases from your favorite authors.

Are you an aspiring writer? Check out www.boroughspublishinggroup.com/submit and see if we can help you make your dreams come true.

Love podcasts? Enjoy ours at:

https://boroughspublishinggroup.com/podcast.